D1600121

THE NEAR DISTANT

BRETT ARMSTRONG
ERIN R. HOWARD
C. KEVIN THOMPSON

Copyright © 2022 by Brett Armstrong, Erin R. Howard, and C. Kevin Thompson

Published by Expanse Books, an imprint of
Scrivenings Press LLC
15 Lucky Lane
Morrilton, Arkansas 72110
www.ScriveningsPress.com

Printed in the United States of America

All rights reserved. No part of this publication may be reproduced, stored in a retrieval system, or transmitted in any form or by any means—for example, electronic, photocopy and recording— without the prior written permission of the publisher. The only exception is brief quotations in printed reviews.

Paperback ISBN 978-1-64917-260-0

eBook ISBN 978-1-64917-261-7

Editors: Erin R. Howard, Elena Hill, and Linda Fulkerson

Cover by Linda Fulkerson, bookmarketinggraphics.com

Scripture quotations are from the ESV® Bible (The Holy Bible, English Standard Version®), copyright © 2001 by Crossway, a publishing ministry of Good News Publishers. Used by permission. All rights reserved. The ESV text may not be quoted in any publication made available to the public by a Creative Commons license. The ESV may not be translated in whole or in part into any other language.

All characters are fictional, and any resemblance to real people, either factual or historical, is purely coincidental.

From Brett:
This book is dedicated the glory of God without Whom there are no words worthy of writing and with Whom home is truly forever found.

From Erin:
To everyone who needs a little more light to outweigh the darkness.

From Kevin:
To all who seek to be free from the bondage of this age.

"If you abide in my word, you are truly my disciples, and you will know the truth, and the truth will set you free."

(John 8:31b-32; ESV)

CONTENTS

PROLOGUE

1

PROLOGUE

The Monolith

"PAST THIS CLUSTER OF TREES, according to the map." Ned pointed off to his left, letting his three friends catch up.

"Don't you think everyone else on Lake Tahoe would have seen Tessie?" Tyler took a swig from his water bottle and twisted the cap back on. "Were there any other reports?"

"No."

"Right. I don't buy it." Tyler turned toward the water. "The so-called witness would've needed a camera with a telephoto lens or binoculars or something, but he claimed he 'saw it with my own two eyes while I was jogging on the Flume Trail.' Come on, man."

Tyler shrugged and raised an eyebrow at the couple lagging behind. "Sounds a bit fishy, if you ask me. No pun intended."

Ned set his backpack on the ground. "Yeah, but he never said it was Tessie. Just that the wake caught his attention."

"It could have been a boat," Everly, the only female of the group, chimed in.

"No." Ned unzipped his backpack and pulled out the newspaper. He flipped the pages around pointing to the article. "See? Right here. 'I knew it wasn't a boat because the creature bobbed in the water with its head sticking out. Like the water turkeys we have back home.'"

Everly peered at her date Carter. Would he come to her defense?

Ned folded the paper back to its original state. "Boats don't bob when the lake is like glass," he said, pointing to the calm water below.

"Uh, sorry." Everly lowered her head, backing away. "I was just thinking logically, you know. I didn't mean to step on anybody's toes."

"Don't worry about Ned's feelings," Tyler said. "He doesn't have any. He aspires to be a robot someday."

Ned feigned laughter, lifted his pack, and threaded his arms through the straps. "When I'm being awarded the Nobel Prize and the Copley Medal, maybe you'll take me seriously."

"If you win either one of those awards, we'll still know *you*. The *real* you." Tyler repositioned the ball cap on his head. "And will we have stories to tell when they come to interview us."

"Ooh, ooh, ooh," Carter finally contributed to the conversation, "I get to tell the one about the chemistry lab last year. I can see the headline now: *Nobel Prize-Winning Recipient Nearly Burned Down Chemistry Lab in Early Days*."

"And then there's the girl from UC-Davis," Tyler said.

"Oh yeah ..." Carter scratched the back of his head. "I'd forgotten about her."

Everly slipped her backpack off her shoulders and dropped it at her feet. "What girl?"

"Could've easily been Gemma Chan's sister. Looked just like her. Was all into saving the environment." Tyler paused and winked at Everly. "And apparently was all into Ned too. She found all sorts of ways to come on campus to see him. It was—"

"Embarrassing," Ned said.

"Embarrassing?" Everly peered first at Tyler and then back at Ned. "How?"

"She followed me around like a lost puppy. Always asking questions about what I was doing, what I was studying, where I was from."

Everly laughed. "What's wrong with that?"

"You laugh. She was intrusive. Overbearing."

"Maybe she simply liked you, Ned. Did you ever think of that? She asked all those questions because she wanted to get to know you better." Everly shook her head, glancing at her own date. "She was probably hoping you'd return the courtesy. Show some interest in her as well."

Ned squinted, looking away from the group. "Yeah ... well ... I don't have time for all that." He left the trail and headed into the small patch of trees off to the left. "Love is for fools."

Everly faced Carter. "I take it she stopped coming on campus?"

"Pretty much."

Tyler jammed his water bottle into the backpack's pouch. "I know I would have, if I was told to stop bothering him."

"He actually said that?"

"I was there when he did."

Everly's gaze oscillated back and forth between Carter and Tyler. "Men."

"What?" Carter said with a sheepish smile. "I didn't do it."

"Hey, guys! Are you seeing this?" Ned stopped at the edge of the cluster of trees. "That reflection. It flashes like someone is trying to get our attention."

Everly followed Ned, with Tyler and Carter behind her. "I see it. Looks like a mirror. Is it signaling Morse code?"

"Nah, not the right pattern. Whatever it is, it's blinding when you look directly at it." Ned ducked under a low-hanging branch, shielding his eyes.

Carter scanned the ground in front of him. "Be careful, guys. This underbrush is the perfect cover for snakes."

"'Snakes ... why did it have to be snakes?'" Tyler said.

"Just a warning, Indiana. No need to be a putz."

"I would think we'd need to be more concerned about a Sasquatch or a mountain lion in these parts."

Ned huffed. "With the way you guys are blabberin' back there, it's a wonder anything is still around."

Tyler rolled his eyes and mumbled. "I take back what I said earlier. I've programmed robots with more social grace.

"I'm not worried about scaring off snakes," Everly said. "And Tessie can't hear us from up here ... *She* is the reason we're here. Right, Ned?"

Ned cleared the final outcropping of trees and came to a small opening. Standing before him was a silver, triangular-shaped pillar. At least eight feet tall, extremely shiny—almost mirror-like—the pillar didn't appear to have any writing on it. The top came to a point at a forty-five-degree angle.

Ned slowly circled the object, examining it from a distance, as the other three approached.

"That looks like one of those monolith things," Everly said emerging from the foliage. "Pictures of them have been in the news."

"All over the Internet too." Tyler pulled his smartphone from his pocket. "I've got an article saved. According to this ... the first one surfaced in a desert in Utah. Since then, they've been seen in Romania, southern California, the Isle of Wight, Spain, Germany, Belgium, and the Netherlands."

Tyler held his phone up and compared the pictures to the monolith standing before them.

Carter slipped his backpack off and opened it. "All those have been proven to be a publicity stunt of some artist in the area. Dr. Wallsay said it was a 'tip of the hat' to the movie *2001: A Space Odyssey*."

Ned inched closer and squatted about three feet from it. "Look at this," pointing at the pillar's base. "The ground's undisturbed. Like it sprouted from the ground. You can't say that about all those other monoliths." He gestured to Tyler's phone. "With those, you could tell someone had dug a hole, dropped the thing in, and then tried to smooth the dirt out."

"Maybe they just did a better job of covering up their tracks with this one." Carter pulled out his camera and continued to rummage around inside his pack. "I'll take some pictures to document, and we can video ourselves."

"Maybe we could be on Good Morning, America," Everly said.

"Why would you want to be on that show?" Ned said, pulling at some undergrowth. "Just to get your fifteen minutes of fame, followed by a lifetime of obscurity? While they use your fame to make themselves rich?" He stood and glanced at Everly. "No, thanks."

"Oh, come on!" Carter dug through his bag with increasing force.

"Forget your lens again?" Tyler asked.

"I'm gonna kill Jamie. He borrowed my camera the other day for his final Biology project. He didn't tell me he kept the SD card."

"Shouldn't you have checked all that before we came all the way up here?"

"I was in a bit of a hurry this morning. Remember?" Carter jammed the camera back into his bag.

"I remember you oversleeping and—"

"I'll be back. I have extra cards in my other bag." Carter held out his hand. "Ned, the keys?"

Ned tossed them to Carter with a shake of his head. "You need to run. It took us almost thirty minutes to get up here. We don't have an hour to wait."

"Why don't we just use our phones?" Everly said.

Ned lifted his hands as if the answer was obvious. "Because you don't shoot scientific evidence with smartphones."

"Why not?"

Tyler dropped his chin to his chest. "Please don't ask that question, unless you want an hour-long diatribe on the pros and cons of smartphones."

"I just wanted to—"

"Privacy, Everly," Ned said.

"With that, I'm leaving," Carter turned to Tyler. "I'll be back ASAP. He'll probably still be rambling when I get back anyway."

Tyler rolled his eyes. "Here we go."

"When you take a picture or a video ..." Ned continued on without acknowledging Tyler's remark.

TYLER, listening to the banter between his friends, circled the pillar. He examined each side from bottom to top, admiring the mirror-like qualities of the material. He paused. Written across the top was a word in a language he didn't recognize. He took a step back, and the word disappeared. Easing forward again, the word reappeared. "I hate to break up the little debate club, but you two may want to take a look at this."

Ned stopped mid-sentence and walked to the other side and stood next to Tyler. Everly joined them.

"You see it?" Tyler pointed at the top of the pillar. You have to stand just right."

Ned peered up. "What are we looking for?"

"A word, maybe? But it's a language I've never seen before."

"Maybe it's Klingon," Everly said with a chuckle.

"I don't see anything." Ned shook his head.

"Here. Let me move. Stand where I'm standing." Tyler sidestepped to his right.

Ned did so and muttered an expletive. "I see it." He kept his feet in place and swayed to the left and then to the right. "That is awesome. When I move, the word starts to fade and blur. Can you still see it now?"

"No," Tyler said.

"What about you, Everly?"

"Nope."

Ned took a step backward. "I can still see it." He took another step back. Then another. "Yes, still there." He took his fourth step back, and the word disappeared. "I lost it." Sliding forward again, the word reappeared.

Ned excitedly directed the others. "Tyler, Everly, circle around each other and stand just so." He pointed to his left and right. "Look up. Are there words written at the top?"

"I see something," Everly said.

Tyler nodded. "So do I."

"Tyler," Ned said, still looking at his word, "is it the same as this one?"

"No. Yours is longer. This one only has two characters."

Ned's finger bounced along as he counted. "My word has eight characters. Everly?"

"Are you calling the square-ish squiggles characters?"

"Uh, no? I mean, mine aren't square," Ned squinted then

widened his eyes as he spoke. "Mine are round. Like crop circles."

"Mine are ... uh, I'm not sure what mine are," Tyler said. "One looks like the lower peninsula of Michigan. The other looks like ... a fried egg. But they're connected by a straight line."

"That's weird," Everly said. "Mine are definitely square."

"Okay, doesn't matter. On three, everybody take one regular step forward. We'll move closer to it in unison to see if the words are still visible. Ready?"

"Ready," Everly said.

Tyler nodded.

"In three ... two ... one ... step," Ned said, moving forward.

Tyler and Everly did the same.

The top of the pillar pulsed with a light. The brightness pulsed faster and faster.

"Are you seeing this?" Ned said.

Tyler grabbed the straps on his backpack. "It looks like we woke something up."

Everly's voice cracked a little. "Maybe we should—"

The throbbing light brightened and shot a beam into the sky. Hurricane-force winds, radiated out in all directions. The energy rocked the surrounding trees and swept loose debris away from the pillar like a small atomic blast.

As quickly as the detonation exploded outward, it inverted the process. The trees swayed violently, but their branches held firm. Leaves fluttered in the air.

In the blink of an eye, the entire event ceased, as if sucked inside the top of the pillar with considerable power. The clearing, with only the monolith standing erect, looked undisturbed and eerily quiet.

BRETT ARMSTRONG

ONE

1

ANOTHER ORBIT

THEY SAY when one is drowning there's a lot of struggling initially. Resistance. Then, gradually, the person gets worn down, the struggles cease. That's how Tyler felt. He was drowning.

For years now he'd lived in another time and place than he belonged. One of his favorite Sci-Fi shows, *Quantum Leap*, ended on an episode where time-traveling Sam Beckett, who just wanted to go home to his own time, was told by God he always could have gone home if only he'd chosen to.

At the start, Tyler imagined he, too, was here for a purpose. To right wrongs in this world or himself. But trying to get back home, to understand it, became exhausting, so he just stopped.

When had that happened? Year two? And here he lay, resisting the start of day one hundred of his tenth completed orbit around this world's primary star.

A chime sounded next to Tyler's head, pulling him from his thoughts. On Earth things like this could be ignored, silenced, or snoozed. Not so on Irizan, a world that functioned much like Earth but wasn't the same.

"Tyler-Zan," a coolly modulated voice that reminded him somewhat of Scarlett Johansson addressed him. "Your sleep cycle is complete. You have forty-five minutes remaining to hydro-debride, garb, and ingest your morning sustenance ration before you must board the shuttle to the launch site."

"Thank you, Irizan," he muttered.

"Forty-four minutes, Tyler-Zan," the planet-wide AI informed him. "This would be the second time in three revolutions you are delinquent in meeting your timeliness obligations."

Tyler sat up from the sleep capsule and pushed off, staggering in the same groggy state he did every morning toward what amounted to a bathroom. Under his feet, the smooth underlit flooring was cool, but not cold. The room was perfectly modulated to a comfortable temperature. As he walked, the walls, which were formerly deep indigo hues, shifted to brighter shades of blue and settled on something akin to a noon sky as they emitted light for him to find his way.

Doors slid open on his approach, and though several yards away from it, the Irizan equivalent of a shower switched on and adjusted the water temperature in expectation of his arrival. If he were to stop now it would shut off until he started moving again and adjust temperature and start time to match his preferences. Early in his exile, he'd tested and probed the AIs precision and decision-making, being fascinated by it. Now it was just a daily annoyance.

In fairness, he, too, was probably much more interesting to the AI, before it quantified and tabulated everything that could be known about him. Even now as he reached the bathroom and approached the analog of a toilet, he resigned himself to the indignity that his urine would be analyzed for mineral composition and charted against his daily, weekly, monthly, yearly, and lifetime trends. While he showered, a breakfast tailored precisely to his biological needs would be prepared for him and waiting, warm, on a counter.

Stepping into the shower after removing his clothes and dropping them into the clothing renewal receptacle, he closed his eyes and let the warm water spray directly in his face. Every day was a struggle, but a launch day twice as much. Not the least of which, because he knew *she* would be waiting to speak with him. As she did every launch day.

"Warmer," he instructed.

"Microcellular damage will occur at temperatures in excess of—"

"Warmer, please?" he tried. However, the AI had originally been designed, such overtures did impact its decisions, and its decisions frustratingly were effective law.

"Temperature increased three degrees Celsius."

"Thank you."

"Water shutoff will commence in 1.5 minutes."

Clenching his jaw, Tyler added an ironical, "Thanks."

True to its word, precise to the nanosecond, the water shut off. A microfiber towel was dispensed to him, which he utilized and placed in the clothing renewal receptacle. On Earth he would've brushed his teeth, but on Irizan the food already contained necessary molecules to keep his teeth a perpetual ivory shade. Not unlike treats he had given his black lab, Geist.

He tried not to think much about her anymore. Not after he realized that even accounting for Irizan's shorter solar years he'd been in this world for a decade now. Geist, about six when he was transported here, was likely dead. With the pandemic and general instability of Earth, maybe the whole planet was gone at this point and he was the last human left. Just very, very far from where he belonged.

"Thirty-eight minutes, remaining. Increase your pace to meet your timeliness obligation."

Tyler slipped on a polymer outfit that was deep black with teal highlights. It wasn't form fitting but also wasn't good T-shirt and pair of jeans comfortable. Addressing the AI in an airy tone he said, "Timeliness modulates discord."

"Parodying Kayli-Zan's accurate recitation of this crucial maxim is inappropriate," Irizan informed him. "Disdain for your life mate does not inculcate harmony nor improve biological longevity."

Slipping on his final article of clothing, a teal jumpsuit of sorts that marked him as a member of the miner's class, Tyler slipped in a dig. "You know you always side with her."

"She is Zan. Her rhythms and comprehension of optimized civilization are more expansive than your own." There was a note of reproof in the AIs familiar recitation of why Tyler was wrong in literally every disagreement he'd ever had with one of the planet's people.

Tyler took a moment to look into the reflective panel on the wall. His hair was already drying, kept short and darker here than it had been on Earth. His face was clean shaven though he had formerly gone to lengths to maintain a steady level of intentional dishevelment and scruffiness in his appearance. He lost the fight on growing a beard early on. Only elites among the Zan were permitted facial hair. Or any control over their appearance. The AI had optimized every facet of life, including ensuring that pre-selected couples would match their partner's preferences in appearance. Kayli-Zan liked him to look what he thought would have been termed "preppy" on Earth.

"Might as well get this over with," he told himself.

"Thirty-five minutes to complete tasks."

All that time dreaming of what it would be like to have a smart home on Earth seemed silly right this moment. "You're a peach," he informed Irizan.

"Peach?" the AI repeated, analyzing the Earth word that

he'd let slip into his now fluent Kaizan, the predominant language of Irizan. Every so often he would use English words that the AI would note and try to perform a philological analysis on.

"No direct matches to this idiomatic phrasing exist. There is the pejorative, 'You're a *ponzo*.' Or the superlative, 'You're a *sheniri*.' Which best represents the meaning of this idiom?"

Having been on the receiving end of the former numerous times and the latter at least once, Tyler smirked. Maybe this day would be better than he expected. "Neither."

"Explain the meaning of peach."

"It's a stone fruit from my home world," Tyler explained, relishing the chance to have one over on the AI. "It means something akin to, 'You're swell.'" He made sure to toss in the English word swell, knowing it would further fluster Irizan.

"The meaning of this word, 'swell,' is also unknown. Analysis of facial expression and tone implies it connotates a superlative. Lexical entries for 'swell' and 'peach' added. Additional analysis determines the use of sarcasm. Critical or congenial?"

Nope not a great day.

"Congenial," Tyler said, amusement fading from his voice. Irizan tolerated a little roasting, but as the arbiter of law and order for the entire planet, flagrant disrespect landed one in reformatory therapy. Something Tyler had twice endured and only just come away with his sanity each time.

"Assessment: Congenial. Proceed with your preparations. You have twenty-seven minutes remaining. Alerting supervisors to probable delay."

Ugh. Definitely not a good day.

"Thank you," he said and hurried to the kitchen. As soon as he crossed the threshold into room, he saw her.

TWO

1

DOMESTIC TRANQUILITY

KAYLI-ZAN WAS ABOUT 5'9", average height for females of Irizan, and curvy with a somewhat athletic build. Today she was wearing a silvery dress that ended above her calves and had cuts that were peculiar to the Zan. Tyler wasn't a fashionista by any stretch, so he never quite managed to articulate what Earth styles it compared to.

As usual, Kayli-Zan's long dark hair, naturally kinked, was straightened. Years ago, he made the idiot comment that his last girlfriend on Earth kept her hair that way. Kayli-Zan's had been straight ever since.

She had almond shaped eyes that were a deep blue and lips artificially tinted the same shade. Her features would have been considered lovely on Earth—beautiful, he had to admit. If they were on Earth, he would've said she was of Asiatic descent. But the absence of tonal accentuations in words and cultural heritage muddied the comparison and left it inapt. Not to mention her faintly purple skin meant she would've stuck out sorely among the inhabitants of Earth, much as Tyler had when he was teleported to Irizan.

Her eyes brightened in a way that stung him when she noticed his arrival. "Tyler-Zan," she said, a hesitant smile parted her indigo lips. "Testing the limits space-time can stretch again, I see."

It was meant as a joke, but the hollowness in her words only scored a deeper wound than if she'd been genuinely critical of him. He rubbed his neck and said, "Yeah, looks that way."

The fractional fall in her expression from hopeful expectation to confirmed disappointment was familiar. "Irizan informed me you will be late again."

He crossed his arms and ran his tongue over his teeth. Some choice things he'd like to say about Irizan right now would land him in reformatory therapy. "I'll do my best to not bring you dishonor again."

There was a slight twitch at the corner of her mouth, and she wrung her hands in an unconscious way. Taking a seat at the smooth white table in the room, she gestured to the other seat. "You should eat. You will need your strength for the launch."

Not wanting to further antagonize her, he took the seat opposite her and sat down. Already a plate, warmed as expected, was there. Right away something was noticeably amiss. The meal, the Irizan equivalent of scrambled eggs and toast, looked ... imperfect. There was browning along the edges the food prep bot never caused and a proliferation of ruddy flakes that most certainly did not appear on the bot's concoctions. "You made these?" he asked, looking at her as he took hold of an eating utensil.

"Yes," she said. "I know you are not fond of launch days. I thought a special breakfast might help."

"Nothing helps launch days," he mumbled and then immediately hated himself for it when she winced. "But this certainly won't hurt. Extra rabica flakes?"

She nodded. "I know this is how you prefer nila."

Spicy food was his favorite before the Event brought him to Irizan. But that wasn't generally considered an approved dietary custom and was something he regularly lost battles with the AI over. "Thank you," he said quietly.

He said a silent prayer and took a bite. It was hard to deny the flavor profile was remarkably like the scrambled eggs his mom used to make him. Instantly he regretted the association. More than once it occurred to him his mom had to think he was dead and could be herself. She didn't handle grief well.

"I'm sorry," Kayli-Zan said, looking down at the nila.

It took Tyler a moment to realize he had a tear forming in one eye and had grimaced. She must have taken it as disgust. "No, no. These are great." He took another couple bites in quick succession and tried to smile, though the heat of the rabica flakes was starting to build.

He coughed and reached for a glass with water in it. One thing that was very much the same as back on Earth. Downing half the glass, he coughed again and gave a self-deprecating smirk.

Kayli-Zan smiled a little, too, though clearly this wasn't the best day for her as well.

"You look beautiful," Tyler commented, and was able to be sincere. "Is that a new dress for your first day?"

Darker profusions appeared on Kayli-Zan's cheeks. "I didn't think you would remember."

This time he did a better job burying his initial reaction—guilt, frustration. "Of course, I remember. It's a significant honor to be placed in charge of the sector's energy consortium. You must be excited."

Her smile broadened, and she swayed in her seat in a way on Earth would have been a coy agreement. "It is an honor. But a little scary."

"Scary, nah. You're brilliant. The consortium was wise to choose you. You should be proud."

Kayli-Zan took in a breath as though she'd been holding hers the whole time. "I am. I can't believe they picked me at such a young age. My father was nearly ten orbits more seasoned when he was given the task for my home sector. I wish he could be there with me!"

It was her turn to look stricken and realize she'd misspoke. Beyond the obvious sore point of him being stranded on an alien world with no clue how to return home, Kayli-Zan's parents had all but disowned her when she agreed to be Tyler's mate. The AI had produced her as the highest percentage match for him, and though Irizan's biological welfare policy insisted committed pairings were a key to well-being, a quasi-law, she had been given a choice in the matter and elected to be with him. Marrying the freak who didn't fit in wasn't the best move for social mobility. Often her friends would say, "You're handling your burden so well." Or quote a maxim, "Those who bear up under the hardest suffering become the noblest of Zan."

The fact that she was the equivalent of an engineering doctorate holder and he was the very lowest vocational wrung on the Irizan ladder only complicated things further. There was no need to remind him that she would have had so much more, been so much more, without him. Effectively, his coming had ruined both their lives.

Rapping his knuckles on the table, Tyler forced down the last of the nila and water in a couple quick bites and a gulp. He stood and knotted his fingers and shook them in her direction. The equivalent of a common courtesy greeting/parting gesture and headed for the door.

"You have three minutes to reach the shuttle stop," Irizan alerted him. Not particularly empathetic in tone, but that it had remained silent during the entire exchange until now meant it had observed every bit of the painful conversation.

Tyler took a few items presented to him by another service bot that were needed for the launch, including his identity validation cylinder and a protective hood to wear when out in this world's sun—neither of which he could afford to forget.

"Tyler-Zan, wait," Kayli-Zan called out to him. She rushed over to their home's exit and grabbed his hand before he could walk through.

A jolt of a fretful current rushed through him. They rarely touched. Zan produced currents that provided an extra form of emotional connection to their mates. That he had no such ability was just one more thing he deprived Kayli-Zan of. Though she never said so, she must have mutually agreed avoiding contact would least agitate them both.

Looking into her indigo eyes, he could tell she was on the verge of tears and holding them back. "I'm sorry," she said, a gentle pulse in her touch somehow enhancing his perception of her sincerity.

"You're not the one who needs to apologize. Ever," he replied and with his unfettered hand pulled up his protective hood. "And Irizan agrees with me on that at least."

"One minute thirty seconds," the AI commented.

Kayli-Zan closed her eyes and shook her head. A sharper sensation pulsed from her hand and he guessed that was anger or frustration. If it was, she managed to keep herself from going too far down that path. The feeling mellowed and she said, "Please, take care. Come home safely."

His first thought was, "If I could really go home, I would." But that helped no one, so instead he said, "I'll try."

The instant she let go, he took off running. Down the street within the densely packed buildings of Hanite City, racing to make it to the shuttle departure point. He was almost certain to be late now and would either have to pay a fine or work an extra shift in orbit. Definitely a miserable start to an already miserable day.

THREE

1

A FRESH BREATH

A FAINT SHUDDER as the gravity wave generator augmented the low natural gravity with artificial enhancement was the only indication of arrival. There were no windows or viewing panels on the extraorbital shuttles. Marezan, the AI for all Zan affairs not on Irizan that sounded a bit like Stephen Lang, had explained to Tyler a view of cosmic magnificence only served to depress the asteroid mining crew members. A look at the dark expanse stretching like a vast ocean dotted with stellar archipelagoes would make them feel small, insignificant. There was also another reason for it that Marezan wouldn't reveal to Tyler.

Around Tyler's chest, the harness securing him released. Marezan's firm and low voice instructed, "All miners of expedition A11-83-245-3139-EH, please stand. You may now disembark and head to your stations for assignments."

Tyler didn't move. He sat stiff in his seat, waiting for everyone else to file past off the ship. Over the years he found this to be the least confrontational approach to the process. Even among the lowest echelons of Zan society, or perhaps even more so, he was tolerated, not welcomed. Not to mention, he was fighting his usual bout of nausea.

Staring at the bland, grey wall section of shuttle interior opposite him, Tyler remembered climbing the tallest mountain in his hometown with his dad. They camped at the top, and as night fell, they were able to look out on the valley below and see the cities along it light up. Even up on that mountain, it was too bright from artificial light to see a true night sky, so the star-like dots spread below was the closest they could get. "Remember, as impressive as this is," his father had instructed, "This is like a school kid's model compared to the real thing. The real thing is more incredible than you can find words for."

"Come on you flerr slug. Move your tiny 'huzan' legs," one of the miners next to Tyler instructed, a smarmy grin on his grass green face. A darker swath, closer to forest green cut across his face in a pattern that marked him as an athletics champion. Hearl-Zan's ribbing was almost worse than the nausea.

Tyler gazed up at the towering hulk of a Zan. The last to exit besides him. Small, intense jade eyes that would intimidate a bear on Earth stared back at him. An injury ended Hearl-Zan's vaunted sports career and landed him in his current place of nonage. Even so, he was the most physically imposing Zan that Tyler had ever seen.

"I have to wait for you sloth-brains," Tyler replied, leveling a cool stare up at him.

The Zan glowered down at Tyler with narrowed eyes. "Sloth-brains, eh?"

After a moment a smirk broke out on his face. "And what exactly is a sloth?"

Tyler snickered and gave a shrug. "A creature that moves so slow it has moss growing on it."

"Ooh, like a nissaru."

"Well except it's a mammal. Um, a vevan."

With a nod, Hearl gestured toward the ramp off ship. "We better move before we get mistaken for these sloths."

"Any chance Marezan will forget about us if we don't disembark?"

"No," the low masculine voice of Marezan responded. "Neither of you are reported as ill by Irizan and have yet to meet your required work quotas this orbit. Please report to your designated muster site."

"Right away," Hearl-Zan replied, though for Tyler he had a glint of exasperation in his eyes.

Hearl was perhaps the only Zan with whom Tyler could be friends. Following him down the ramp, they both walked across the wide docking area—enormous, flat and faintly blue from specialized lighting, which bustled with loading of ores and other mined elements and the unloading of equipment. Reaching their group on the far right of the space, nearest the lively unloading activity, Hearl crossed his arms over his chest.

"Brace yourself," Hearl warned.

"Mhm," Tyler mumbled in agreement as he caught sight of Pophtne-Zan standing at the head of their crew pointing to a holographic display of what appeared to be work assignments mapped onto the physical structure of the asteroid's interior. Physically average in size and coloration for a Zan male, but disproportionately irritating by Tyler's estimation, Pophtne had more than once found ways to complicate Tyler's work life.

Pophtne glanced their way and immediately soured in expression. "Good of you both to join us," he fussed petulantly.

"Congratulations on your promotion," Hearl replied, nearly succeeding at deflecting the implicit ire and accusation. He even smiled broadly.

"You may congratulate me after your rotation is

completed," Pophtne shot back. "You should thank Marezan that I didn't list you as a deserter for being so slow."

The last was drawn out and from the arch to his eyebrow it was clear the Zan was taking a swipe at Hearl's washing out as a star kebny scorer in which speed and reflexes are crucial. Whereas Tyler might tease, Pophtne aimed to wound. Hearl was wise enough to let the criticism go.

A semblance of disappointment flickered across their supervisor's expression when no challenge was forthcoming. "Very well, you'll be making up for it with laser alignment and refuse disposal duties."

"On which level?"

"All of them," Pophtne replied sounding as if he were exasperated with a child.

Tyler glimpsed Hearl's fists clench at his sides. Those were objectively the least desirable jobs in any launch rotation. Which meant that Tyler was likely to receive something equally annoying.

"You, Tyler-Zan," Pophtne turned his attention without even looking up from a handheld display he was suddenly concerned with. "You'll be evaluating resource distribution and excavation quantities."

Shaking his head, Tyler blurted out, "What?"

"Don't play ignorant," Pophtne answered. "Do as you're told and perhaps you will succeed in not convincing everyone you're irreparably sub-Zan."

"Yes, sir," Tyler replied. He was even able to mask most of his annoyance and disdain for the other, because oddly, he had been given one of the most important tasks available. Glancing out of the corner of his eye, he tried to gauge how Hearl had taken this development.

At that moment something else, besides Hearl's frustration caught Tyler's eye. There was a shuttle unloading some cargo.

It wouldn't have piqued his interest, except the rotations Tyler belonged to were always in the middle of a mining operation's lifecycle. Excavation for new areas that would require large equipment loads like this should already have been completed.

Hearl bumped Tyler with his elbow. Everyone was dispersing, having received their instructions. Now Tyler didn't bother to veil his curiosity and shot a look over at the mystery unloading. The crew handling it was almost finished. It wasn't possible to tell from here, but he had the vague suspicion they weren't part of the normal work crews either.

"Marezan summons to Tyler," Hearl said waving a big hand in his face.

Tyler blinked. "Sorry, thought I saw ... something."

"Yeah, well you better see the inside of your workstation, fast. Pophtne set your start time to five minutes from now," Hearl said with a mirthless chuckle.

"Argh, I should have known he'd never do me a favor," Tyler grumbled and dashed to the nearest open lift.

"That makes two of us," Hearl called after him.

A minute later, the lift Tyler rode halted and allowed him to dash past other Zan disembarking on the same level he'd been assigned. Rushing around this way earned some snide comments, as Zan, who had super AIs to guide their time management, were seldom faced with issues of tardiness. Yet another reason Tyler was often a pariah. If he got another bad mark for lateness, he'd have to attend mandatory performance improvement training in his few off hours.

The door to his assigned workstation slid open, and Tyler leaped in with thirty seconds to spare. Huffing in deep gulps of the low-density oxygen circulated in the asteroid mining facilities, he looked up just in time to almost bump into a technician.

"Oh, my apologies," Tyler choked out breathily.

Grunting something, the technician shouldered past and exited the small enclosure of the workstation. Tyler expected to hear Marezan chide the Zan for rudeness, but there were only the occasional sounds of the devices projecting the holographic displays around him.

Thanks for nothing, Marezan.

Standing in the circular command position for the station, Tyler immediately noticed something was off. Technicians regularly inspected each station before new workers commenced their shifts, albeit usually hours before hand, but it appeared to Tyler as though the tech had left his station in open mode. A restricted state in which the underlying codebase with which Marezan interfaced to each physical device of the mining operation was accessible.

Tyler spun around to call to the tech, but he was long gone. In the scuffle, he hadn't managed to note the tech's identification tags, or anything distinguishable about him. Other than he had been hunched and in a hurry.

Turning back to the station, it occurred to Tyler that this might be why Marezan was silent. He'd long hypothesized that the AIs had been designed to give some degree of separation from their active involvement with their own underlying code. A sort of safeguard against helpful tyranny, in which they already regularly engaged, in Tyler's opinion. They didn't control updates to themselves, though to Tyler's knowledge, no such things ever happened apart from ephemeral and far-edge inclusions of newer devices that were developed.

Part of him warned he was seeing something forbidden. But another part, long dormant and quickly awakening, wanted to look further. To examine the code. When he'd first arrived among the Zan and explained his education and planned career on Earth, he had been shown samples of the code used by the AIs. Over time and consolidated conviction that Earth was far less sophisticated technologically than Irizan, those privileges were revoked, and Tyler had been given assignments more akin to Hearl's. Grunt-labor with heavy doses of tedium and perhaps unnecessary risk. This was his chance to see something more akin to his old life.

This could be a test.

Gnawing on his lower lip, Tyler dithered. It was strange he'd been given the assignment he had. It certainly wasn't for his impressive career history. Honestly, he was subpar and deserving of his demerits when received. Though it was possible Kayli-Zan's advancement had led to a recalculation of his social worth, and he was riding on the resultant waves of her success. If so, he owed her a thank you.

Maybe they're also giving my access back because of my improved score.

For better or worse, the notion had become fixed in his mind. Fully justifying his curiosity's ravenous hunger. He dove in, so-to-speak, to the code without hesitation. There was no resisting it—for the first time in longer than he could remember, he felt like he was breathing freely. Hours rushed past as they never did, and it was only the aching of his eyes and the growling of his stomach that drew him away from the depths of all he had explored.

By the end of it, he'd learned how to activate open mode on his own. More than that, he stumbled on some strange subroutines that stood out as different from the rest of the code, as if hastily added in recently. Accessing them was a bit tricky, so he decided to leave that for the next few days.

Backing away from the station, Tyler realized he needed to get some of the actual work related to his new assignment completed. He called out, "Marezan, I'm ready to begin."

The coloration of the displays changed by darkening a few

shades. Marezan's voice echoed in the small space, "Tyler-Zan, you are late."

"What, no, I made it to the workstation in time," Tyler began to protest.

"I am aware you made it to your station on time. Your duties were all completed on schedule as well for the first time in two rotations. It is, however, three standardized hours past time for your evening meal. Nutritional balance is important for overall wellness and biological stability," the AI chided.

"I'm sorry, I must have lost track of the time while working," Tyler replied, though he had no idea how the AI could have thought he completed any actual tasks. Or why the AI didn't alert him to dinner time like normal. Then he remembered he was in open mode so the AI couldn't talk to him. But that still left the question of his tasks being marked as complete.

"Work is a vital component of Zan wellness, but psychological elements of wellness must be balanced by physiological necessities."

"Yes, Marezan," Tyler agreed readily out of concern that the AI would suddenly realize his greater malfeasance.

"You may consume a light meal before reclining for sleep. I have alerted the automated kitchen devices to prepare it for you. Please proceed to the commissary at once."

"Yes, Marezan. Thank you," he said and headed out the door and toward the commissary without delay. He got the meal and ate it with little attention to what it was or how it tasted. His mind was already abuzz with parceling out the mysteries before him. The strange shipments he'd seen, his surprise work assignment, the open mode, and now his tasks being marked complete for him. Something was going on and he would figure it out.

FOUR

1

BLINDSPOT

TYLER TAPPED on the virtual interfaces, scrolling through the usual readings on pressure, depth, device integrity, and precision estimates. The composition analyses continued to show positive results from the areas being mined. High yield, low impact to total mass removed. That was something he had learned quickly. Mining asteroids required some conservation of mass or it could change the trajectory of the asteroid. For the bigger asteroids, that was important. The smaller were mined almost to oblivion, and whatever remaining particles were left were used to keep the mass of the bigger ones close to pre-mining. It was about as close to not sending ripples through the pond of millions of rock shards surrounding the system as possible. Whether any of it was necessary or not was immaterial. It was a meaningful task, which Tyler realized some time ago was possibly an end in itself. In a society so advanced, anthropocentric labor wasn't essential, but the act of work itself helped on a psychological and physical level. The Zan, much like humans, Tyler imagined, needed work by design.

And by design, Tyler had not been able to suppress his curiosity once he'd given in to it. Swiping aside the figures still trending well within the green, he began tapping as fast as his fingers could move across the virtual display. Seconds later, the hidden portion of the monitoring system he'd uncovered two weeks ago was displayed. In spite of what Hearl-Zan warned after he'd told him what he was on to, Tyler perceived none of this was normal, and with an AI that for centuries kept things in impeccable balance, this level of divergence was something.

The trick was to figure out the big picture from all the smaller parts. As best he could tell, someone was using this blind spot in Marezan's field of vision to do something pretty big. There were all sorts of shifts in manifests and personnel that had been happening as early as a year ago.

Workers were being reassigned in what smacked of random patterns, but Tyler understood from years of coding, random errors almost always had a consistent cause—one just had to find the commonality.

Gotcha.

There was a common element. It took pulling back and looking at the spiderweb of intersections in subsequent trees of work orders, but he found it. Everything was focused around two locations. One was in a newly opened digging site and another was on the far side of the asteroid field.

Wait—that can't be right. Didn't they say nothing was allowed past the asteroid field?

Tyler thought he remembered that being a law, though he couldn't recall why it was in place. Running the data again, he came to the same conclusions.

Maybe I have that wrong about the asteroid field thing.

Guilt for not knowing something like that for certain galled him until something else caught his eye. There were no video or audio streams coming to Marezan from the new digging area of the mining complex.

Tyler closed out open mode by calling out, "Marezan, I'm ready to begin."

"Yes, Tyler-Zan," the masculine voice responded.

"I noticed there are no readings coming from equipment in Level Hazos-6-2. I'm concerned there is something wrong with the sensors, could you please evaluate them directly?"

Almost instantly after he requested it Marezan responded, "There are no sensor malfunctions in that level because it is presently undeveloped. No excavation efforts have been started there."

Tyler tapped his fingers on his knee, feeling the hairs on his arm stand on end. "Are you sure? I thought for certain progress would have reached that level by now."

"You are correct. Level Hazos has been excavated, but not in sublevel 6. There are 2 sublevels currently engaged. Those sublevels need not concern you. They are assigned to Psorn-Zan's supervision. You are under Pophtne-Zan."

"I'm sorry for wasting your time," Tyler replied, trying to stay focused on Marezan's words. Already his mind was at the starting blocks to race through the possibilities of what the mystery work could be doing.

"No time is wasted when learning takes place. You were mistaken but now are more fully aware of the division of labor within Asteroid Z43-21-99."

"That is an excellent perspective," Tyler commented. His whole body was tensed, waiting for the right moment to begin his search afresh.

Several seconds elapsed and there was a slight flicker of his workstation's holographic display, indicating Marezan was no longer directly interacting with him. Immediately, Tyler resumed the open mode querying. The impossibility of it weighed heavy on him, and he couldn't shake the feeling that something very wrong was going on. And apparently Marezan, the near all-seeing AI, was clueless to it.

FIVE

1

MATTER OF CONCERN

THERE WAS no such thing as sneaking out of your bunk at night. Marezan had continuous views of just about everywhere in the mining complex. That meant Tyler telling Hearl-Zan about what he had found had to wait for morning. It wasn't worth it to risk being caught and sent to reformatory therapy.

It also wasn't as though he could just tell Hearl-Zan about it. Someone was up to something nefarious and doing an impressive job keeping it hidden. Who was to say they couldn't co-opt Marezan's observations and use them to safeguard their secrecy? Going against such an individual or group was an incredibly dangerous proposition.

This is a terrible idea.

Tyler gnawed on his lip as he waited by a lift for Hearl-Zan to walk up. He traced the lines of the smooth grey construction along the walls and floors of the asteroid which released continual levels of breathable air and partially magnetized the boots every worker wore. It was an interesting blend of incredible technology and the natural sorrel stones of the asteroid. At length, his eyes found their way to a tall Zan approaching, a scowl on his face.

"Marezan said I had to meet you to go to Level Kyawa-1-8. Scrap equipment disposal? What did you do to mess up this time?"

"The usual," Tyler replied, trying to sound casual.

From the brief side glance Hearl gave him, he understood something was off.

The lift doors opened and both stepped on. Marezan announced, "Remain stationary to prevent injury and allow for maximum transport velocity."

As soon as it began to whoosh across the vertical travel axis rail, Tyler reached over and quickly tapped into the holographic display a string of code. There was a slight jerk and then the tram moved faster but changed junctions early and dropped several stories deeper before coming to a stop. Marezan was silent as the tram opened to let them off.

The cavern was larger than Tyler expected and filled with steely gray containers, some opened and others still electronically locked. Lighting and interactive displays were set up along the far wall. A laser drill was on the near side, which only made sense for carving out the space.

There were no observation devices or sensors in the room that Tyler could spot. Meaning Marezan had no eyes or ears into the room beyond the tram they rode, and it was already a wraith to the AI.

Hearl grabbed Tyler's shoulder as he exited the tram. "What did you just do?"

"I wasn't being carried away by my imagination. Welcome to Level Hazos-6-2, which shouldn't exist."

Hearl's nose crinkled up. "Huh?"

"Those anomalies I was tracking." Tyler gestured with a sweep of his arm. "It turns out this is what it was all about.

Marezan doesn't know this place exists. That code I entered on the tram was embedded in the transactions that brought all this equipment here and personnel who shouldn't have been reassigned."

"Are all humans crazy or just you?" Hearl grumbled. "You're going to get our pay docked. Or suspended. Or us sent to reformatory therapy."

Letting out a low whistle as he examined the contents of some of the crates, Tyler replied, "Marezan is the biggest glitch ever written. It's the worst program composed by an ignorant backward species of moonbats."

Hearl craned back aghast. "What did you just say?"

Tyler shrugged. "I said enough to set Marezan off times ten. Note the complete silence?"

Scratching at the back of his head Hearl searched around them. At length he nodded. "Okay. Yeah, this is weird. So, what's going on master investigator?"

Picking up and putting down a variety of devices, Tyler replied, "I don't know yet. But I needed you to see this. Something is very wrong."

Hearl walked over and opened a new crate and whistled. "They sent enough fuel canister matrices down here to power the whole mine operation."

"Fuel?" Tyler questioned.

"Yeah. You know, to start a fusion reaction? It's how everything runs."

Tyler shook his head.

That earned an eyeroll from Hearl—Something Tyler had taught him. "Isn't your life mate a regional power grid supervisor or something?"

"Director for the Hanite City Sector's Energy Consortium," Tyler corrected under his breath. He was looking at a variety of parts and had a strange sense of familiarity with them. The connections were frustratingly close. Like the thoughts were on opposite sides of window. So close, but blocked from linking.

"Whoever ordered all of this has a strange sense of utility. This is a daekun switch. They don't use these on anything anymore."

Hearl handed the small metal box to Tyler. Examining it for a moment, he asked, "So what is a switch like this used for?

"Setting off explosive charges. But we use laser drills, so these are pretty pointless, except to make a big boom."

All at once it hit Tyler what this was. He put the switch down and backed away a few steps like the thing was a snake ready to strike.

Though he wasn't into it much, he remembered his friend Carter was very knowledgeable about bombs and munitions. He talked for over an hour once about nuclear weapons. In fact, he'd brought it up on the drive to Lake Tahoe on the day the Event landed Tyler here .

Though no one else was listening, Tyler barely whispered the words back. "They're building bombs."

"Bombs?" Hearl waved his big hand dismissively. "They didn't even use bombs for mining back in my great-grandparents' lifetimes. What makes you think this is to make explosives?"

"Because these are essentially the parts you would use to make a nuclear bomb back on Earth."

Snorting Hearl retorted, "My Mosha-Zan is barely five orbits old, and she could build a more sophisticated device."

Hearl caught Tyler glowering at him and amended, "With the help of Irizan, of course."

"Yeah, well neither Irizan nor Marezan are aware of this," Tyler retorted and tossed the switch back at Hearl.

With impressive reflexes, Hearl caught the part. Bouncing

it between hands, he asked rather casually, "Fine. Then what's the purpose of bombs like this?"

Tyler sat down on a crate and rested his chin on his fist. "That's a good question," he muttered.

"Mhm," Hearl replied. "Don't overthink this. We have three more rotations on this launch. Just let it go."

"And if I don't?" Tyler inquired, looking up at Hearl.

The tall Zan shrugged, another gesture he had learned from Tyler. "Still keep cool till we end the launch. Then you can ask Kayli-Zan about it."

Brows furrowed in confusion Tyler stared at Hearl like he was speaking English all of a sudden. "Huh? Why would I do that?"

"Well, besides her being your life mate and concerned about you, these crates have markings from Hanite City's Energy Consortium. They must be the ones providing the fuel cells and switches."

Hearl zipped the switch back at Tyler. He caught it, but just barely and his fingers stung from the impact. "Right," he said nodding, but his thoughts were already millions of miles away.

What is Kayli up to?

SIX

1

HAUNTED

WITH A SLIGHT JERK, the lift slowed to a stop and returned Tyler and Hearl to their floor. Only half conscious of it, Tyler disabled the override code he'd used. They parted ways for their respective workstations.

Once at his, Tyler jumped as his console flashed blank. Marezan's voice rebuked, "Your productivity has slipped Tyler-Zan. I am adding one standard Zan hour to your remaining work shifts."

"Of course. Thank you, Marezan."

"Genuine gratitude and relief noted. You are welcome. Do you require any assistance?"

"Can you run a simulation of the impact of a 0.5 million terajoules nuclear fission device on the asteroid's integrity if set off at these coordinates?" Tyler located the points and said, "Level Hazos-6-2?"

"Certainly, but why do you require such an analysis?"

"I'm just concerned is all. You know what could happen if someone mistakenly set something like that off."

"Such devices are no longer manufactured by Zan. It has been four hundred orbits since one was utilized."

"Yes, but someone could accidentally create one, couldn't they?"

"The probability of this is low."

"Please, Marezan? Tell me about the scenario," Tyler pressed, trying hard not to tip off the AI by seeming too insistent. He didn't need to spill everything to it, yet.

"The damage to a celestial body the size of Asteroid Z43-21-99 would be catastrophic, and deflect its orbit an amount within compensatory ranges, but create a shower of meteors that could strike Irizan. Any personnel within all substrates of Levels Gera, Hazos, and Inzaet would be instantly killed, and life support systems across the asteroid would be comprised beyond restoration resulting in death of all Zan present within minutes."

"That's terrible," Tyler murmured, his heart rate picking up again.

"Indeed. But you need not worry. Such an event is impossible. As discussed yesterday, Level Hazos-6-2 has not been excavated yet and is not scheduled for any activity during extractions from this asteroid."

Tyler's stomach roiled. Now that was the impossible scenario. He knew what he had seen.

"Measurements of your vitals indicate you are in need of palliative care. Please travel to the medical bay. Instructions will be sent ahead."

His first impulse was to argue, but Tyler managed to keep himself together. "Right. Thank you, Marezan."

"You are welcome, Tyler-Zan."

Out in the main corridor of the level, Tyler felt oddly exposed. He had to be more careful. Getting sent to the med bay with unexplained anxiety and inquiries into non-existent levels was a good way to get caught. Though violence wasn't something the Zan believed in, they were capable of it. And if some of them were plotting to blow up the asteroid and smart enough to evade Marezan, there was no telling what they were intending to accomplish. Nor what lengths they would go to realize their goals.

With a faint whir, the light blue door to the medical bay slid open as Tyler approached. Across the low-lit room stretched twenty cylinders that were effectively hospital beds. Each was under a bright light focused on that particular spot. Robotic assistive devices were in each capsule for taking vitals, administering treatments, and even performing surgeries as needed. The medical bays for each level could effectively manage and treat everything from hiccups to life-threatening trauma.

Early in his stay on Irizan, he had needed many visits to such sites for doses of special serums to help him acclimate to the particles emitted by the Zan system's primary star. It had also served as an opportunity for them to sample and map his genetic makeup. The Zan scientists had been near giddy with such a rich vein of utterly novel information to process and analyze. By now, Tyler had no doubt they, with Irizan's help, understood more about human anatomy than was known on Earth.

An older attending physician noticed his arrival, and with a sneer, nodded to a nurse. The nurse, a thick built Zan male around forty revolutions in age, walked over and addressed him. "Ah, Tyler-Zan. Marezan detected levels of acute stress in you without known etiology. Your mineral study this morning appears fine, though it was noted your sleep was irregular and fitful." He glanced up under his bushy brows and said, "At least the note says for your species it was abnormal." There wasn't any condescension or congeniality in the assessment. This Zan was probably in that group with mixed feelings toward Tyler and, well, his existence.

"Records from reclamation services indicate you did not consume your waking nor afternoon meals. I will need to check your glucose levels for a deficit. Please present your palm."

Tyler complied and the Zan gripped his hand to apply the sensor. Much like Hearl-Zan, this one did not convey any additional emotive charge from their skin contact. Perhaps it was something reserved for close acquaintances or simply discomfort at interacting with his alien tissues. Whatever the case, the nurse strode away and minutes later returned with a nutritional supplement drink and instructed Tyler in stress management and proper eating habits, then released him. It was, on the whole, not the worst thing he could've endured.

Once he was back out in the corridors of the asteroid, the mood relaxing compounds released into the medical bay air dissipated, and he remembered his worry.

No, keep calm. You have to hold it together or Marezan will just send you back.

Willing his heart to slow, and wrestling his wild thoughts to a still, Tyler took a swig of the drink he'd been given. Then he took several breaths and walked back to his work site.

Three rotations till I go back to Irizan. Just three rotations.

There was no sneaking off before then and no shirking his duties locked up in his room. He had to be on stage every day giving the performance of his life. Anyone who noticed him would have to believe he was totally fine. Or at least normal. For a human. As far as they knew.

Why couldn't I have been a theater major instead of computer science?

Worst, he normally avoided everyone, even Hearl, ninety-nine percent of the time. That meant he wouldn't have anybody to confide in or lean on for support. The sensation of being lost at sea and utterly without hope he'd had during his first year when it hit him that he couldn't get home pressed down on him as if he was Atlas holding the weight of the Earth.

"Your heart rate is stable but your demeanor continues to reflect distress," Marezan chimed of a sudden, startling Tyler. He was alone in the corridor in front of his workstation.

Scrambling for anything he grabbed hold of, "I miss Earth."

The door to his station slid open and on the display screen instead of readouts for equipment was a display of Earth. From how long ago was difficult to say. Some of it was simulation based on Tyler's sketches and descriptions for the Zan astrophysicists. With it they had discovered Earth's location and were able to tell a number of things about it from their advanced techniques. Ultimately, this wasn't much more than a computer-generated imagery stand-in. Even so Marezan's attempt was something. "Thank you, Marezan. That helps."

"You are welcome, Tyler-Zan. If you provide sufficient data on your world's music and cultures, more comprehensive sensory treatments could be applied."

Tyler just managed to repress a sigh. This always happened if he showed any homesickness. The answer was always the same. "You know I'm not a musician, Marezan. I would not do it justice."

"Justice is in upholding the well-being of each Zan corporately and individually such as can be balanced between the two."

Thanks for reminding me of your Core Directive No. 5.

Truth be told, Tyler probably could give enough for Marezan to simulate some songs and even provide interactive simulations of people and places on Earth. But it was all fake. Ghosts from things long past.

He couldn't live always grieving his home. Nor could he forget what he'd lost when these absurd AI programs wouldn't leave him alone. Never mind making the best of it—they had to make it impossible to even exist.

"Your vital signs and body language indicate you are angry," Marezan observed, a fatherly reproving tone employed.

Gritting his teeth, Tyler opted to be honest. "Yes. I would like to just focus on my work."

"This does not address your underlying emotional stressor. It will not result in sustained mental wellness."

Now Tyler did sigh. "Please, Marezan. My work?"

There was a long pause. "Incident passed to Irizan and logged for subsequent follow up with mental health physician two rotations after arrival on Irizan. You may return to your assigned duties."

The holographic displays returned to normal, and Tyler tried to focus on doing his work. Having a psych eval wasn't going to make him reporting what he'd found easier. They might not listen to him at all. It occurred to him that he had taken for granted he would report it. He had no obligation to these Zan who poked and prodded and preened and plied him with images of home and false hopes of fitting in.

For some reason Kayli-Zan's face from the morning of his last launch came to him. The sincerity in her eyes and the hopelessness. She at least was trying. The same Kayli-Zan who might be trying to destroy Asteroid Z43-21-99, and with it an untold number of Zan.

Those two pieces of Kayli didn't fit together any better than did his pretending he could be so cold as to just let others die. Perhaps everything of his old life was dead and gone and only a specter haunting him, but he did still have the kernel of himself left. And that was worth protecting.

SEVEN

1

EXPECTED

THREE DAYS PASSED like three hundred, but Tyler was never so thankful to board the shuttle back to Irizan. Keeping a steady heartrate when he expected to be discovered any moment was the most difficult thing Tyler had ever done. Whether he was discovered by Marezan, Irizan, or those intelligent enough to create means of exploiting blind spots in Marezan, the end would be bad. Until now, he had not felt pressure to succeed, but lives were literally at risk.

Disembarking, he had made it about ten meters down the street toward a public shuttle when he was jerked to a stop by a strong hand holding him back. "Where are you going, friend?" Hearl asked.

This time Hearl did send a charge that carried with it concern and a high dose of annoyance.

Tyler turned and scowled up at him. The primary star's rays were in his eyes from this angle, so it helped him keep from having to put on a pleasant face. "I'm going to see my life mate," he replied, his tone as congenial as if it was a commonplace thing for him.

"Are you sure you want to surprise her at work?"

The way Hearl had emphasized the last made it clear what he was meaning. Surprise her with accusations and be wrong, it could damage both of their reputations. Be right, and he wasn't likely to leave the office alive. Tyler gnawed on his lower lip for a second and answered, "I don't think I can wait to see her. Too excited."

Hearl nodded and turned to leave. Hesitating as though he realized that was an odd way to leave things outside their conversation's true meaning, he added, "Give her my best."

"Of course. Be well, Hearl-Zan," Tyler replied and hurried down the street to where the public shuttle would pick him up. It wasn't until he was onboard that the hovering vehicle arced into the air and zipped past the soaring buildings and mid-air skyways of Hanite City. The off-white spires intermingled with verdant forests, some suspended along skywalks between buildings looming over him.

They were fascinating feats. Some forests were suspended hundreds of feet in the air and from a distance looked like narrow beams of blue and green. In truth, they were bigger and more immersive than Central Park on Earth. The Zan created vertical nature spaces, and, through reflection off the windows of their spires and unbelievable urban planning, ensured both the ground-level wooded spaces and those above each received the solar rays, rainfall, and nutrients needed to thrive. With so much of the planet settled and urbanized, these planned, nature lands hosted the biomes of the respective city planetwide and were an integral component of Irizan's holistic wellness approach for the Zan. The attention given to the ground level's nature spaces also made them impeccably lit and tended for the urban development surrounding it, such that the Zan of the lower levels in cities didn't appear cast into an increasingly forgotten and seedy underbelly. They were of equal status and vibrance to those above.

Tyler had always wanted to inquire how this harmony of nature and civilization happened, but he wasn't sure he wanted the answer. Because if it was Irizan's designs, then that meant all of the good was tied up in something he could not embrace. Resignation of will from sapient peoples to a sentient machine.

Tyler shuddered a little as the shuttle approached the energy consortium facility. The consortium was in the heart of the city, an enormous focal point that loomed over all other structures.

The enormous transparent front building of the energy consortium rose in front of his shuttle portal. The huge crystalline center tower glowed with a bluish light, which cast shadows of special Zan script onto parts of the structure and wrapped around it like an angular mantle. The words were simple, "The future is formed from the energy and efforts of all that is past."

It occurred to Tyler as he began mounting the semi-circular stairs up to the building's entrance that this wasn't a well-formed plan. He was going unarmed and uninformed into a potential confrontation

This is Kayli-Zan we're talking about.

Part of him couldn't attach something so sinister and surreptitious to her. Though he was always at arm's length from her, she had never once shown the kind of malevolence a plot like this required.

Tyler hesitated halfway up the stairs.

I'm being silly. Those crates were probably for something else.

He turned and went down several stairs before stopping again. Part of him insisted if he took one more step away from confronting Kayli-Zan about this, that would be the end. He would really have finally drowned. Every vestige of who he had been when he arrived, who he wanted to be, gone.

Swallowing hard and glancing up at the sky, he understood. There was no escaping this. He had to do it. Come what may, he needed to follow through on this as much as he needed the air he was breathing.

Tyler jogged up the stairs and entered as the doors to the Energy Consortium's main entry slid open. Immediately he was intercepted by two security personnel. Both Zan towered over him and flanked him, though without actually grabbing him.

"Tyler-Zan, Irizan has informed us you intend to meet with a Zan of social status more than four degrees of separation from your own. This is not permissible."

Tyler ground his teeth. The soft caste system of the Zan was usually more a generalized annoyance than an acute hindrance. "I'm sure Irizan also informed you that my intention is to see my life mate? Social degrees of separation do not apply to such a meeting."

As he tried to walk on, one of the guards tossed a tiny device onto his chest. A jolt ran through Tyler as the device emitted a current that paralyzed the skeletal muscles of his arms and legs. This was the more extreme form of restraint available to the Zan. Usually, they would simply attach an electric restraint band on his arm. Akin to the ankle monitors placed on earth convicts, it would give him an uncomfortable shock if he attempted to enter areas designated off limits, which he guessed would be most of the city for him. That they opted for a more potent deterrent meant they were deadly serious about him not going a step farther.

"That exception is superseded," one of the two other Zan explained coolly. Director Kayli-Zan is in a meeting with a Degree One Zan."

This brought Tyler to a halt. Degree One Zan were the most elite and socially accomplished on the planet. Whether that was something comparable to Earth like political leaders and industry titans to the very best waste repurposing officers. Notably, miners such as Tyler, could not become Degree One, no matter how effective they were at their job. Even so, Tyler deduced immediately who was seeing Kayli-Zan. "Her father is here."

The two security personnel cast wary glances at one another. Lines of annoyance bunched on their brows. Tyler had guessed everything up to this point, in spite of their attempts at secrecy. It was predictable. Most Zan expected that a Degree Twenty-Five alien such as himself would be oblivious or incompetent. Normally, Tyler relished their vexation. Right now, it was just another delay.

"Actually, I have concluded my meeting," a deep voice announced from across the wide entry space.

Tyler flinched reflexively. Kayli-Zan's father, Qirep-Zan, was striding up to him. Whatever vague notions he might have had about a future father-in-law on Earth, they would never have converged to something so bleak as Qirep-Zan. Superior, successful, physically imposing, and beguiling. Qirep had over the years found myriads of ways to torment Tyler for being selected as his daughter's mate. Perhaps for simply existing at all. Kayli did not know, but there was a proceeding instigated by him early on to have Tyler terminated. Something which had not been done on Irizan for centuries.

"Venerable one," Tyler responded with what he believed were the best imitations of sincere and societally dictated welcome for such a person. "You are looking well and bring joy in your wellness."

Qirep was near enough that Tyler could see him smile. The smooth lime green of his skin was broken by the laser precise cut of his black circle beard and, in spite of his age, he bore almost no wrinkles or age marks. In general, there was scarce even a twitch of his face at Tyler performing the obligatory verbal obeisance.

Odd.

"Your own wellness, beloved offspring is my joy," he replied with a gracious tone, highlighting his required reciprocal response.

Very odd.

Formalities concluded, Qirep gave a dismissive gesture to the security guards, who nodded without word and disabled Tyler's restraint before bustling off to another part of the room. "You must be here to congratulate Kayli-Zan on overcoming adversity to achieve her new position," Qirep surmised.

"Yes," Tyler replied, doing his best not to begrudge him the subtle dig. "Much as you are, venerable one."

"Why did you not express yourself sooner? She has been in the directorship for more than a month," Qirep pressed.

Why didn't you?

Rather than speak his mind foolishly, Tyler tried to be diplomatic. "My launch for duty on Asteroid Z43-21-99 kept me away. I just arrived on Irizan once more and have immediately come to do so."

His demeanor stolid as granite, Qirep replied, "Dutiful of you. Perhaps you are becoming Zan after all." Qirep paused. "And a Zan knows his place. Including when to stop looking beyond his occupational assignments."

Tyler tried to keep the surprise off his face but knew he didn't completely succeed.

Does he know I've been accessing Marezan's source code?

Realizing he was in danger of reprimand from Irizan for social rudeness, Tyler replied, "I will bear your wisdom in mind."

The stony impassivity of Qirep's face softened by a fraction into his look of superiority. "Do keep it, and be sure to lavish my daughter with praise. She—"

"Has overcome great adversity," Tyler completed for him. To complete his humiliating charade of veneration, Tyler knotted his fingers and shook them in Qirep's direction in the Zan formal farewell gesture.

For the briefest moment, Tyler thought he glimpsed satisfaction flicker over Qirep's face before it became unreadable stone again. "Indeed." He then walked past with a pair of security Zan following him that Tyler had failed to notice. It was possible they had invisibility technology of some kind, but given his current state, it was more likely Tyler just needed to pull it together.

After Qirep-Zan departed, the security from earlier escorted Tyler to a lift that took him to Kayli-Zan's office level. Approaching the door, Irizan announced for him, "Kayli-Zan, your expected visitor has arrived."

EIGHT

THE BINDING TIE

IT STRUCK Tyler that he hadn't really thought this through to any degree. What would he say? Furthermore, since he was expected, what kind of covering up could she have done in advance?

The doors slid open. Kayli-Zan wore an ankle length black dress and sat on the front edge of her wide smoothly curving desk that glowed light blue from the variety of displays of communications and performance indicators displayed. The faint light highlighted a mostly inquisitive expression, and her hands were folded in her lap.

She's so calm.

"I thought Irizan was mistaken for the first time, when I was alerted about your coming," Kayli commented. Her tone and expression difficult to read.

Once more Tyler wrestled with the absurdity of believing her guilty.

"I try to not interfere with your work," he replied with a dose of honesty. "You have enough to deal with in the social sphere." He left off "from me," because he wanted to offer, not receive, sympathy.

Kayli nodded her lips pursed. "May I ask what changed that for you?"

Again, the innocent inflection to her words disarmed him. She had every right to be icy toward him, he had set the temperature of their relationship firmly in the polar regions. But she wasn't taking advantage of it. There was no way she was caught up in something so fraught. He must have misunderstood something. It wouldn't be the first time.

"I guess I just needed to see you," he replied. "I'll go now."

There was a furrow in Kayli's brow as she replied, "Okay." A second later she shook her head. "Actually, no. It isn't okay. We aren't close, perhaps not even friends, but I've been around you enough to know when something is wrong. I would have been home this evening as normal. You've never before needed to see me so badly that it could not wait."

As she spoke some heat entered her voice. Kayli was standing now. "What is going on?"

"Kayli-Zan, I ..." he began and faltered. How was he supposed to delicately tell her he thought she was plotting mass murder? And to what end? He was an idiot.

"Shall I allow you a privacy interval?" Irizan spoke up.

Kayli's cheeks flushed. "No, I do not think that will be—"

"Privacy interval of 30 minutes initiated," Irizan announced.

Though there was no visual change, Tyler peered around for them anyway. "Privacy interval?" he asked at length.

Kayli scowled and crossed her arms at the elbows. "It's meant to offer couples time without observation from Irizan to be ... um ... intimate."

Had Kayli not winced as she said it, Tyler might have burst out laughing with incredulity. Instead, he just said, "Oh. I never said anything that should have … I mean that's definitely not why I'm …" He sighed.

Kayli looked like she wanted to curl up in a corner and ball.

Tapping his foot anxiously as the minutes of silence stretched on, Tyler at last admitted, "I discovered something while on launch that I wanted to talk to you about. Something that didn't make sense."

Kayli-Zan's eyes widened. "The other miners weren't cruel again, were they?"

"No, not cruel," he answered and then hesitated. There was no point in continuing when this all added up to foolishness. Another couple minutes of silence exacted a toll on Kayli-Zan's momentary brightening. Why did it matter to her?

Because she's your wife.

The thought caught Tyler off guard. He had never really thought of Kayli-Zan that way. After all they had been forced together by an AI. By all accounts he was an anchor weighing her down. He had always assumed she was cordial and compassionate. But was it that she did take their pairing genuinely and what he perceived as pitying kindness was in fact her overtures at genuine love and warmth?

If it was, then he owed her honesty, messy as the truth might be. "I noticed some weird things," he continued. "There were shipments arriving at odd intervals. Then my workstation was updated, but the technician forgot to close the interface to Marezan, and I was able to see into some of its source code."

He could see the last bit had sparked something akin to wonder in her eyes. But he pressed on, "I figured some things out and began looking into the shipments."

"And?" She encouraged when he stopped to sort out the most tactful way of saying the next bit.

"I discovered they were being sent to a sublevel of Asteroid Z43-21-99 that Marezan doesn't know exists. The shipments came from the Energy Consortium. Fuel for reactors among other things."

"That's odd, the mines shouldn't need additional fuel. Which sector sent them? Perhaps I can look into what they were for."

"They were from this sector," he said quietly.

"Oh!"

Now it was Kayli-Zan who became silent in her thoughtfulness. After a few moments she called out, "Irizan?"

"Yes, Kayli-Zan? You still have three minutes of privacy remaining."

"Could you please extend it by another thirty?"

There was a pause. "The maximum extension I may allot under the current circumstances is fifteen minutes."

"We'll take it," Tyler called out trying to sound enthusiastic.

Irizan seemed to ignore him. "Is this acceptable?"

"Yes," Kayli-Zan replied. "Please."

"Privacy mode extended," Irizan confirmed.

Kayli-Zan waited a few moments before commenting, "Only one who addresses Irizan directly in privacy mode is acknowledged for communication. It's one of its rules."

"Hm, sort of like in 'open mode,'" he commented, mostly to himself.

She motioned for him to come around to the backside of her desk. Before he could comply, she began touching a number of holographic display points.

As he strode up beside her, she commented, "I did notice some oddities in the last reports from my predecessor. They weren't shipped to the asteroids though. They went to the orbital construction yards. At the time I didn't think much of it ..."

Looking down at her, the blue light played off the lines of consternation on her face. "What is it, what's wrong?"

"I found the shipments you were talking about. Crude fuel cells that should have been disposed of but were sent to Asteroid Z43-21-99. There's no record of acceptance or the shuttle's return. It's almost as if Marezan didn't acknowledge receiving them."

"Wait, Marezan has to let Irizan know a shipment is received?"

"Yes, or that one is incoming. Anything extraorbital is Marezan's domain. Orbital resources are shared to a degree."

Tyler ran a hand through his hair. "So, hypothetically, you could send something to Marezan and in the hand off from orbital to space, it could get lost?"

Kayli-Zan shrugged. "If I wasn't looking at exactly that, I would say no."

Tyler frowned. This was bad. Suddenly all of his concerns from before reawakened and doubled in intensity. Could it be a coincidence that the parts needed for bombs were unloaded in an unregistered sublevel of the asteroid taking advantage of a blind spot in Irizan and Marezan's handoff?

"Are you okay?" Kayli-Zan asked. Her hand had drifted closer, betraying her desire to reach out and take his hand.

He cleared his throat. "I think someone is building bombs on Asteroid Z43-21-99."

Kayli-Zan leaned back and regarded him for a moment. Conflict overtook the concern in her expression. Not that he blamed her. In an enormously peaceful society like Irizan's, it had to sound insane.

Swallowing uncomfortably, he reached out slowly and laid his hand on hers. He gave it a squeeze. "I know I haven't given you many reasons to think well of me, but I really believe something awful could be happening."

Kayli glanced down at his hand on hers and gnawed at her lip. No emotive current flowed from her. After a few seconds she withdrew her hand and turned away. Tyler felt an unexpected wrenching within. "Kayli-Zan, I—"

She spoke up, "I'm checking to see who sent the shipments." Glancing up from her typing, eyes glassy, she added, "We are life mates. Your worries are my own."

Before he realized what he was doing fully, he bent down and kissed her on the lips. Not a quick peck, but a real one. The kind he had always imagined giving a future wife.

There was a sudden jolt midway into it, as if he jostled her careful control and he experienced what he imagined was joy.

When they parted, Kayli-Zan drew in a shaky breath and then laughed. "Unexpected, but not unwelcome."

Tyler chuckled, "Same here." Growing more serious he gave her hand a squeeze. She had stopped holding back transferring sensations and he felt a cautious hopefulness. Curiosity at what he was about to say. Before he could say what was on his heart an alarm sounded.

The doors to the room slid open and several security personnel filed in. Over them Irizan announced, "Kayli-Zan and Tyler-Zan, you have each violated Zan Sedition Laws 33257, 445876, and 1998765. Place your hands on your heads and lower yourselves to your knees. You will be taken into custody for judicial processing."

NINE

1

CORRECTIONS

TYLER WAS silent until the security personnel loaded him and Kayli-Zan into the back of a transport. This wasn't his first such experience since being on Irizan, but Kayli-Zan's face was pale, her dark lips pursed, and cheeks taut as she followed him into the back of the transport. Her eyes were so distant, he didn't know if he would be able to bring her back.

As the panel slid shut, locking them in, he took her hand. "Hey, it's going to be okay."

She barely seemed to register it. And the sensation from her was chaotic, unintelligible to him. Under her breath she mumbled, "I almost had it, I was almost able to find out who sent those shipments." As if discovering a lost item had been in her pocket all along, Kayli turned to face Tyler. "Do you think this is because of the shipments?"

Tyler let his hand drop. That was exactly what this must be. How many rules had he broken in his pursuit of whatever this was? "I'm so sorry. I've never meant to make things worse for you. I should have realized that from day one on Irizan that's what I've excelled at."

He didn't have hopes for forgiveness, so he didn't begrudge Kayli when all she had in response was distracted mutterings.

A shudder signaled to him that the transport had lifted off the ground and was shooting toward the reformatory therapy processing center. The automated piloting was seamless in its weaving into the steady traffic far above the ground.

With a huff he said, "I'm an idiot. Tilting after windmills."

"I don't understand what that means," Kayli answered, her voice choked. She fussed a bit with her hair, twisting it in anxious curls around her fingers and finally said, "You aren't an idiot. Whatever is happening, it's like nothing I've ever seen. Someone has planned—"

"Please remain silent until the shuttle arrives at the destination," Irizan instructed. "All conversations and comments are admissible in the judicial process and are likely to exacerbate the penalties assessed."

Kayli-Zan put her head between her knees, and Tyler could see little tremors run through her. She had never been in any substantive "trouble" before. Something about her vulnerability, her hurt snapped something long held back in him. He scooted over to her side and put his arms around her. "I'm going to make this right," he whispered to her.

"Please remain silent—"

"I don't care," he bellowed raising to his feet. "Whatever the charges are, Kayli-Zan is innocent. Any laws that were broken—"

A piercing squeal cut through the space and assaulted his ears. "Remain silent," Irizan instructed.

Kayli grabbed his arm and with reddened eyes shot him a look of pleading. It was reinforced by the sensations pulsing into his arm. Fear, not just for her, but for him.

Jaw clenched, he nodded and settled down beside her. After a minute she leaned against him, the tremors from sobs giving him gentle shakes every so often. Again, her emotions were too chaotic to sort out from the pulses traveling to him via their contact.

Tyler could understand her turmoil. Irizan had never purposefully hurt Tyler before. He didn't even know it was allowed to use something like a sonic burst to enforce compliance. These charges must be serious. Which meant whatever he'd uncovered may have been pinned on him, and by association, Kayli.

Looking up, he offered a soundless prayer, his first of that kind in a long time. Strength for himself and rescue for Kayli-Zan.

TEN

1

JUDGEMENT RENDERED

ALMOST THIRTY MINUTES passed by Tyler's reckoning before the transport came to a stop. The doors did not slide open, and after several minutes longer, Kayli mouthed, "Is this normal?"

Tyler shook his head. The other occasions his processing had been swift and efficacious. This was peculiar. Perhaps greater crimes required something additional. He just hoped a thorough inquiry would reveal their innocence. Though Irizan did not second guess itself that he was aware of.

"Kayli-Zan please exit the transport. You are free to return to your home as travel conditions permit."

The relief on her face made Tyler smile. His prayer had been answered. And to a degree he could look past his own impending suffering to relish that fact.

Relief faded to confusion and then concern. "Irizan, what about Tyler-Zan? Is he free as well?"

"No."

The brevity of the answer was punctuated by an

undercurrent of criticality. He wasn't just about to be punished —this would be unambiguously just in Irizan's estimation.

Kayli looked towards where the sound of Irizan's proclamation issued. "But what has he done?"

"Sedition Laws 33257, 445876, and 1998765 have been violated," was all Irizan offered in response.

"Kayli-Zan, it's okay," Tyler tried to persuade her. "You should go ahead."

Waving a hand to indicate he should stop, she asked, "What are the punishments for the alleged crimes?"

"Immediate execution by a duly appointed Zan authority."

"What? No, no, no!" Kayli protested and launched into a series of arguments and questions that Tyler barely heard. He was too stunned to focus in on them. He had never seen capital punishment trials among the Zan. Qirep-Zan's inquest to have him terminated had been mocked out of consideration by Irizan and judicial Zan officials alike. Whatever the sedition laws consisted of, it had to be hideously awful.

He was minutes away from death now. Death, on a strange planet, surrounded by beings who hated him. Apart from Kayli-Zan, at least. It was a pity he took so long to recognize the genuine affection she carried for him. Even more so that he had, until now, failed to show any reciprocal signs of it for her.

A thought occurred to him. Could the Zan go to Heaven? Were they outside redemptive grace? Was that why Tyler was pulled here, because he would no longer be counted as human and therefore be equally cut off from eternal hope he'd so long, if quietly, carried?

He heard Kayli-Zan growl in frustration and watched her tug at her hair as the sonic waves forcing them quiet were leveled against them again. The burst was shorter at least, probably aimed at curtailing Kayli's arguments.

"This makes no sense," she insisted to Tyler. "Irizan and Marezan are forbidden from killing a Zan."

Irizan interjected, "Tyler-Zan is not a Zan biologically. Therefore, his punishments do not conform to statutory limits applied to Zan."

The irony that Irizan had still referred to him as Tyler-Zan even as it insisted he was not Zan almost made him laugh. It was Kayli-Zan's crestfallen expression that grounded him too firmly in the moment for madness to take hold of him.

She glanced at him, her deep blue eyes like the sky at the close of a day, and he saw the close of his life in them. "It's okay," he insisted, surprised he was still able to say it without having to struggle. It was purely for her benefit. At another level he would happily have done everything possible to escape right now if he were alone, but he wasn't. Kayli was still in stormy seas, and her rescue not set until she left this place. Tyler couldn't be brave for himself, but for her, he would. After all this time, he owed her that much.

"He is Zan in all the ways that matter," Kayli challenged, her voice ragged. "And Tyler-Zan is my life mate."

"That fact does not mitigate the judgement rendered against Tyler-Zan."

Kayli stared at him for several seconds, gnawing at her lip. Her expression was conflicted, but what she was thinking, what the look meant was impossible to discern. Closing her eyes, she said in a rush, "Very well. If he must die, then so must I. A Zan rises and falls by her life mate's side."

"Kayli," he said, sudden fear rising in him. She had pierced the veil of his peaceful surrender with the threat of harm to herself. "No. I'm not from your world, don't throw your life away. Please, this is your chance at a fresh start. The life you were born to enjoy."

There was an intensity in the gaze she leveled at him. Not

anger, but determination, a fury that banished any tears that he could tell would freely come if allowed. "I know you did not choose me, Tyler. You did not choose any of this. But I did.

"You keep me at a distance, but I have seen enough to know you have a compassionate heart. It is buried under layers of bitterness and sorrow, but there are glimmers of someone I have come to care about deeply.

"'Life mate is more than a trite title, and the experience beyond a random pairing. It is a lifelong discovery of love's expression and quality.'"

"You are quoting an ancient treatise on the nature of love," Irizan observed. "Is it your choice to suffer the same punishment as your life mate with consideration to his current sentencing?"

"It is, I only ask that the nature of our crimes be explained before the sentence is rendered. Tyler-Zan is noble. I cannot imagine him committing a crime befitting this punishment."

"Negotiations are not part of the sentencing process. Verdicts are delivered based on multivariate analyses of tangible evidence. Do you waive your pardon and commit to sharing Tyler-Zan's punishment?"

"Kayli," Tyler protested.

She waved him off. "I do."

The door out of the transport slid open. "Please disembark in preparation for application of penal measures in accordance with the judicial findings."

Kayli took Tyler's hand. There was fear, but over it rode something fierce and vibrant that he understood to be love. As if he needed the sensations to understand now the depth of her feeling and commitment to him.

He thought about shaking loose her hold but was too numb for that. As much as to himself as Kayli-Zan he muttered, "I'm not worth this sacrifice. I was barely polite to you before. You deserve more. Your career, a family, and love. All I did was keep you from all of them."

"Love does not require reciprocation to endure," she replied. "I have known love, because I loved you. There are things I lost, but you lost them first. We are mated, you cannot have a loss that I do not feel. So, I have grieved for the other things already."

"I ... you ..." Tyler rubbed his face with his free hand. He contemplated arguing, fighting to make her see reason. In every imagined scenario he failed, and no words could be coerced into coming.

Finally, he gave her hand a squeeze. "I think if I had one more day to live, I would spend it showing you the love I should have all along."

"You must proceed off the transport immediately," Irizan insisted.

Wrapping his arm around Kayli-Zan, Tyler sucked in a pained breath, thinking about death and life ever after. He did not know what his faith he'd carried with him meant for a Zan, their pace was too quick, the doorway too near. They were outside before he'd resolved to halt to explain it all to Kayli-Zan.

They both came into a chamber with a round, sloped dais. Standing on it, a light shone down on them. Scanning them by appearance. Before he could say another word, gas filled the chamber and he knew in a wholly abstract way he was dropping to the floor, the world swallowed by darkness. The last thing he carried with him was emotive sensation of Kayli-Zan's love abruptly ending.

ELEVEN

11

AT THE CORE

"UGH," Tyler rubbed at his head and raised up. Through bleary eyes he recognized a modest lab was set up around him. Some robotic drone assistants tethered to Irizan were at work.

His eyes went wide when he spotted Kayli-Zan laying nearby. As feeling and cognition improved, he scooted himself to Kayli and checked her pulse. She was alive!

But why are we still alive?

"You have regained consciousness thirty-five seconds earlier than calculated," Irizan noted. "Kayli-Zan will awaken in thirty-two more seconds."

"What?" Tyler asked, the throbbing in his head making Irizan's words doubly difficult to parse.

"Human anatomy still presents some unknown variables. Your wellness has suffered as a result, for that the Zan will compensate you," Irizan stated.

"Compensate me? Will that be after you kill me or before?" Tyler snapped back.

"Irritability is not an intended effect of the delusion." Irizan paused. "Greetings, Kayli-Zan. You have awoken at the precise instant calculated."

"What happened?" she said and then with a shake of her head, her eyes brightened, as they found a focus that eluded Tyler. She spun to face him, relief displacing the concern that had jolted through her. "You're all right!"

"Mostly," he replied, wincing. The headache and fuzziness were fading but still potent enough to make it hard to concentrate on smiling back at Kayli.

"Tyler-Zan appears to not be responding to the sedative as calculated. However, indirect biological indicators suggest he will be back to normal consciousness in forty to one hundred twenty seconds from now. Please reserve questions till that time."

Kayli-Zan pursed her lips like she wanted to say something and started to but ended up respecting the injunction to keep silent. She passed the time rubbing Tyler's back gently and looking at him with an expression that mirrored the currents of hope and barely suppressed indignation she sent to him.

As his head cleared, both fascinated Tyler. How is that he had so woefully misunderstood her feelings toward him? Or was he misunderstanding now? A pang of concern followed that line of thought ,which in itself was startling.

"Markers of wellness indicate you are restored to average cognitive function for your respective species," Irizan announced. "Assessment of your facial expressions and body language indicate you have questions."

"A few," Tyler retorted.

"Sarcasm and double-meaning in discourse do not serve social wellness," Irizan reproved.

"These are unusual circumstances," Kayli pointed out, somehow finding levelheadedness in the midst of this. Tyler admired her calm, her graciousness. Envied it.

Colorations in the lighting shifted to softer tones, the air became slightly cooler with the sound of ventilation suddenly noticeable. "Adjusting environmental factors to accommodate comfort and tranquility."

From the pulsation's sent to him, Tyler doubted Kayli-Zan was any more comforted or tranquil by all this than he was. They shared a look that confirmed that just before Kayli pressed, "Why are you doing this to us, Irizan?"

"Your inquiries earlier into the order history for shipments to and from Marezan revealed anomalies. These anomalies do not have precedent within recorded Zan history. Analysis of evidence available suggests a conspiracy to commit large scale violence against Zan society."

"Why did you arrest Kayli-Zan then?" Tyler challenged. "I know I'm a mystery to you, but you've observed Kayli-Zan her entire life. You know she has a good-heart."

"Physiological assessments confirm that Kayli-Zan's cardiac wellness is above average for a Zan."

Kayli had a quizzical expression and with some shame, Tyler realized he had never used this phrase in this way. Not even for Kayli, to whom he had long known it applied.

"It's a saying from my world. It means Kayli-Zan is virtuous. Noble. Compassionate. Someone to admire."

"Making note of idiomatic phrase and indicators from tone and context to differentiate from medical assessment.

"Would a comparable idiom from the Zan be, 'Kayli-Zan is part of the whole'?"

On Earth, that phrase would probably be negatively applied, meaning you are a worthless, featureless cog. In Zan society, it meant so much more. It was representative of all they valued and aspired to. Timeliness, which meant dependability. Dedication, honor, respect for their role in the greater network of their culture, contributing to the wellness of others, and service to something greater than one's interests. All of it was wrapped up in that phrase. Even with all that meaning, it fell short of the patient, kind, enduring love she had shown him. There were no Zan phrases to cover that.

Kayli's eyes revealed that an abundance of questions lurked within her. She released her hold on him, letting the current drop between them. Probably to protect herself from showing him disappointment if he declined.

"Yes," he replied. "It is equivalent. And absolutely true of Kayli-Zan."

The question in her eyes morphed to one of restrained delight. Quietly she mouthed, "Thank you," as Irizan announced over her, "Entry for 'good heart,' 'good-hearted,' and 'has a good heart' created."

Without missing a beat, Irizan pivoted back to Tyler's question. "Subterfuge requires a sufficient level of prudence to mitigate. You and Kayli-Zan were brought to these chambers as a safety precaution. You were moments away from triggering subroutines coded to catch any investigation into the seditious activities taking place."

"You were protecting us?" Tyler surmised, feeling his nose crinkle as dubiousness overtook him.

"Correct. Qirep-Zan is in the top 0.01% of Zan in terms of intellect, drive to succeed, and resources. His critical thinking and planning scores are noteworthy. Analysis of the records available and extrapolation of missing information leads to the conclusion that Qirep-Zan has been targeted through the staging of an attack, with the intention to assign all guilt to Qirep-Zan and those close to him."

It took Tyler a few seconds for his shock to abate enough to trust his face to not show concern, given how close Kayli was to him. A quick glance at her expression was more puzzling than what Irizan was alleging. She emoted neither sadness nor anger nor incredulity. It was a mix of surprise and stoic brooding.

"There must be a mistake," Tyler replied haltingly, as much to Kayli as Irizan.

It was Kayli who spoke up first, "Why would someone do this to Father? What potential goals have you identified?"

"Kayli?" Tyler asked, forgetting in his puzzlement to append the "Zan" ending.

"End goals are not determinable with a high degree of confidence. The limited goals in the greater framework include assigning blame, utilizing the dangerous materials transferred to Asteroid Z43-21-99, and mitigating the resultant crisis to enhance general trust and reliance upon the perpetrators."

"They're building a bomb to make themselves popular?" Tyler blurted out, sure he must still be unconscious. Perhaps this whole bizarre scenario was a dream from start to finish.

"Your assessment is a simplistic summarization of the apparent aims."

"Why did you mislead us into believing Tyler, er Tyler-Zan, would die?" Kayli challenged. "Why not explain this to us plainly?

"Facial expression analysis indicates a need for calm," Irizan noted. "The primary objective of the arrest and filing of the judgement met the need of required public visibility to mislead the conspirators into believing falsely that their aims have been achieved. A secondary objective was to prompt each of you to better understand the nature of your relationship as life mates and to determine the viability of your pairing given the immediate danger faced."

Tyler peered at Kayli-Zan and was pretty sure her cheeks flushed deep violet. He gave her a crooked smile. "So, I take it we did well or you wouldn't be revealing all of this to us?"

"An astute observation, Tyler-Zan. Review of your

behaviors indicate that your bond is successful and will result in mutual wellness improvements.

"Should the current crisis be averted without casualties, the probability of meaningful spousal relationship is extremely high."

"Wow," was all Tyler said. Though he didn't say it, something was off about Irizan's confidence in their relationship. It could observe and generate extremely accurate hypotheses, but thinking back on what would have been observable from the outside, Irizan's conclusion seemed incredible to him. Knowing the thoughts and intentions of the heart, particularly those so buried he hadn't known them within himself, was beyond Irizan.

Kayli took hold of his hand, and the intensity of warmth and welcome in her indigo eyes suspended his silent inquest. She was happy, and a second later the currents of it reached him. She had known her feelings. Perhaps even confided them to Irizan. Her love was what kept the tie between them alive, and there was an undeniable stirring within him for it. He had never been in love before. Had he stumbled into it unknowingly in spite of his intended apathy?

He found himself leaning toward her. Her dark lips were parted slightly as if in search of partners beyond themselves. Every sinew suddenly became ensnared to the notion that his lips had to end that loneliness. As if paired in a musicless dance, Kayli shifted closer, facing him directly. Her other hand brushed along his chest with a tender delicacy. Tyler closed his eyes and leaned forward, the image of Kayli doing the same in mirror seared into his mind's eye.

"Pheromone levels indicate the potential for physical romantic expression between you. Lowering temperature in room by five degrees and increasing air flow. Disruption of this is essential to expedient resolution of the present crisis."

Every cell in Tyler's body raged against the pronouncement. Even if objectively it made sense. There was something truly wrong happening. He hadn't been paranoid or merely desperate.

When he looked at Kayli, he saw the briefest flicker of mischief in the way she bit at her lip. He had never seen that from her before. Quick as a blink she leaned forward and kissed him. It was maddeningly brief but shockingly satisfying.

"Unexpected but not unwelcome," he said, reiterating Kayli's choice of words from earlier.

"Preparing flight materials and arranging for transport," Irizan called out, voice steady and undeterred by the couple's rogue act.

"Flight materials?" Kayli-Zan questioned.

"Correct. You must both travel to Asteroid Z43-21-99 to prevent the impending disaster, which by estimation will begin in half a standard planetary rotation."

Which meant, if Tyler converted correctly, less than twelve hours from now, hundreds, thousands even, would die.

TWELVE

1

CHECK

"SO, this is what a launch is like for you?" Kayli-Zan asked observing the interior of the interplanetary shuttle Irizan had provided them.

Tyler's impulse was to snort and respond with a decided, "No." This shuttle had comfortable seats, artificial gravity, gyroscopic and inertial compensation taking place, and overall stability of the craft. It was perhaps the same size as the smaller shuttles that did not also carry or load cargo, but otherwise, the sleek silvery lines and contours of the ship's primary cabin and the availability of numerous displays for entertainment and requesting service made this more like a cruise ship than a freighter. "Not exactly," he managed to say.

Scowling, Kayli replied, "With how much you dread launches, this must be disgustingly lavish."

Tyler couldn't help looking surprised. As he understood it, this would be normal or perhaps even substandard levels of comfort and trappings for her, at least prior to their pairing. He tried to remember another Zan he'd met with as much empathy and awareness of others. "On the positive side, I'm usually nauseous by this point in the trip and feel totally fine right now."

She smirked at this and then her expression mellowed into a somber one. "I don't like Irizan's plan. It feels risky for us to sneak onto the asteroid without notifying Marezan. All the more since you had to exploit the back-end access to facilitate it."

Tyler grimaced. He had hoped that it had only rubbed him the wrong way. "Irizan is trustworthy though, right? It knows the lines of sight that have been exploited so far and can give us the best chance of success?"

She shrugged and peered out at the pinpoint stars stretching into multicolored lines. "You would know better than I. Maybe better than anyone."

"What do you mean?"

"There aren't many of us who know how Irizan and Marezan work, but you do." She paused and with a light laugh said, "I suppose this is the closest you've come to living the life you were meant to have on Earth."

When he arched his brows in question she clarified, "Chasing criminals who exploit others using programming."

There was an unmistakable note of wistfulness to the comment. "Yeah, I suppose you're right," he replied for want of something to say. Was she worried now that his positivity toward her was only a byproduct of his finally feeling like he was keeping above the surface, taking in much needed air? More importantly, was she right? His perceptions were so very different ever since stumbling on the enigmatic code and transactions.

He reached across and laced his fingers with hers. "I'm glad you're with me for this."

Though he'd wanted to say something so much more

profound and was almost terse, Kayli-Zan responded with a smile. A jolt of sensation that magnified it ten times followed.

The ship shuddered. There was a moment of calm, and then as if on stormy seas, the ship rocked. The groan of its hull echoed within the air-filled interior. A few seconds later, the calm returned.

"I'm beginning to see why you aren't fond of this," Kayli-Zan commented drily.

Tyler grimaced. "That was a first for me." Examining the holographic displays, he scoured for some indicator of what had just happened. Nothing stood out at first, and then he spotted it.

"No, no, no," he said hands hovering over the displays, but completely ignorant as to how to fix it.

"What's wrong?" Before he could answer she spotted it. "Wait, we've changed course. We're not headed to the asteroid."

He nodded and checked the display again. He almost missed her asking, "How did this happen?"

"I don't know," he answered, trying the system logs on the auto-pilot to find answers.

"Can you fix it?"

He shrugged, scanning through the hundreds of lines of system notes on minor corrections, steady state operations, and other standard observations for the one aberration. Just as he found it, another round of tremors rocked the vessel.

Kayli, sounding as shaken as the ship, asked, "Where are we headed now?"

Tyler shrugged. "I'm not sure, but it looks like someone hacked into the flight plan and altered our destination coordinates."

"'Hacked'?" Kayli questioned, looking like the word alone was a terror.

"Sorry. On Earth it means someone forcefully accessed the computers on this ship and used some code to change what the ship was doing."

Leaning closer to the displays he was accessing, Kayli's brow furrowed as she scrutinized it. "It looks like it's sending our path around the asteroid." She sucked in a sharp breath. "There's nothing there but interstellar space!"

Looking over the last lines of the rogue commands entered, there was specter of familiarity to it for Tyler. He tilted his head a bit as he examined it.

What is it about this?

"Wait, no. We're not going to interstellar space. Among the things I uncovered was evidence that they're building a station just outside the asteroid field. I think we're being directed to land on it."

"That means whoever is behind this knows we're coming," Kayli lamented.

"Looks like it. At least they didn't send us on course to crash into another asteroid or something. They're drawing us in."

"Can we stop them?"

As if in answer, the streaks of light resolved back to pinpoints as they came out of the special slip drive state into regular propulsion. Tinkering with the displays, Tyler got it to show what was directly in front of the ship. An enormous silver ring with mirror-like planes angled along its surfaces loomed ahead. In a way, the gleaming surfaces reminded him of the monolith that had brought him to Irizan, only in a circular form. Marring its sleek lines at the bottom was a large, duller gray, trapezoidal prism constructed with what was evocative of a long antenna jutting downward. As Tyler watched, the ring and its "stand" grew until it became obvious they were headed toward the stand.

"Tyler?" Kayli-Zan pressed.

"I'm sorry. There's nothing we can do."

A few minutes later, the ship coasted through a gigantic airlock which sealed behind them and began its landing routine. Of its own, the ramp to the ship slowly descended and the sound of footsteps from a boarding party echoed to them.

Tyler feverishly worked over the controls for the piloting cabin to see if he could lock their portion of the transport off from those boarding the ship. From his right a gruff voice intoned, "That's enough you ponzo."

Turning his head, Tyler just managed to glimpse a Zan dressed in a security uniform ripple into the visible spectrum before being thrown to the deck by the guard. A restraint band was slapped onto his arm, and from where he lay smashed to the floor, Tyler noticed that on Kayli-Zan's left another such guard appeared and more gently restrained her.

I guess they do have invisibility tech.

The realization came with some chagrin. But more quickly, genuine horror gripped him. Those Zan had been onboard with them the whole time. Which meant whoever was behind this had known Irizan was sending them. Whomever they were up against was one step ahead of not just them, but both of the Zan super AIs.

THIRTEEN

WARM WELCOME

TO TYLER'S ANNOYANCE, the device placed on him was again not the kind that simply shocked him for waywardness, but of the paralysis-inducing variety. Apparently, the device was programmable, because instead of his legs and arms being limp, the signals it blocked were for his arms and jaw. So, he was able to march mutely along with their captors.

He couldn't tell if Kayli-Zan was similarly paralyzed or if she was simply stunned into silence. Kayli had a neutral expression, what would be called a poker face on Earth. If it was from her own composure and control, he had to envy it. Were he free to express himself, anger and heated challenges were too readily available to keep him so stoic.

The guard detail led them off the ship and across a bright blue-lit floor that was glassy smooth in appearance. They passed through a maze of bland and remarkably similar slate corridors, which Tyler instinctually memorized, more from watching adventure movies than his limited cyber forensics and criminal justice education.

Right, left, straight, right, right, straight, left, straight.

A large double door automatically slid aside as they approached it, though Marezan's usual salutation on their behalf was notably absent. Before them stretched an enormous room filled with Zan at various stations monitoring displays and interacting with them. Tyler recognized one of them to be Pophtne-Zan, which should have surprised him at least somewhat.

At the center stood an imposing and lavishly attired Zan. He clutched his hands behind his back, which was to Tyler and Kayli, as he admired a visual of the asteroid field. Asteroid Z43-21-99 was highlighted in the display with statistics scrolling past on its orbital speed and some angular measurements for which Tyler couldn't guess the purposes. A timer also displayed its micro and millisecond decrements as a yellow blur of digital motion.

"I must admit, you both surprised me," the central Zan commented. He lifted a dark blue spirited drink from a small platform hovering beside him and took a sip, before releasing a contented sigh. He spun to face them, and Tyler was relieved his facial muscles were paralyzed because he would have gaped at what he saw. Qirep-Zan stood there, an imperious look on his face, highlighted by the satisfied smirk he beamed.

Tyler's eyes were able to move freely and shot to Kayli-Zan. Her face remained unaffected, but tears streamed down her cheeks leaving rich plum trails, and he could tell she was paralyzed too. If he was stunned, she was heartbroken.

Waving a hand at the guards, Qirep instructed, "Bring them to my offices and disengage their facial controls. I need to have a chat with these inquisitive *offspring*."

A FEW TAPS were delivered to the band on Tyler's arm once they were in Qirep's office. An enormous viewing screen out into the depths of space framed the center of the room. Also at the room's center was an expansive console desk of contemporary Zan design. It was framed and contrasted by a variety of artifact and art pieces along each wall. As a low degree Zan, he'd seldom had opportunity to look at what passed for high art in their culture. Particularly if it were from the long past as their accompanying designations suggested them to be.

There was, however, a collection of holographic displays that stuck out to Tyler. These depicted things more familiar to him. Scenes he had described to Irizan over the years. Places. Some of them famous, some personal. These were the sources for the simulations that both AIs had tried to use to comfort him. Those efforts were abysmal failures. Seeing them here sent a chill running down Tyler's spine.

"Well, you have finally reached the end," Qirep said once he entered from an adjoining room. He gestured to the guards to leave. Their soundless compliance kept Tyler from immediately launching an offensive of insults.

It wasn't until he heard, Kayli-Zan choking back a sob, her face tight from constrained emotion, that Tyler found his voice, however cracked it may have been. "Why?"

"Rather blunt and obtuse today, are we human? What happened to your sense of formality from our last encounter?" Qirep still had his dark drink, and he sipped it with the pleasure of a cat having caught its mouse or perhaps a child with a new toy. In either case, it further wreaked havoc with Tyler's nerves. His heartbeat quickened.

Belatedly, he realized once more Marezan, which should have chimed in and commented on his state, was silent. Meaning this place, much like the missing sector on the asteroid, was completely beyond its sight. Dread over what that meant, what all this meant, was just catching up to him. This was so much more real and terrible than he had anticipated when he'd begun his surreptitious inquiries.

While Tyler struggled to find his footing, Kayli-Zan spoke up. "Venerable one, Papa, if you will not tell Tyler-Zan, will you hide the meaning of all this from me?"

Qirep cocked his head to the side and regarded her with a more troubled gaze. "Indeed, I would not hide anything from you, child. Everything you need to know is already displayed in this room. I had hoped you could elucidate the purpose of this venture from these clues alone. If you cannot, perhaps it's more understandable why you are so easily taken with this husk of sapience you pine after."

This time Qirep took a grudging drink, as if chasing away a bad taste from his mouth. Tyler's attention focused mainly on Kayli, however, and the way her face tensed under her lavender skin. He imagined she was clenching her jaw. Whether in anger or shame it was difficult to read.

"You are surrounding yourself with the least favorable art from antiquity. The early Zan period, before which we were little more advanced than Tyler-Zan's species on Earth. A mocking contrast?"

"Hm," Qirep replied, giving a slight frown. "Perhaps it is dually effective. But no. That is not the primary purpose."

Leveling his jade eyes on Tyler with a furious intensity he added gruffly, "And do not disrespect me or the heritage displayed before you by referring to this creature as a Zan. I have trained erspecs more like a Zan than he."

For whatever reason, being referred to as less than what was equivalent to a dog got under Tyler's skin. Though more likely it was Qirep's condescension toward Kayli. Tyler had seen Qirep as something of a helicopter parent, but the level of coolness he showed now seemed out of place. "Is it like a Zan to torment and berate his child in front of a Degree Twenty-Five alien?" Tyler sniped.

Qirep sat his drink down, his glacial gaze hard on Tyler. "What would you know of parenthood among our people? What would you know of what a true Zan is, human?"

Glancing at the artwork assembled around them, Tyler did notice a commonality. They all, like the office had broad stellar vistas. A sense of looking out, beyond. Almost for himself, Tyler commented, "More than you, I suppose. Given you've gone to great lengths to hide your love of the forbidden regions beyond a Zan's reach from Marezan and Irizan. Cowardice and rebellious zeal don't usually go together well."

If Tyler had expected to get a rise out of Qirep, he couldn't have been more surprised when the Zan burst into laughter. He and Kayli exchanged puzzled glances before Qirep's humor subsided, and he said, "I suppose even a fool finds a kernel of truth on occasion. Even if he bandies about with it like a child holding his father's gun."

The last word and phrasing weren't Zan. Qirep had said, "gun." It had a bit of affectation from Zan accenting, but Tyler stared at Qirep as though that could make clearer what he had impossibly heard from him.

"What is a *gun*?" Kayli asked, though it was ambiguous who she was speaking to, because it appeared as if she was studying the things in the room, perhaps hoping that solving her father's puzzle would offer escape.

"Would you like me to explain it, or shall you, human?"

Though it would be far more enlightening to see how Qirep imagined the term, Tyler understood that given their precarious position, he was obliged to follow subtle instructions of this sort. "They are primarily projectile weapons on Earth. Humans have used them for centuries for hunting and defense."

"And for conquest," Qirep added, clearly unsatisfied with Tyler's sanitized description. "Slow speed projectile weapons for taking by force that which you will."

"I need to sit, Papa," Kayli said, her voice sounding strained. Tyler could tell from the way her face had lightened almost to the color of a pale lilac that she was feeling faint. Whether it was from comprehending the brutality that Qirep implied humans to possess or something else, Tyler couldn't tell.

"The paralysis current will keep you on your feet," Qirep replied with little remorse.

Tyler noticed beads of sweat forming on Kayli's brow and wanted to move to comfort her. If only he could move his legs! He wiggled his toes in frustration.

Wait, I can still move my toes!

In the other instance when his legs and arms were paralyzed the immobilizing current reached to the tips of his fingers and toes. Had the guards forgotten to reset the devices to freeze their legs in place? Looking at Kayli-Zan, he understood now the sweat wasn't just from whatever was sickening her. She was faint enough from that, but the sweat was from her effort to stay totally motionless. At some point during the conversation, maybe when she started feeling faint, Kayli had perceived that they could move their legs. Much like her, Tyler now struggled with the burden of concentrating on such stillness, because in it they had one possible advantage and chance at escape.

"Still no idea what these images depicting our glorious past are intended to instill? Nor the brutish simplicity of these humans? Of where you stand?"

It hit Tyler with the force of a slap to his face and he almost lost his rigid hold on his footing. "You've built a gateway for reaching other worlds."

Turning with a slow purposefulness to glare at Tyler, Qirep shook his head, his lips pursed. He sighed. "Well, my child, it looks like the sub-erspec has bested you in a test of wit. Though I might add, this station, while configured to reach any number of known habitable systems, will first be applied to reaching your world in particular, human."

FOURTEEN

1

MALEVOLENCE

TYLER GAPED. "You're going to travel to Earth?" he mumbled stricken with shock. A somewhat optimistic part of him hoped that all this meant was that he would be cast back to Earth in what the Zan would have seen as exile.

"Have I gone to such lengths to unshackle the chains our ancestors laid on us—Irizan and Marezan—to do any less?" Qirep retorted. He gestured to the displays of the ancient art. "Long ago our people dreamed of interstellar empire, but some feared our own internal strife might collapse our civilization. There was civil war, and to our people's shame, the isolationists won. They implemented Irizan and Marezan to imprison us in our own system. Subsisting off the scraps of what this system offers and hiding the wonders of Zan civilization from the universe."

Shaking his head, Qirep drained the last of his drink and all but snarled at the kick it gave. "I should thank you, human," he added darkly. "When you arrived, it awoke many of us to how complacent and weak we had become. Few of us even understood how our 'beloved' Irizan and Marezan worked.

Some have worshiped them as divine. And yet here was an outsider who, given time, could enslave them with his knowledge. Enslave us. A fool. Less than an erspec, conquering the Zan.

"Your arrival shook us from that sleep of death and allowed us to remember our strength. Soon, precious soon, we will have the resources needed to claim the destiny lost to us millennia ago."

Qirep glanced at his daughter as if to get her thoughts on it. She was extremely measured in her words, "Irizan and Marezan would never allow us to build warships and leave the system."

Nodding, Qirep turned stony, "No they would not. Which is why we need the impending disaster on Asteroid Z43-21-99 to force off their chains. When the fuel cells detonate, they will disrupt the asteroid field, raining shards significant enough to destroy 5% of our cities on Irizan. Irizan and Marezan's creators did not leave us wholly undefended. They have a trigger sequence for a root mode in the event of an attack. Once in that state, we can activate the defense modules in each that will allow us to begin military production once again.

"More than that, we can access their source code directly and rebuild them in such a way as to create fleets of sentient ships which can be sent to wage war and claim new lands without endangering our people. We can conquer worlds hospitable to us and use the AI to understand the worlds at subatomic levels before risking colonists to govern our new dominion."

"But why Papa? Why do we need to enslave other worlds at the cost of Zan blood? Can't you see you're killing us to reign over lesser species?"

"These lesser species will be shown true civilization as a reward for ensuring that the universe will never see a single moment without the Zan," he replied as easily as if providing his name and birth date.

"Starting with my life mate's species?" Kayli-Zan all but wailed.

Qirep shuddered with barely suppressed rage. "I brought you here for one last chance to prove yourself a true Zan ..." Shoulders rising and falling, teeth gritted, Qirep snarled, "That Irizan paired you with such a waste of matter is proof that neither Irizan nor these humans should persist a moment longer than they must. When we come to Earth, it will be to cleanse that planet and establish on it a new Irizan. The first monument to our destined empire."

Tyler was almost catatonic at this point. Numbness spread throughout him, warring and winning against his will to resist. To live. Much as Qirep predicted a swift and merciless end to the rest of humanity. All these years squandered in feeling sorry for himself. Now, because of him, all of Earth and so much more of the universe would suffer and die.

The elder Zan tapped something on his desk's holographic controls, and the back display shifted from that of space beyond to the asteroid field, centering on Asteroid Z43-21-99. In the distance, the bright orb of Irizan could be faintly seen.

"I had hoped to surgically separate you from this parasite, child," Qirep addressed Kayli. "Everything was laid in place for you to finally ascend to the role you deserved in life. But you chose this, this, argh!" Qirep slammed his fist down and seethed.

After a few moments, he straightened, seemingly having restored the temperature of his veins to that of ice. "Now, you will wait and watch here as we true Zan reclaim our birthright." Pressing another series of commands, the main doors slid open and a group of guards entered.

"Take the human to the transport. Make sure to unload him

in his own workstation and to set Marezan to regain access to his station just before the detonation."

Still too stunned to resist, Tyler allowed the guards to essentially carry him out of the room. He watched Kayli-Zan straining over her shoulder, still hiding her mobility, no tears left to be shed for the tragedy of humanity.

Before he was taken out the doors, Tyler heard her shout, "If you value me so little, Papa, then why let me live? Do you think killing my life mate in front of me will make me a true Zan? Watching you lay the foundation of your insane plans with his blood will only insure I despise and fight you to my dying breath."

Before, his barely controlled fury had manifested outwardly, but this last salvo from Kayli-Zan appeared to have far greater effect and created an implosion within the Zan. "Very well," he said, his voice as frigid as space behind him. "Leave her with her 'life mate.' She will be sacrificed as a symbol of all the foolish vanities of the past, which have hindered the true Zan from rising."

With that he turned on his heels and faced the display, the replicated countdown and angular assessments of before projected for him. The guards glanced at each other and retrieved Kayli-Zan.

As they were carried down the hallway Tyler could see the apology in her eyes. But he was plunged back under the surface again. Seeing her love and commitment from beneath the waves, he could only lament that she would be just another futile casualty of the horror to come.

FIFTEEN

1

DESPERATE MEASURES

IT TOOK the full flight to the asteroid before Tyler began to feel anything again. Unfortunately, what he encountered first was grief. Through it, he rediscovered fear as one of the guards struck him when tears rolled down his cheek. "Keep presentable or we kill your life mate here and now," the guard had threatened.

That stopped the tears and carried him to the offloading. They arrived at a secret port on the asteroid, one Tyler hadn't even uncovered in his code snooping. The guards never altered Tyler or Kayli's restraint controls. Instead, they were placed on hovering medical gurneys. From the banter between their captors, the cover story for their arrival would be that they were being transported to the medical bay on the level where Tyler's workstation was located. Since his station was nearer to the landing site than the medical bay, Qirep's goons could surreptitiously sneak into his workstation.

From end-to-end, he could see now how the whole thing was a set up. He had played his part well. The questions to Marezan combined with the sequence for detonating the devices at his workstation would be enough to make even a skeptical juror feel hard pressed not to convict him. And there would be no jury. Just Marezan rendering verdict. Though he couldn't be sure, he felt certain that being a human, an alien, and setting off the detonation was essential to the plan. They had thought of everything. Even covering up Kayli-Zan's face, who should never be on the asteroid, in a protective face helm while leaving Tyler uncovered.

Tyler could feel himself reaching that point where all drowning men do when the struggle ceases. Dark was enclosing him, and it wouldn't be long until he faced the end of this life. His sentence not commuted from earlier but delayed. Except this time, it wasn't just him. It was the beautiful, even-if-alien, woman he finally realized he might love. It was everyone he had ever cared about, or their children, or grandchildren, or whatever generation awaited at the other end of time and space's door. How does one even begin to process a genocide of that scope?

The lift's doors opened. Tyler barely registered the curses their guards muttered as they tried to push out onto the level. Faintly interested in the disturbance of the surface above him, Tyler gave attention to his surroundings and his eyes widened. This level of the asteroid was packed with Zan. "They recalled all of the miners?" one of Qirep's lackies mumbled, gruffly reciting Tyler's own thoughts.

"The Nabu thought it would heighten the tragedy and ensure the people's support," the other replied under his breath.

Tyler recognized that term as one from the old Zan history he had half listened to. It had stuck out in his nerd mind because it sounded just like the planet Naboo from *Star Wars*. Except for the Zan it was a term related to dictators, essentially their word for emperor.

"As wise as the Nabu is, would anyone shed a tear for the dregs of society?" the other replied.

"Leave it be," the second scolded. "Let's just get these two in position and off this thing before it's obliterated."

They made it all of ten meters before a tremor ran through the gurney, jarring Tyler. Someone called out, "Ow, you sloth-brain, watch where you're going with that!"

As recognition rippled through him Tyler imagined someone reaching to him from the surface. *Hearl-Zan!*

Sure enough, when he cast his eyes down to the end of the gurney there was the hulking form of his friend. It was at once the best and worst news he could get at the moment. If he played this right, maybe, just maybe, Hearl could help them.

"Watch it yourself you ponzo!" One of the guards snapped back.

"Hey, Ornth-Zan, isn't that him? The Kebny Meteor?" the other said slapping his compatriot on the arm.

"Oh, right! What was it? Hel ... um ... Hurl? Uh ... Hearl-Zan! Hearl-Zan who lost half of Irizan's wealth in blowing it at the kebny finals. I wondered what happened to him."

With deep belly chuckle the other replied, "Looks like he found his way to where he belongs."

"Yeah, well at least I can walk a straight line and not crash into every Zan I see," Hearl retorted. His gaze drifted down to Tyler and lingered for a moment. He opened his mouth to speak. But Tyler quickly mouthed, "Don't. Not yet."

"Ha, you're one to talk. Isn't that how you lost the first five points of that game?" Ornth-Zan challenged.

"He did. Ran straight into Wync-Zan like pszic bird a window!"

Hearl's gaze shifted up from Tyler to the two guards, his brow furrowed in anger. "How about I smash you two like a pszic bird on a window?"

"I'd like to see you try you flerr slug," Ornth retorted and reached for what Tyler guessed was a weapon or more of his paralysis restraints.

The other grabbed Ornth's arm. "Hey, focus. We don't have time for washed out kebny players. We have to get these two to, uh, medical bay."

"Right," Hearl replied and shouldered past them towards the lift. "Better hope I don't run into you alone before this rotation ends, Ornth." Hearl spun and cracked his knuckles for effect and then was out of Tyler's line of sight and onto the lift.

Suddenly Tyler worried Hearl had misunderstood. And just like that his hopes faded, and he slipped back down deeper than ever.

A COUPLE MINUTES later they arrived at his workstation. How they managed to unload Kayli and him into the station without drawing suspicion, he couldn't begin to care enough to ponder. When they put him into the station control ring, he didn't resist. Not even when they set everything up as intended to pin the detonation on him.

Tyler didn't even process them yelling insults and curses at him as they both bolted out of the station to get back to their transport. It wasn't until he registered that Kayli-Zan was screaming his name that he came back to the moment.

"Tyler, please!" she begged.

He peered over at her, finding her indigo eyes vivid, panicked. She was no longer hiding her ability to move her legs. Dimly he thought it extra tragic that he would die without even being able to hold her in his arms once with the tenderness she deserved. "I'm sorry," he murmured. "I'm sorry I've cost you everything now."

"You haven't cost me anything yet," she protested. "We have to find a way to stop this. Please, Tyler, look at me! I know we can stop this."

His gaze had dipped, and he did look at her, at the almost wild hope simmering in her. She certainly hadn't given up. Maybe this had been her plan all along. Not to die with him, but to try desperately to find a way to live.

"I can't. All of it was a set up. Your father was too good, anticipating every move I made. He played me to the end."

"We aren't at the end—yet," Kayli insisted. "And father didn't anticipate everything. He didn't anticipate me loving you."

Tyler glanced at her. She nodded enthusiastically as he finally really saw her. "He couldn't conceive of it as possible. And he also didn't anticipate his lackies running off without manually setting Marezan back on. They set it on a timer instead. That has to be helpful."

He glanced at the display. Sure enough, she was right. In their panic to escape through the crowds they hadn't expected, they had entrusted a programmed counter to be what activated Marezan again. It would be trivial to edit the counter and re-execute the command so that it never woke Marezan. Might he then have time to disable the bombs?

Shaking his head, Tyler stiffened against the breakers of guilt and shame and sorrow he'd been protected from, all of them hitting him at once. "No. I can't. This is all my fault. I've killed you. I've killed them all by selfishly trying to hold onto something I couldn't."

"No. Tyler, please, listen to me."

"It's my fault," he countered.

Kayli-Zan shrieked in frustration and yelled, "No, it's not! What if you were sent to us for this very moment?"

For such a time as this.

As though he'd been yanked coughing and sputtering to the surface, Tyler suddenly snapped out of his stupor. Those words, he'd heard those words before, so long ago now. Read them, studied them, hoped in the One Who was behind them.

Drawing in a shaky breath, he steadied himself mentally and physically. He recited to himself, 'If I perish, I perish.'"

Kayli's head drooped, her eyes were filled with defeat and turmoil, not understanding his outburst. Eyeing her shoulder restraint and his in turn, he felt strength flood his limbs and in one swift movement that had as much prayerful hope of success as practical expectation, he leapt into her, raking his restraint against hers.

With a yelp of pain, his restraint tore free. He lay on the workstation floor for a few seconds as control of his limbs slowly was restored to him. Getting to his feet, he moved to Kayli-Zan, grabbed her face in his hands and gave her a full, wild kiss. When he pulled away, feeling the current of her surprise and pleasure running from her face through his fingers, she mumbled, "Unexpected, but not unwelcome?"

"Definitely. Thank you, Kayli-Zan."

Then remembering himself, he disabled her restraint using its interface. The device fell away and she shook out her arms. As soon as the feeling returned to them she sprang into an embrace with him.

Just as quickly though she pushed away and said, "Later. How much time is left?"

Tyler clambered back into the control ring and began searching. "Minutes," he mumbled half to himself.

With a flurry of touches, he disabled the timer they had set for the countdown to re-alert Marezan to his station. He tried sorting through the coding for the bombs and cried out in frustration.

"What is it?" Kayli-Zan asked, standing close beside him.

"The code for the bombs. It's too intricate, and it's littered with ancient references that I'm sure meant something to the programmers creating it, but, thanks to me not paying attention to my Zan history lessons ... It's got too many foreign terms to know exactly what I'm changing."

"What if I help you through them?"

"There's too many of them, it will take too much time to work through them all."

"What do we do then?" she asked, the edge of fear creeping into her voice.

Panic was starting to set in when he spotted something. "Would the power supply to trigger the detonators be hooked into the mining level's core station?

"It might be," she replied thoughtful.

"So, I could disable the station from here!"

"You could in theory, but that will cut off the lights, gravity, and life support." Kayli assessed, wincing.

"Right. And the subsystems will take too long to parse that out and protect everyone individually." He tapped his foot rapidly on the floor and then got what on the surface was a bad idea. "They have a laser drill down there. I could just go down and cut the power lines directly."

"But what if you accidentally cut off power to the life support systems in that part of the asteroid as well?"

He nodded. "'If I perish, I perish,'" he recited again for her.

Before she could argue, he leapt up and bolted for the door. He'd have barely enough time if he ran.

As the door slid open, he crashed into what amounted to a wall and fell backward. Staring up from the ground, Tyler blinked, stunned. In the doorway loomed Hearl-Zan, arms crossed over his broad chest.

SIXTEEN

SACRIFICE

"HEARL-ZAN," Tyler said with a groan.

"Yup. Where exactly are you about to run off to?"

Tyler shot a look up at Kayli-Zan suddenly worried Hearl might be a traitor too. He hoped she understood to grab the restraints the guards had used on them. They might need both for Hearl.

"Kayli-Zan?" Hearl suddenly exclaimed with such genuine surprise that it defused Tyler's worries. "What in Irizan is going on? How are you in here?"

Glancing down at Tyler and then back at her, his eyes narrowed in suspicion, "Did Tyler not say 'Marezan, I'm ready to begin' yet or is this an intimacy thing?"

"Hearl, no!" Tyler shouted.

"Tyler-Zan," Marezan's voice broke into the conversation. "Your workstation activities indicate actions that could result in catastrophic harm to Zan. You are in violation of Sedition Laws 33257, 445876, and 1998765. You will be placed under arrest and delivered to appropriate sentencing."

Tyler rubbed his face with his hands. The nature of the

sleep state was such that any voice could reactivate it and Hearl had just inadvertently done so.

"Uh, Tyler, what is Marezan talking about?" Hearl-Zan asked.

"Tyler-Zan has placed thermonuclear devices in a portion of the asteroid to which there is no access," Marezan informed him. "Evidence indicates that he intends to detonate the devices and destroy this asteroid within 724 seconds.

"Please stand aside so the workstation may be locked until Tyler-Zan can be apprehended by security personnel."

Hearl glanced down at Tyler then up and said, "Um, I think you have this wrong. Tyler didn't do any of that, it's a misunderstanding."

Marezan was silent but the door suddenly started to close. Hearl gripped it and with a feral growl, pushed it back open. "Hurry," he shouted.

Tyler peered up at Kayli-Zan and mouthed, "Pray." He leaped up and tumbled through the doorway just as Hearl was forced to back away from it.

Rotating his arms to work out the kinks, Hearl started to ask something, but Tyler interrupted him, "No time to explain, follow me."

He took off running for the lift that he knew would lead down to the sector in question. As he jumped on the lift, Hearl nearly barreling him over, he caught glimpse of a black device whirring down the corridor.

"Was that a drone?" Tyler asked somewhat surprised, having rarely seen drones in use among the Zan. They emphasized personal efforts and participation in society over robotic ones in just about every situation.

"Marezan must think you're too dangerous to let Zan pursue," Hearl replied with a shrug.

"Are you sure it's not you that's too dangerous for pursuit, Incredible Hulk?"

Hearl glared down at Tyler. "That's the fifth time since we first met that you've called me *Hulk.* When are you going to explain to me what that means?"

The lift came to a sudden halt, having reached the room with the bombs. "Ask again when we're not in danger of being blasted to bits?"

Tyler stepped off and ducked as a rush of air from the drone swooping down into the room traced along his neck.

"Tyler-Zan, you must submit to arrest at once. You are in violation of Sedition Laws 33257, 445876, and 1998765."

"So, you've told me," Tyler replied as he ran off the lift and looked around the room for the power lines to the detonator. All of the shipping crates they had seen in the room previously had been emptied and now, with the entire device set up, there were large cabinet-shaped boxes, fifteen total. In each, Tyler guessed there were fuel cells. Except there were no wires in sight.

Argh, the Zan even have wireless power transmission on the asteroid! This would be a great time to have Kayli-Zan with me. I'm sure she'd know how to handle this. There's no time to go back for her though.

An idea struck him.

What about the receivers, maybe all we need to do is break the detonator's receiver?

The drone hovered in front of Tyler again. "Tyler-Zan, you must submit to arrest immediately."

"Hearl, get ready on the laser drill," Tyler pointed to the device across the room. "I'm going to find the detonator, and you'll need to take out its power receiver."

"Tyler-Zan, you will submit to arrest or use of deadly force will be authorized."

Tyler hesitated just a moment. He had concluded that Irizan's threat of execution had been part of the test. If it wasn't then ...

"Deadly force authorized. Eliminating threat to Zan security."

Hovering to eye level, the drone spun to reveal a compartment Tyler hadn't seen before. It began glowing with an ominous red color.

On instinct, he leapt to the side and rolled clumsily behind one of the fuel cell containers. He didn't even see the laser as it raked across the ground centimeters from where he'd stood. Tyler barely had the chance to catch his breath before he heard the drone whir to over his head.

He ran out and leapt behind another of the cabinets. This time the laser came close enough to cut off the corner of one of the gleaming metals blocks. Tyler held his breath in wait, but the cells seemed stable.

That drone is going to get us killed. Either by running out time or by releasing the fuel within the cells.

There was no time to think of how to stop it. Tyler dashed for safety behind another cabinet as the drone took another shot, this time it just grazed the back of his leg. Pain exploded through him as he tumbled along the metallic surface of the room. Smoke roiled from where the laser had burned through his suit and injured his leg. He couldn't feel the injury itself, but from the unreliability of his leg he knew he wouldn't be getting away again.

"Tyler, which one of these things do I blast?" Hearl bellowed.

"The drone!" Tyler yelled back. "Blast the drone!"

The sleek black extension of Marezan hovered above him, and Tyler feebly skirted around the edge of the fuel cell block to keep it from having a good angle, but he could only do that maybe once more before it would out maneuver him.

"I can't get a clear shot!" Hearl called out.

Narrowly avoiding another blast that melted a groove in the floor beside him, Tyler took a breath. Saying a silent prayer, he leapt out completely into the open.

Not even bracing for the landing he hit the ground and rolled into one of the fuel cell cabinets. The air rushed out of his lungs as he slammed hard into it. Tyler lay there gasping, his heart pounding in his ears. He couldn't hear or even see the drone anymore. All he could do was tense himself for what would surely be a swift death.

Closing his eyes, he fought for just one more breath before the end. It came to him and in the same moment, he felt himself being hoisted into the air.

Looking around, he saw Hearl holding him up. "No time for napping right now," he chided.

"You got it?" Tyler asked.

"Of course, my aim is legendary," Hearl retorted with a smirk. "Now, which one of these do I need to hit?"

Tyler shook his head as Hearl lowered him. "I ... I don't know. They all look the same."

"Do we have time to try all of them?"

"No. It would take too long to cut them as delicately as needed. Marezan's drone ate up all of our time. You'll have to just rake them all."

"That'll release the fuel into this room," Hearl said, his tone as dead pan as Tyler had ever heard it.

"Yeah. It'll stop the detonation," Tyler replied, knowing the Zan already understood.

"Well, then let's not waste everyone else's seconds."

Hearl turned and as he did, Tyler caught sight of the drone, smoking and hovering shakily over the ground using only half of its four Zero-G rotors. Marezan announced, "Eliminating security threat."

Faster than Tyler could blink, Hearl tackled him out of the way. They both landed, with Hearl's huge mass laying across Tyler's legs, pinning them. Tyler tried to move and immediately his head swam. He must have banged it as they went down. Reaching to it he found a knot already forming. His fingers came away damp and stained red.

Tyler wanted to be grateful to his friend for the save, but Hearl was taking too long to get up. "Hearl, move it, that thing is going to be coming around again."

Hearl lay still. Only then did Tyler catch the scent of burnt flesh and noticed that the laser hadn't missed totally. It had caught Hearl square on.

From around the far side of the fuel cell block the drone wobbled into view. Even if Hearl's weight wasn't holding him down, Tyler's thoughts were too fuzzy from the head trauma. And beyond it, the crippling paralysis of witnessing his only Zan friend, so massive and strong, having been silenced in an instant. A moment ago, they had both been ready to sacrifice themselves to save everyone, and now Marezan would inadvertently ensure no one escaped their fate.

SEVENTEEN

1

END GAME

TYLER SWALLOWED back the fear that was potent enough to break through the haziness plaguing his vision. Watching as the drone continued to wobble there in front of him like a cat toying with a mouse. He hadn't realized Marezan could be cruel. This was the end.

But the end did not come as quickly as Tyler expected. In fact, the seconds dragged on without anything happening. No brief, searing pain. No being called out to the wondrous light of eternity. Just the throbbing of his head and the thrum of Marezan's drone which bounced off the floor once as it tried to maintain flight with erratic success.

"Assessing Hearl-Zan's injury," Marezan called out.

"He's dead," Tyler found himself mumbling though it sounded like it came from someone other than himself. "You killed him."

"Assessment accurate. Zan life has been ended. Entering hibernation state. Transferring control."

"Transferring control?" Tyler parroted, unsure he was

hearing things correctly. There was a building ringing in his ears.

The drone dropped to the ground with a metallic clunk. It remained still.

What just happened? Did the drone malfunction?

Tyler extricated his legs and got to them, shakily. His injured leg had been tweaked by Hearl crashing onto it and threatened to give completely. Leaning against the fuel cellblock, Tyler stared at the drone. It had a clear line of sight to blast him through the chest but didn't whir or blink a light or anything. Hearl must have irreparably damaged it. The tragedy that it hadn't gone down sooner rested heavily on Tyler. All the more because the drone had been intending to kill him. Not Hearl. Not a Zan.

The bombs!

"How much time?" Tyler asked aloud before remembering no other Zan were there to answer.

His eyes traveled upward and fixed to an odd light above on the dig room's wall. A semi-spherical gray protrusion was bathed in the greenish sheen the light emitted.

The power transmitter.

Dimly registering the fact, suddenly the significance struck him.

The power transmitter! If I can knock it out then the wireless power transfer to the detonators will be cut off. All I have to do is hit it.

Hobbling around the fuel cell block, he spotted the laser drill across the room and made for it. Aches shot through him as he tried to force his contused body to reach it before the unthinkable began. He had to make it. Once more he uttered a prayer for help, this time aloud, fervent, desperate.

His hand gripped the frame of the laser drill's housing.

"Tyler-Zan, stop. Step away from the laser drill."

Tyler felt as if he had been speared through and through with an icicle. Turning his head to look over his shoulder he glimpsed Marezan's drone once more hovering with its determined flutter. The thing had somehow rebooted. Only the voice sounded off.

"I have to stop the bombs," he called out and climbed into laser drill's control pod.

"Tyler-Zan, stop. Using the drill on the fuel cell blocks will kill you."

Tapping at the holographic controls, Tyler aimed the laser drill as best he could at the power transmitter. He wasn't nearly as experienced with the device as Hearl. "I'm not going to blast the cells ..."

Come on. I have to make it. Just one more second to align it. Hopefully the door on this thing will block the drone's laser long enough.

"Assessing strategy. Target identified. Blocking power transmission to detonator and fuel cells."

Tyler's aim faltered. What had it said?

He looked out and the drone was hovering just outside the drill laser pod. It addressed him. "Threat neutralized. You may exit the pod."

"I'm still alive," Tyler countered, unwilling to step out. What sort of mad short circuiting was going on that it thought he was already neutralized. Could Marezan lie to bait him out?

"Your evaluation of your current well-being is accurate. Though you have suffered considerable injuries. Preparing medical bay to provide appropriate care."

"What?" Tyler said putting his hands on his head. This wasn't making sense. "I thought you had to eliminate me. Aren't I a threat, Marezan?"

"Marezan is currently offline. All control for extraorbital operations was passed to Irizan in accordance with Protocol 0."

Now Tyler knew he had to be going insane. "Protocol 0," he repeated, leaning away from the drone and bracing himself up on the far side of the drill laser's pod.

"No artificial intelligence may perpetrate fatal harm upon a member of the Zan race. Upon such action taking place, the responsible artificial intelligence must execute the subroutines corresponding to this protocol such that all operations and controls will be diverted temporarily to an uncompromised artificial intelligence. The responsible artificial intelligence shall also be placed into hibernation state to allow manual intervention and correction of source code errors precipitating the fatality."

"Marezan is offline?" Tyler tried to summarize, though it sounded impossible.

"Correct. Marezan fatally wounded Hearl-Zan and has executed Protocol 0."

"You're Irizan? You have control of the asteroid now?"

"Correct."

Tyler tried to work moisture to his mouth. Hesitantly he pushed off on the pod wall and stumbled towards the door separating him from the drone. "And the bombs?"

"The mission to which you were assigned has been successfully completed. Thc powcr transmission to the detonators has been blocked.

"Your alternate plan of disabling the power transmitter was much improved from damaging the fuel cell blocks, which would have contaminated the chamber with radioactive isotopes."

"The bombs are stopped?" Tyler verified again, ignoring the dour assessment of his attempt to stop the cataclysm.

"Correct. The signal to the detonator is jammed. It is unnecessary to continue with the destruction of the transmitter."

Tyler opened the pod door and stumbled out. He dropped to his hands and knees for lack of energy and will to support himself. He felt as if he were coming up on a shore, every bit of him physically and emotionally exhausted. "We did it."

"Sensors for vital signs damaged. Readings of current physical wellness reaching critical thresholds."

"We did it. We stopped him," Tyler murmured as he collapsed and a dark swell crashed on him.

EIGHTEEN

1

MENDING

TYLER BLINKED; his eyes irritated by an overbright light. Had he died and was opening his eyes to take in Heaven?

No. There was too much pain for that to be true. Several seconds of the pained blinking passed before the light was dimmed and he began to make out a face.

"Tyler?" a concerned voice spoke to him.

He recognized Kayli-Zan by her voice long before the soft curvatures of her face sharpened. The first thing he was able to hold onto visually were the striking indigo irises fixed on him with such concern. She gripped his hand in both of hers rather tightly.

"Ugh, I guess we didn't get blown apart?" he mumbled and tried to sit up. He found some restraints kept him from doing so and caught sight of a doctor at work applying some sort of treatment.

Kayli laughed, drawing his attention back to her. "We are safe. You and Hearl were able to stop the detonation."

"Hearl," Tyler recalled with a groan. "He's gone."

The hopefulness in Kayli's face faded into something more somber. "I'm sorry, Tyler. Irizan told us he died saving your life. I wish I had known him better. That I could thank him for what he did."

Tyler closed his eyes and blinked back some tears. Hearl would've taunted him for being an emotional human. Zan of course cried, but that was just Hearl-Zan. Able to lighten the moment with a well-timed jibe. Suddenly the tiny face of Hearl's daughter Mosha-Zan seared into Tyler's consciousness. His own regret and sense of loss became pale and small by compare. "What about his family? How do we tell them he died defending me? A human."

"Hearl-Zan's family has already been notified," Irizan's clear voice intoned. "They have been informed that Hearl performed an act of heroism thus saving millions of lives in addition to your life specifically." Did Tyler imagine the edge of sympathy interlaced within it?

"How will they make it?" Tyler asked and then realized he was too ambiguous in meaning for the AI. "How will they subsist without his wages?"

This time Kayli-Zan spoke up. "Zan are taught from a young age to care for neighbors. They will be aided by those who care most about them."

"In addition to a regular stipend as a reward for the act of heroism on behalf of the Zan race," Irizan added. "His social rank was also amended to Degree One."

Taking in a deep breath and letting it out slowly, Tyler settled down onto the relatively soft confines of his medical bedding. "That will change everything for his family." School, housing, and a host of other options would now be open to each member of the family previously closed to them.

A chime sounded, startling Tyler. The physician walked around from behind him and announced. "The last of the therapies in accordance with treatment of Tyler-Zan's species have been completed. By Irizan's estimation he should be ready to leave the medical bay within the next hour."

"Thank you," Kayli-Zan said for both of them.

The physician's eyes darted from Kayli-Zan to Tyler and the emerald colored Zan of at least sixty orbits age seemed conflicted. Stroking his white beard, at length he addressed Tyler rather formally and said, "Thank you for your service. The whole is greater for your part in it."

Tyler's eyes widened and he watched the physician as he quickly stalked away. "Did he just say what I think?"

"You are part of the whole," Kayli confirmed and kissed him on the forehead.

"The same notification of Hearl-Zan's heroic actions also informed Zan on Irizan and throughout orbital assignments that it was you who uncovered the conspiracy and ultimately prevented the unspeakable damage that would have resulted," Irizan informed him, this time with the intonation of a proud parent. "You have also been confirmed Degree One status."

Shaking his head, Tyler replied, "They'll all hate me even more for it. And Qirep-Zan, what will he try—"

"Qirep-Zan and his conspirators are currently isolated and will shortly be placed in indefinite stasis," Irizan informed him. "Because of the unique nature of their transgressions, a judicial review panel will determine how many orbits will be required before they can re-enter society."

You don't forget hate and ambition like that because you're told to, they'll come back more vicious than ever.

Kayli must have sensed his reservations, or perhaps he wasn't disguising his misgivings as well as he had in the past. She rubbed his hand gently with hers, sending sensations of pride and relief and hopefulness to him. Though mixed in were notes of sadness and bitterness that couldn't be masked. After a minute she said, "There's something else. My father," Kayli hesitated and grimaced. "Qirep-Zan and the other rebels completed the interstellar conduit. In fact, it will be used to keep Qirep and the others trapped. Not quite in our system, not transported beyond the system."

"That sounds terrible, but fitting given what he planned to use it for," Tyler replied. He tried to keep his face neutral unsure whether celebrating the punishment or decrying it would do more harm to her after what she'd endured.

Clearing her throat, she added, "Before Qirep's sentence begins, there is one more thing. Irizan has already confirmed that the conduit is capable of sending you home as soon as you are ready.

"Though Irizan also said that you will have a preeminent role in amending the shortcomings in both Marezan and its own code base if you stayed. There is no Zan so trustworthy to such a task as you."

Suddenly at a faster clip, she added, "But I would not ask you to stay. So, Irizan will also schedule your launch, if that is what you choose.

"Tyler?"

"Do not be alarmed. Tyler-Zan is not going into medical shock. Behavioral and physiological indicators suggest he is intensely surprised and reacting within expected parameters for his species," Irizan explained.

Brows knitted, Kayli first squeezed his hand, and when he failed to find words for a few minutes longer, released his. She gnawed at her lower lip and finally said, "I will give you some time alone."

Tyler barely noticed her leaving. Barely registered anything in the room. He was pretty sure Irizan tried to say something to him, but he totally ignored it.

Is this real? After everything that's happened, the years of longing for it. I can go home.

He tried the word out, whispering it for the silly fear that just by speaking it aloud he could shatter the precious and assumedly tenuous circumstances according the opportunity. "Home."

NINETEEN

1

HOME

ALL AROUND THE evening air of summer wrapped everything in a wonderful balance of warmth and coolness. The sky was near cloudless with the slow burn of daylight blending into night to transform the horizon into an artist's muse of orange, red, and fuchsia bands. There was a charge to it all that enlivened the various amphibians and insects in the long expanse of swaying grasses and tall trees in the distance to cry out in an organic symphony. Much the same as it would on Earth. The only thing it lacked was the lightning bugs or fireflies, whichever one would choose to call them, providing earthbound starlight to complete the scene.

Tyler rested his elbows on the railing surrounding the veranda of the new Degree One home Irizan had assigned. And Irizan had thought it prudent to provide one that was at the edge of Hanite City. It was stunning inside and out. Not unlike Kayli-Zan.

He tapped his foot on the ground with anxious energy. More than a month had passed since arriving back on Irizan. Tomorrow he was scheduled for launch. Not to another mining expedition, but for a trip to the interstellar conduit. The lone passenger to pass through it to its destination of Earth. Before tomorrow came, however, he had a number of goodbyes to say. And apparently the biggest of them was to be delivered now, dressed in this dark midnight suit that was perhaps the fanciest clothing he'd ever worn.

"Irizan was correct, you do love this view," Kayli-Zan called out from behind him.

Without turning he replied, "It reminds me of my childhood home." Taking a deep breath, he turned around.

Kayli walked toward him draped in a flowing dress with the texture of silk and the rich indigo hues of deep twilight. Little points of some other fabric invisible except at the proper angles gave the impression of stars dotting the night sky. She stopped beside him and offered a tight smile. "Soon you'll be there again. Irizan says it is summer there as well. You can touch and smell and taste the Earth you've missed so dearly."

"Well, maybe not taste," he said with a chuckle.

She gave a little laugh. "I was being a bit too figurative."

He nodded, but said, "I won't criticize. You inspire poetry with your grace, compassion, and honesty. I would never fault you for allowing it drift into how you speak of things as beautiful as you."

Her cheeks deepened in color almost to true purple and she looked away. "It sounds as if you are accustomed to the language yourself. It will not be easy to find someone for whom it comes so readily in either person or speech."

Wincing a bit, Tyler reached out his hand placed it on hers. "Kayli-Zan, I—" This wasn't how he intended for this moment to be. It was too formal, too melancholy. He told Irizan not to dress them both in fine clothes and stage this at sunset. It was a little forced.

"You do not ... You don't have to say anything, Tyler. I

already said goodbye to you in my heart when we arrived back on Irizan. I started the moment I learned that Irizan told me you could leave."

Tyler swallowed with some difficulty. Unsure how to respond. What could he say to that?

Kayli-Zan didn't give him a chance to try. She added, "You did not choose this world, and I will never begrudge you for leaving it for where you belong. It is enough that on a night like this I will be able to remember what has passed between us and how you changed my world for the better."

He let out a pained sigh. He had never taken himself for the emotional type, but this was new waters for him, and he was only now learning to swim them. "Kayli-Zan—"

She put her hands on his arms, rubbing them. "Please, you don't have to say anything. Irizan told me you have something you must share. If it can be left as a note instead, I think I would handle it better in time. Later, when I'm missing you and need something of you to hold onto, I could turn to the note."

There was a tremble to her lip and her eyes glistened with tears ready to fall. Like splintered glass, one wrong touch would shatter her. But he had to get through this. It would tear him apart if he didn't.

Taking both her hands in his own, he could feel the barely contained pulse of sorrow and grief coursing through her. "Kayli." He paused just a moment to arch his brow to make sure she didn't interrupt him again.

She took in a shuddering breath and nodded.

"Growing up back on Earth, there was this televised story I really enjoyed. It was about a man who had traveled through time, leaping from point to point in history, driven by an unknown force to change things for the better. 'Striving to put right, what once went wrong, and hoping that each time, his next leap, will be the leap home.'"

He paused smiling to himself as he remembered the words of the show he'd just quoted. Kayli-Zan however had no frame of reference for this and at best could be described as crestfallen. This had gone so much better in his head.

"And I understand how he felt. Being trapped away from the one place he wanted to be. Unable to return home. It was unbearable to see it as out of reach. Until now, I never understood how the story ended."

Kayli-Zan started to pull away and he held on. "Please, Tyler, let go," she begged.

"Kayli, please, just give me a few more moments. I promise I'll be brief."

She heaved in another shaky breath. Though she stayed a step farther back, she didn't fight to get free and gave a nod.

He continued, "The man never went back to his own time. He chose to continue leaping from time and place to time and place for the rest of his life. I never understood that choice, till now. He did make it home."

The tension in Kayli-Zan's arms went slack, and she stared at him, confusion in her expression and coming in waves through where his hands touched the sleek skin of her bare arms.

Tyler licked his lips and chuckled, the planned words having gotten lost in the moment. "Um, Kayli, I had something better planned than, well, this. All my life I was told that this would happen. This saying and feeling and thinking the same things so often but expressing them in totally different and wrong ways. It's natural. And I never believed it till now." He chuckled again and the coughed to cover it, worried he was coming across as glib. Or insane.

"This? What are you talking about Tyler?" she asked barely over a whisper.

"I love you," he said simply. With a hefty sigh to clear the emotional weight so he could speak again, he added, "And beyond that, I discovered the purpose for my being here. So, I, um, I'm going to stay Kayli. If you'll have me."

Kayli's eyes widened and her hands flew to her mouth. Unfortunately breaking his direct line to how she was feeling. "You're staying?" she repeated.

He nodded and glanced up before dropping to one knee. "On Earth we have a custom, when a man wants to mate with a woman for life. He gets down like this and offers a token of the bind that ties them together in love." Producing a ring Irizan had provided him with two gems intersecting in the center to represent their two worlds, he held it aloft. "And if the woman accepts, he places it on her finger."

Shaking her head, mouth still covered with her hands, Kayli asked, "Why are you telling me this?"

Tyler grimaced. Definitely not what he expected, but what had been in his life these last ten years? Blinking he tried not to laugh at the humor of it but couldn't hold back at least one more wry chuckle as he said, "When you told me that I may have come to your world for a time like this, I realized you were right. I don't think my time, my purpose here, is finished.

"And, I mean, I'm choosing you, if you still choose me. No leaving, whether in good or bad, better or worse, sickness or health. Those are the vows that come with a life mate, a husband to his wife, on the home of my childhood.

"This past month sealed it for me. If you still choose me as your life mate in the way your people view it, I want you to understand I will choose you in the way my people view it. And through it, instead of two views, there will be one. One us."

It had all definitely sounded better in his head. Especially as the seconds stretched on without response from her.

At length, Kayli-Zan lowered her hands, which trembled slightly, smoothing the sides of her dress. She said in a soft voice, looking him in the eyes, "Unexpected, but not unwelcome." And offered her hand.

Sliding on the ring and standing, Tyler had to steady himself. This moment, so different for context, was as ethereal as he'd ever been taught it would be. Taking Kayli-Zan's face in his hands he kissed her and was transported to an entirely other world on the currents of her love and joy. One he could call home for the orbits remaining in his mortal life. No longer adrift, struggling to keep afloat, he had come ashore and was breathing freely.

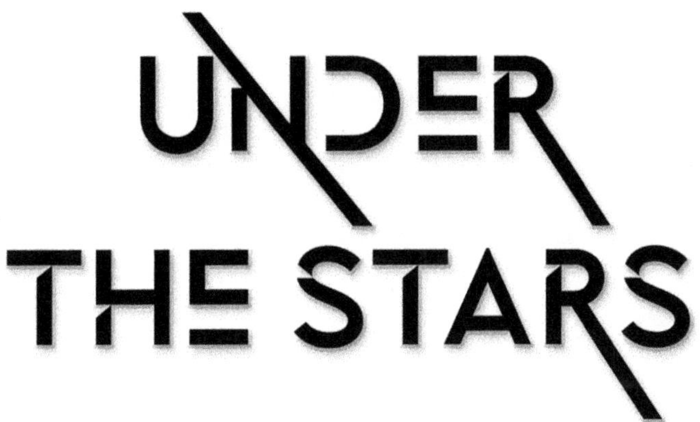

ERIN R. HOWARD

ONE

1

WHITE LIGHTS DOTTED EVERLY'S vision, blurring everything until she couldn't see the monolith or Ned and Tyler standing by it. She gripped the strap of her backpack as she waited for the light to fade, but instead, it intensified.

The air buzzed around her, building and strengthening, until a blast erupted from the monolith, knocking her backward. The force of the explosion sent her sprawling on her back, her vision swirling and dancing around her.

What just happened?

She rolled over to her side, waiting for the dizzy spell to fade. Squinting against the bright light, Everly tried to make out the shapes of the others. Did they fall as well, or was she the only one on the ground?

"Tyler? Ned?" Everly moved to a sitting position, straining to hear a response, but all she could hear was the ringing in her ears—as if she were at a rock concert, standing too close to the speakers.

Everly drew in a deep breath and exhaled. Waited for her sight and hearing to return to normal. But nothing changed.

She sat as still as she could, shielding her eyes against the light until it became so bright, she forced her eyes shut.

She opened her eyes again and immediately regretted the decision. They stung, bringing tears to the corners. She drew her knees up and buried her face in her hands, too much in shock to do anything else.

What was going on?

Just as fast as the light had intensified, it diminished, and she was able to open her eyes. Everly placed both palms on the ground, ready to push herself to an upright position when a deep rumble came from underneath her. Vibrations reverberated throughout her body, and she sank back down to the ground as she tried to figure out what to do next.

"Tyler?" Her voice came out in a hoarse whisper. She cleared her throat and tried again. "Ned?"

Nothing except the rumbling. She half expected the ground to split in two. A nervous laugh escaped from her lips at the direction her thoughts turned. That couldn't happen. Could it?

Were they having an earthquake?

She stood, her legs shaking. Even though the light had dimmed, it was still bright and her vision hazy. Her meager breakfast threatened to come back up as the blurred images of her surroundings whirled in a frenzy and then suddenly became crystal clear.

The monolith still stood in the center of the clearing. Normal sunlight filtered through the trees, casting shadows on the stone structure. Her eyes darted from the fixture to the area surrounding her. Her breath caught in her throat.

This wasn't the clearing.

She scanned the area again. Her heart beat out of control as her mind tried to make sense of what happened. Ned and Tyler were gone.

How could two people disappear? Well, three, if she counted Carter. But he wasn't even at the monolith when the light appeared.

There must be a logical explanation. She simply needed to get in touch with the others. Everly reached in her pocket for her cell phone, but all she found was lint. She must have stashed her phone in her backpack instead of her jeans.

Dread curled in her stomach as she lifted her hands to her shoulders. No backpack. No phone. No Ned, Tyler, or Carter. Vanished. All of them. Tears threatened to spill over, and she blinked them away. But what if it wasn't the others who left? What if it was her who had disappeared?

Even though the monolith stood in front of her, nothing else was familiar. The wooded trail was gone, replaced by a landscaped garden with stone walls bordering the perimeter.

The garden was exquisite. Instead of green leaves, the trees boasted purples, pinks, and even teal. Manicured grass, mixed with rose bushes, wildflowers, and perfectly trimmed hedges graced every inch of the ground around her. Ivy grew up the sides and along the top of the stone walls.

Everly's gaze drifted back toward the monolith, but it was what stood behind it that caught her focus.

A castle.

She let out a nervous laugh and whirled around. This was some sort of joke, right? Ned and Tyler were pulling some sort of elaborate prank on her.

Except, how could they pull off such a complicated joke? Everly reached out and touched the silky leaves of a green shrub, listened to the melodious chirping of songbirds. Laughter and chatter drifted from the pathway toward the castle.

This was real.

She tried to clear her head and investigate the garden. A

cobblestone path led through the mixture of shrubs, flowers, and bushes. There had to be a way out of here, but where was she? And what would she find if she were able to escape? The walls were too tall to climb, and she couldn't just march up to the castle and tell whoever lived there that she suddenly appeared by the monolith.

The monolith. Whatever happened must be because of the strange structure. She whirled around to return to the monument when she collided with a hooded figure.

Everly nearly screamed, but the stranger lowered her hood and gave her a small smile. The hooded person's voice was gentle but held a hint of unease. "I'm sorry. I didn't mean to startle you, but I've been calling after I noticed you by the statue."

Everly gaped at the stranger unsure of what to say. She didn't hear anyone calling out to her. Her mind scrambled to come up with something—anything at all.

"Did you get lost?"

The question seemed to clear Everly's head enough that she nodded. The girl's worried expression relaxed, and she waved her hand.

"It happens all the time. There's always some girl getting lost in the Garden of Tranquility before the Royale."

"The Garden of Tranquility? Royale?" Now that Everly found her voice, she couldn't stop the words from rushing out.

"So, you're not here for the Royale?" The girl tilted her head to the side. "Come to think of it, you're not dressed like the others." Her gaze ran down the length of Everly.

Everly couldn't help but look down at her tank top and jeans. Her right knee had a rip, and her arms were dusted with dirt. Other than that, she looked normal. But as she shifted her gaze from her hiking boots to her companion's sandaled feet, she knew she appeared anything but normal.

The young woman—probably not much older than herself—waited for Everly to answer. But her mind went blank again. She had to come up with something, some explanation, but what could she say that would make any sense? She would end up sounding like a crazy person. A wave of dizziness wafted over her, and Everly lifted a hand to her rub her forehead.

"Are you all right?"

"I'm not sure." There. An honest answer, and her voice even sounded halfway coherent.

A hint of skepticism and fear filled the girl's eyes before she looked away, tucking a strand of golden hair behind her ear. She glanced around them and then turned back to the Monolith and frowned.

"Come with me, and don't say another word." Her voice lowered to a mere whisper. "You're clearly not here for the Royale, and everyone in the palace will know it as soon as they take one look at you."

"I'm sorry, I don't know what's going on."

"I know." She pulled Everly into the shadow of the trees, off the cobblestone path that ran along from the monolith to the palace. She shrugged out of her emerald velvet cape and turned it inside out, with the black lining on the outside. "Put this on."

Everly did as instructed, shivers racing up her arms as the velvet tickled her skin. "Why are you helping me?"

"Take down your hair and turn around." The girl barely looked at her as she untied a black satin ribbon from around her neck. "What's your name?"

"Everly."

She met her eyes. "Turn around, Everly."

Everly pulled the ponytail down and put her back to the girl. The girl separated Everly's hair into three sections, making quick work of a braid, weaving the black ribbon through one of the sections. "It's not very good, but maybe it will buy us some time."

"Buy us time for what? What is going on? Where am I?" Everly didn't care anymore about trying to act like she understood what was happening or where she was. She was scared and needed to know what she was up against.

"Buy us time to get you to my room and have my servant dress you and fix your hair."

Everly finally took the time to study the girl's appearance. Jewels adorned her wrists and neck, and a delicate tiara graced the top of her blonde hair.

"You're a princess."

The girl finally smiled. "Yes. I'm Princess Kaitlin of the Kingdom of Lux. We are out of time. The Royale is about to begin, and if we do not get you changed, you will have to join them."

"I don't understand. What is a Royale, and why would they make me join?"

Kaitlin's smiled faded altogether, and she narrowed her eyes. "You picked the wrong day to stumble into the kingdom. Every year, girls are brought in from the surrounding lands, and they must go through a series of tests."

The princess reached out and looped her arm through Everly's. "I will explain more, but we have to go. Now."

"You didn't answer my question, though." Everly turned around to face the girl. "Why are you helping me?"

"Because I think I'm the one who brought you here."

TWO

1

"DON'T SAY anything to anyone. Smile, and talk to me like I'm your best friend in the entire world." The Princess looped her arm through Everly's again, this time forcing her to walk with her.

They made their way from the trees and back to the cobblestone walkway. She did her best not to gawk at the beautiful surroundings, but it was hard to pull her eyes away from the majestic garden.

"Everly!"

Kaitlin's voice broke through her thoughts and she nearly stumbled on the uneven pavement. "Yes, I'm sorry."

"Keep the cape closed." Her eyes trailed down to Everly's boots. "I can't do anything for your feet. But hopefully, no one will notice."

"I take it that jeans and hiking boots are not in style here."

A frown pulled on the corners of the princess's mouth. "I'm not sure what *in style* means, but usually only men wear boots."

They reached a set of double doors, and Kaitlin paused.

"We will go in here and up to my chambers. No one should stop us. Just smile and act like you are happy to see me."

Everly took a deep breath and then plastered on a grin as double doors opened. Two guards on either side bowed to the princess. They passed the men and went through a massive hall with marble floors and colorful tapestries. Servants in green and blue clothing flittered around them, cleaning, holding trays of food, and arranging vases of flowers.

Kaitlin kept a firm grip on Everly's arm, and she was grateful. It helped her concentrate on the charade she had to play instead of taking in everything happening around her. Wherever she was, it wasn't like anything she'd ever seen before. It was as if she'd stepped into a fairytale. Kaitlin tugged her across the large floor, through a door to the left, and into a hallway.

Instead of the tapestries, giant portraits—no doubt of the royal family—graced both sides of the walls. They were almost to a staircase, but the princess never stopped rambling, and it became increasingly hard for Everly to keep up with the story. Something about how excited she was that Everly finally accepted her invitation to visit.

They reached the top of the stairs and made a right, followed the long corridor, and then went through another set of doors and another hallway before the princess finally stopped her prattling. Everly had long before given up on trying to remember which direction they came when they passed an open door and a figure nearly fell out of a chair, doing a double-take as they walked by.

"Kate!" A deep voice called out, and footsteps echoed behind them as the princess walked faster, nearly running down the long hallway to the last door on the right. "Where have you been, Kaitlin, and who is that with you?"

The princess pushed the handle down and nearly threw Everly through the doorway before shutting it behind her.

"We have to hurry and get you changed." She rushed across the sitting area to another room almost as large as the one they were in.

Everly gasped as she took in the rows of dresses, shoes, and accessories lining the walls.

"Are you always going to have that look on your face?"

"What look?"

"Like you're surprised by everything." The princess pulled out a purple dress and held it up before placing it back on the rack. "I'm not good at this sort of thing. I need Tori." She reached for a rope hanging on the wall and gave it a quick tug.

"I can't help it. I keep thinking this is all a dream, and I'm going to wake up any minute."

"You look like you're about my size." Kaitlin pulled a light blue silk chemise from a hanger and tossed it. "Put this on. Tori can't see you in those clothes."

Everly wanted to laugh at the girl's words. While they were almost the same in height, Everly was not the same size. Kaitlin was petite, and Everly—well, she wasn't overweight but curvier.

A knock tapped on the bedroom door and a gentle voice called out. "Your Highness?"

The princess's eyes darted to Everly's feet before she left the closet to meet Tori. "Hide your boots."

Everly bent down to unlace them, her heart racing as she kicked them off and searched for a place to put them. Finally, she decided on the floor beside a pair of fur moccasins and then laid her clothes on top of them. Her dark jeans and cotton tank stood out in stark contrast to the satin and exquisite dresses. She scooped them back up in her arms and stuffed them under a cushion of a nearby sofa.

Who had a sofa in their closet? Her mind raced as the

princess entered, followed by the servant, whose eyes widened in surprise.

"Tori, this is Lady Everly, a friend of mine from boarding school. She's going to need some help getting ready for tonight's Assessment Ceremony."

"Of course, Your Highness." The servant surveyed the room in confusion. "Where's Lady Everly's trunk?"

The princess's smile faltered for all of two seconds before she recovered. "Unfortunately, there was an incident on the way, and her trunk was damaged. She lost everything."

"Oh, my." Tori's face paled. "Well, we should be able to find something that will work until we can get some more dresses made for her."

Everly bit her lip to keep from saying anything as the girl pulled a dark blue dress from the rack and put it over her head. Surely, it wasn't necessary for Tori to actually dress her. But one glance in Kaitlin's direction, and she closed her mouth.

Once the empire-waisted, sapphire dress was on, Tori's hands set out to fix her hair. The servant's lips pursed at the sight of the lopsided braid, but she took out the hair tie and shook the braid loose. Putting half of her hair up, she twisted blue and black ribbons along the sides and then let them dangle down the back of Everly's head. Once Everly's hair was secured, Tori fastened a bracelet to her wrist before handing her a pair of black satin ballet flats.

The princess beamed. "Very pretty, Tori. Thank you."

Tori curtsied to Kaitlin and slipped out of the room without another word.

Everly waited until she heard the door click shut. "Do you think she was suspicious?"

A clock chimed in the sitting room and Kaitlin glanced at it. "It's not Tori I'm worried about."

"What do you mean?"

"It's my brother we have to convince, and we are out of time."

"Was that who tried to stop you in the hall?" She continued at Kaitlin's nod. "Why are we out of time?"

"Because the Royale just officially started."

"And?"

"It's custom for me to meet with the girls before the Royale and accompany them in." Kaitlin reached over and grabbed her arm. "How good are you at pretending?"

"I'm a drama major at college."

The princess frowned. "I'm not sure what that is."

"I take acting classes at my university." Everly's mind raced for another explanation. "Like the theater."

The princess's eyes lit up. "Good. You're going to need it."

THREE

1

IF FINN BOWEN could rip the velvet curtains from the theater box, he would. The luxurious fabrics did nothing but add to the warmth of the small enclosure. What he wouldn't give to sit down below with the rest of the kingdom. To listen to the crowd's cheers and sit close enough to hear the sizzle and pop of magical currents flowing out of the contestant's fingertips.

But the royal box seat was moved from the ground floor years ago, when a young girl sent a flurry of lightning bolts across the stage and hit his great grandfather square in the chest. Stopped his heart, and none of the healers could get it restarted.

This time, nothing could go wrong. The twenty contestants would battle and show off their Gifts of Lumen, and someone would win. Finn would finally be able to announce a winner, and he could set out to do what he promised his parents and his people he would—heal the dying land.

A shudder swept down his back, causing the hair on his arms to stand up. There was too much riding on this year's

Royale. He was the king, and two years into his reign, the darkness that danced along their borders during his father's rule now blanketed the entire Kingdom of Lux.

Voices came from behind him, and he nearly bolted from his chair. Tradition dictated Kaitlin would be the one with the contestants, and she was a stickler for the rules.

"My lady, in here."

Finn turned at the voice of his steward, Reece, who held the door to the royal box open. A wide-eyed girl walked through the door, decked out in blue and ribbons. Her eyes swept across the room before landing on him. Finn cleared his throat and stood, buttoning his suit jacket.

"Pardon me, Your Majesty. This is Lady Everly, a friend of Princess Kaitlin." The servant bowed toward him and then turned back to the lady. "Lady Everly, may I present His Royal Highness, Finn Bowen."

Curious, he crossed over to her and bowed his head. "Pleasure to meet you, Lady Everly."

The girl gripped the side of her gown and hastily curtsied. A tendril of strawberry blonde hair fell across her cheek, and she quickly brushed it away. "The pleasure is all mine." She rose, meeting his gaze.

Finn momentarily forgot his manners. "Please, join me." He stumbled over his words before gesturing to the empty chair beside his throne.

"Thank you."

"I didn't know Kaitlin was expecting company." He waited for her to sit before he took his place beside her. The girl's face flushed, clearly uncomfortable.

"Yes. It was sort of a surprise."

"Ah. Well, that explains it then."

Lady Everly turned to look at him. "Explains what, Your Majesty?"

He leaned back, angling his body so he could see her better. "Kaitlin is not one for surprises."

"That makes two of us, Your Majesty." Everly shoulders relaxed, and a grin spread across her lips.

He turned back in the direction of the stage, his thoughts a mixture of worry and humor. Who was this girl? He shuffled back through the courtiers that he knew, but he would remember someone named Lady Everly. Especially one who had tiny flecks of gold in her eyes and made him stammer over his words.

A trickle of doubt stopped his train of thought. What if she wasn't who she said she was? There was something he couldn't quite put his finger on. But this girl almost seemed insecure in her title and standing.

"Lady Everly, would you like a cup of tea or perhaps a Marsh Cocoa?" Reece asked, wheeling in a cart from the hallway.

"What is a Marsh Cocoa?"

If Finn were already holding a cup of his own, he would no doubt have dropped it. "I'm sorry—Lady Everly—do you mean to tell me that you have never had melted chocolate and marshmallows?"

Lady Everly laughed, a shaky one she tried to cover up by clearing her throat. "At home, we call it hot chocolate."

"That's not very creative." Finn frowned, not wanting to offend her, but more doubts of her identity took hold.

"Well, you're not wrong." She rose from her chair. "I would love a cup of Marsh Cocoa, Reece."

What in the world was she doing? He jumped up from his chair in time to see Reece's horrified expression. She must have seen it as well because she suddenly stopped and clasped her hands together.

"I'm sorry, Your Majesty. I ... I am used to ... I really love hot chocolate, so my servants at home keep it in a Thermos for me to get whenever I want."

Getting her own drinks? A Thermos? Finn couldn't make any sense of what Lady Everly was talking about.

"Lady Everly, forgive me, but where did you say you're from?"

The young woman accepted a mug from the steward and turned around to face him. "Oh, it's a small place, much smaller than your kingdom."

He accepted his own mug of cocoa and went back to his seat. Did this lady ever fully explain anything?

"How do you know my sister?"

"We went to boarding school together."

Finally, something that sounded correct. He blew on his drink before attempting a small sip. Kaitlin attended a few different schools before coming back home and settling into her position at the palace. But that was the extent of his knowledge. He never thought about asking her about her friends other than the ones who attended court.

Before he could ask her another question, the lights dimmed in the theater, and the chatter from the crowd ceased.

Everly leaned forward in her chair, eyes alight with curiosity. A few seconds later, Kaitlin walked across the stage to grand applause.

"Citizens of the Kingdom of Lux, welcome to the Royale." Another round of cheers. "Twenty girls were accepted into the Royale. Twenty of the best and brightest. Twenty of the strongest, most unique masters of the Gifts of Lumen that the Villages of the Stars have to offer."

Cheers erupted, filling the theater with loud voices and clapping. Too wrapped up in Kaitlin's words and the weight of finding a winner, Finn forgot to watch Everly's face. He wanted to see just how much she knew about the Royale. He stole a glance at her, but she was just as mesmerized by Kaitlin as the crowd.

"Now, please help me welcome your host for the Royale, Mateo Jackson." Kaitlin clapped along with the audience as Mateo walked out on stage.

"She knows how to command a stage, doesn't she?" She whispered, meeting his eye.

"Yes, she does." Finn forced his eyes away from the delight on Everly's face back to his sister, giving himself a mental shake. One smile from the girl beside him, and his unease subsided.

Heart beating fast, he took another sip from his mug, glancing as Lady Everly took a drink and then promptly sneezed.

Lady Everly whispered, "I sort of sneeze every time I have chocolate."

"And yet you continue to eat or drink it?"

A grin lit up her face. "Your Majesty, it's chocolate."

She turned back to the stage as if that was the best explanation she could give him.

"Indeed." He took another sip, trying to hide his amusement. He had a feeling getting to know Lady Everly would be a welcome distraction from the pressure of the Royale.

FOUR

1

WHAT IN THE world was a Royale? Everly longed to jump up from her seat and run back to the monolith. Somehow, it had brought her to this strange kingdom, so surely it could take her back.

Right?

Finn—King Finn that is—sat beside her, every so often glancing in her direction, curiosity and doubt on his face. Did he know she was a fake? Lady Everly indeed. She pulled out every ounce of acting skill and movie knowledgc she possessed to play the part. But would it be enough? He kept staring at her, as if waiting for her to mess up and be forced to come clean.

And don't even get her started on her sneezing fit. Why, oh, why did she have to say that she kept hot chocolate by the Thermos? She loved the rich drink, but her allergies did not. Hopefully it would stay with the sneezing and not turn into a reaction of hives. If a hole could open up right now, she would gladly let it swallow her.

What was Kaitlin thinking, leaving her all alone with her brother? Her very cute, *royal* brother with his perfectly styled mahogany hair and chestnut eyes that seemed to observe too much. But there was also a hint of sadness and mystery. One she found herself wanting to know more about.

King Finn rubbed his hand over his neatly trimmed beard—more stubble than beard—concentrating on the stage below them. Everly had to force her attention away from him and back toward Kaitlin. Her stomach churned, and she gripped the skirt of her borrowed gown. There was no way she would be able to pull this off. Closing her eyes, she inhaled, relying on the sound of her breathing to calm her.

"Are you ready?"

Everly jerked her head up to find King Finn standing before her, his hand held out. When did he stand? Her eyes flickered back the stage, but it was empty.

"Ready?" She scrambled to come up with some sort of indication of what he referred to but came up blank. She'd been too distracted in her thoughts to notice that the crowd was already leaving.

"For the feast." He frowned, letting his hand drop to his side.

"Of course." She got to her feet, plastering on a smile. "I got caught up in the excitement of it all for a moment."

"Ah. I suppose it is rather exciting." He extended his arm for her to grasp, and she quickly looped her hand through hoping he wouldn't notice her trembling.

Everly didn't reply again, in case he would further elaborate, giving her some sort of clue to fill in the missing blanks. Acting like the she knew everything about the Royale and the Kingdom of Lux was exhausting, and she had no idea how long she could keep up the charade.

Finn escorted her from the royal box of the auditorium and to the elevator, where an attendant waited at the doors. The servant pushed the down arrow and bowed to Finn as the doors slid open.

The king let go of her arm and ushered her in, following behind her. He gripped a handrail hanging from the top of the elevator. "Aren't you going to hold on?"

Before she could process his question, the elevator dropped so fast her stomach lurched, the contents threatening to come back up. "Oh, my!" She lunged to grab ahold of the rail and then covered her mouth with her free hand.

Another frown flickered across the king's face. "You've never been on an Ascension?"

"Ours do not go so fast that your meal comes back up."

Finn narrowed his eyes at her words, and then burst out in laughter as the elevator came to a sudden stop. The doors slid open. "Lady Everly, you are very funny for a courtier."

Finally. A word she understood. Checks burning, she tucked a stray curl around her ear and forced her fingers to move from the bar.

He offered his arm once more as he stepped out of the small enclosure. She took it, grateful for the stability. How could anyone get used to those speeds without getting sick each time?

"I will take that as a compliment, Your Highness."

"You should." His grin faded as they moved down the hallway toward another metal door with another attendant guarding the exit. The man bowed his head and opened the door, revealing a strange-looking car. The feast must be back at the palace and not at the theater. She would have to ride in the strange car once more. Everly did her best to mask her shock. If she didn't get control of her facial expressions, they would give her away. She wasn't supposed to be surprised by anything here. But while they had similar technology to her own, it was different enough that she couldn't keep from gawking. The sleek silver car idled in front of them as the servant hurried to open the back door.

"Lady Everly." The servant's voice was quiet, but polite as he gestured for her to get in. Should she slide across the seat? She stiffened, debating what to do, when the voice of Queen Clarisse telling Mia that a queen never slides echoed in her mind. She stifled a giggle as she tried to maneuver her dress and climb into the vehicle.

The door closed behind her and a few seconds later Finn climbed in beside her, an amused expression on his face. Did she get it wrong? Again?

There wasn't time to debate her actions because the car took off with such speed she didn't even have time to look for a seatbelt.

The car weaved through the traffic effortlessly, and it wasn't until they were getting out that she realized there wasn't a driver.

Ever the gentleman, Finn offered his arm again, and she grabbed it, willing her legs to cooperate and her heart to return to a normal rhythm. They entered what she assumed to be the back entrance of the castle. A mixture of pleasant aromas filled the air the closer they came to the banquet room.

Servants stopped whatever they were doing as they passed in the halls, bowing, and avoiding eye contact, but Finn acknowledged each one with a small tip of his head in their direction. It seemed significant somehow—another blank filled in on her assessment of the king.

He was kind.

Floor-to-ceiling wooden doors graced the middle of the hallway, with intricate carvings of leaves, stems, and daisies.

"It's beautiful."

The servant at the door started to pull it open, but Finn held up his hand to wait. "It is, isn't it?" A smile tugged on the corners of his lips, but sorrow lingered in his eyes. "My mother loved daisies."

Loved. Past tense. Tears pricked her eyes at the anguish in his voice, and her own grief rushed to the surface. She did the best she could to keep them at bay. "So did my sister."

Finn stared at her, understanding dawning across his face. He reached over and patted her hand. "Remind me to show you the gardens tomorrow. There's a whole section of Gerbera daisies."

"I would love that."

"Good." He nodded and cleared his throat. "Shall we?"

"I'm ready if you are."

The servant pulled open the double doors, and Everly's breath caught in her throat. The delicate flowers that graced the doors continued on into the elegant dining room. Wooden beams stretched out across the ceiling, and an extra-large, handcrafted table took up residence in the center of the floor. More daisies were carved into the moldings around the baseboards and windows. Colorful lace curtains covered the windows in a range of hues.

Then her eyes landed on the crowd.

Who were all staring at her holding on to the king's arm.

"Finn ..." Her shock momentarily blocked her mind from addressing him with the appropriate title. She scrambled to make it right. "Your Highness, they are all staring at us."

"They are indeed." He whispered back to her. "Ignore them if you can." He gently tugged her forward, and everyone seated at the grand table and nearby smaller tables stood at his approach.

"I don't think that's possible."

"I believe, after tonight, you will have to." His voice carried a hint of amusement.

"What do you mean?"

"Well, Lady Everly, you will be all that anyone talks about during this year's Royale." He walked her over the table and pulled out a chair for her and then leaned toward her ear. "Don't sit until they do."

Murmurs carried across the hall as he pulled away. There was no way they could know what he whispered, but they would definitely be able to see her red cheeks.

Finn waited as a servant pulled out his chair and then took his spot at the head of the table. The courtiers moved, taking their places, and Everly did the same. She lifted her gaze from the elegant place setting to a wide grin on the face of Princess Kaitlin sitting across from her.

FIVE

1

GETTING out of the palace was trickier than Everly anticipated. She tried to leave early, but just as she was about to get dressed, four servants entered, each one with their arms full of dresses, hair accessories, shoes, and personal items. There wasn't any way to shoo them out of the room. She had to sit and wait as they picked out her dress, styled her hair, and selected the perfect jewelry to accessorize her outfit.

Now, she skirted around each corner of the palace trying not to get sidelined by curious eyes. How was she supposed to slip out of the castle unseen and go back through the monolith? The castle bustled with activity—even at the crack of dawn. Everly hurried as fast as she could toward the garden doors. But she would have to pass the dining room, which was already filling up with courtiers eating breakfast. Did they not have anything better to do at this time of day? Everly would much rather be curled up under the down feather comforter that reminded her of her dormitory bed.

What would everyone say when they realized she was gone? How long would her roommate wait to call her parents to tell them she was missing? And why weren't Ned and Tyler here with her?

She pushed the questions away and focused on getting past the dining room without being seen. The last thing she needed was Finn or Kaitlin spotting her. A smidgeon of unease settled in her stomach about leaving without saying goodbye. Especially to Finn. Would he be upset in a few hours when he realized she'd left?

It shouldn't matter—she'd known him for less than a day. But for some reason, the thought of leaving without talking to him felt like the coward's way out.

A servant opened the doors to the garden and gave her a nod as she passed. If it were unusual for guests to leave, he didn't act like it. She hurried down the cobblestone pathway, winding her way through the flowers and roses bushes toward where she remembered the monolith standing.

It was still there.

Relief flooded her at the sight of the statue gleaming in the morning light. Part of her feared it might have disappeared. She pulled up the edges of her dress to keep from dragging the hem and jogged the remaining distance to the structure.

Stopping in front of it, she dropped her dress and stared at the stone, trying to calm her thoughts. How would this work? Last time, she didn't even touch the monolith, it just lit up and then sent her flying backward.

Just touch it and go home, Everly.

She took in a deep breath and touched the stone with her fingertips.

Nothing.

She closed her eyes and pressed her palm against the monolith, preparing herself for the bright light and blast.

The silence was deafening. Slowly opening one eye, Everly glanced at the structure before hastily closing it again.

She waited.

Finally, she cleared her mind of everything but her desire to go home.

Still nothing.

Frustrated, she lowered her hand and took a step back. Why wasn't it working? Was there something she missed? Did she have to be standing in the same exact spot she was before? She moved to the other side and repeated the whole process again.

"You missed breakfast."

Everly dropped her hand and whirled around to find Finn watching her. "Oh? I must have lost track of time."

He clasped his hands behind his back and walked toward her. "That's certainly easy to do out here."

"It's beautiful."

"I thought you were going to wait for me."

Panic welled up at his statement and she scrambled to remember what he referred to. The daisies. "Oh... I uh ..."

The disappointment on his face was evident, but he waved a hand as if it weren't a big deal. "It's all right if you didn't want to go."

"No, I did." She gestured to the monolith. "I noticed this yesterday and wanted to get a closer look."

He narrowed his eyes at the structure. "Ah. You've found the prophecy." Disdain dripped from his words.

"Prophecy?"

"I figured Kaitlin would have told you all about it at boarding school. Most people can't wait to hound us about it."

"I don't like to bring up things that are not any of my business." The truthful statement burst from her lips before she could mask her tone. Too many people had done that very thing to her over the years, their curiosity over her sister's death outweighing their manners. And their prying questions.

Finn sighed and walked around the monolith, bending down to push grass away from the base. "She will come from Under the Stars, during the seventeenth moon. The one with the power to illuminate the kingdom from the darkness."

"Who is she?"

"That is the question." Finn rose from the ground and gave her a slight shake of his head. "We do not know. Every year we hold the Royale in hopes to find the one who will keep the darkness at bay, and every year, I fail. And with each failed Royale, the earth dies a little more, creeping its way to the capital."

His words cut off her reply, the pain in his voice stopping her from being able to speak. The burden he carried cast a pall over the garden, and she had to work to clear the thickness in her throat. "I'm sorry, Your Highness."

"It's not your fault." He gave her a shallow chuckle. "How about I escort you to the Royale? Let's get this disappointment over with for the day?"

Her eyes drifted back the monolith. So much for going home today. Sadness tried to overwhelm her, but she somehow managed to pull herself together before she turned to look at the king. "I doubt very much it will be a disappointment."

"Well, you're new here." He held out his arm. "There's still plenty of time for you to take a front row seat."

SIX

LIGHTNING EXPLODED out of one of the contestant's fingertips, knocking three of her opponents flat on their backs. Finn leaned forward in his seat, anxiously waiting for them to regain their feet. It had been many years since he'd witnessed that much power from one girl. Lightning was a common gift of the Lumen, but the force and brightness that came from the redheaded girl—Angeline—was enough to send the other six young ladies scurrying for a hiding spot.

Twenty girls entered the outdoor arena fifteen minutes ago, prepared to showcase their magic abilities while somehow trying to stay within the perimeter of the game floor. It wasn't an easy thing to do. The ground of the arena was elevated on a tall platform built specifically for the purpose of the Royale. Go off the edge, and you were disqualified from the competition. But keeping both feet on the Royale floor was harder than it appeared. Obstacles covered every square inch of the arena.

"What do you think, Lady Everly?" His sister's question interrupted his thoughts, but he glanced over in time to catch Everly's eyes light up.

"It's completely terrifying and exciting at the same time."

Kaitlin laughed. "Each year, the arena changes. That way the contestants do not know what to expect."

"Seriously?"

"Of course. If the contestants know the obstacle course, then they will have an unnecessary advantage." He frowned, looking back at the stage. "We can't take any chances."

"Please ignore my brother's rudeness, Everly." Kaitlin got to her feet and clapped as Angeline summersaulted away from a blast of ice heading directly at her. "He forgets that not everyone holds Royales in their kingdoms." She pointed to Angeline. "I think she may be my favorite this year."

"It's too early to tell, sister."

Another contestant, with two black braids dangling down to her waist, sent a rush of wind swirling around Angeline, engulfing her in a twister of leaves and dust.

"No!" Kaitlin gasped, and Finn couldn't hold back a smile at his sister's angry scowl but stopped when Everly's worried eyes met his. He leaned over to her and lowered his voice. "Don't worry, Lady Everly. No one is allowed to maim or kill another contestant."

Relief flooded her face. "That's good to know."

"It can happen though." Kaitlin returned to her seat on the other side of Everly. "It's rare, but some have died competing."

"That's awful."

"Not everyone has the best of intentions." Finn sighed. "They are all vetted before coming, but sometimes—well—we can't always prevent what happens in the Royale."

"How many days do they compete?"

"It depends on how many last the first day. But each day has a newer and harder task. They will eventually get down to only one."

Finn turned his attention back to the stage. The three ladies who were knocked down from Angeline's bolts now successfully hid in different spots. It was almost impossible to remember who was who from this vantage point. But number five—the tallest of all the girls—had her arms raised, moving the water in a pond on the other side of the platform.

"Did she just pick up that water?" Everly reached for the binoculars in front of them. "Who is she aiming for?"

He scanned the arena, searching for the girl's target and flinched when he found a short, curly haired girl standing with her back to the pond, in a duel with another contestant. Both of them were trading short bursts of electricity. Finn flinched as number five thrust both her hands forward, sending a stream of water to smack the girl square in the back. She screamed as the pressure of the liquid pushed her along the floor and toward the edge, her electricity halting with a hiss.

"Oh no." Kaitlin groaned. "We are about to lose our first one."

"I don't know. She may surprise you." Finn leaned forward in his seat, waiting for the girl to fight back.

"How can either of you stand to watch this?" Everly got to her feet, walked over to the balcony rail, and leaned over. "Are you sure she won't get hurt if she falls? And why isn't the water hurting her? Shouldn't she be electrocuted?"

Finn jumped up and grabbed her arm to pull her back. "Quite sure. Falls are cushioned to prevent injury. We, however, well, we are up rather high. Why would Lumen give her a gift that would harm her? The water may stall her gift, but it's not going to hurt her."

"Do you not like heights, Your Highness?" Everly gently freed her arm from his hold.

"No. Nevertheless, there's no reason to tempt fate."

"Look!" Kaitlin pointed to the stage, and Finn turned in time to see the girl who was getting drenched by the water somehow turn enough to send a series of sparks to a tree near the water girl. The tree fell over—right at the feet of the attacker. It was just enough to divert the attacker's attention and lessen the water stream so the girl could jump out of the water's current.

"Told you!" Finn cheered with the rest of the crowd. This year's contestants were the best he'd seen in years. A spark of hope ignited at the thought. Maybe this would be the year. He didn't know how, but something felt different.

"You seem happy, brother."

He glanced up to find Kaitlin close to his side, clapping with the other spectators.

"It seems like there are loads of potential this year." His eyes drifted over to Everly, who was accepting a plate loaded with cheese and fruit from one of the palace servants.

"Ah, I see." The meaning behind her word were hard to miss. She had noticed him staring at Everly.

"Everly has nothing to do with it." He frowned. Finn loved his sister, but she had an annoying habit of trying to marry him off. And all she had to show for it was a trail of brokenhearted courtiers. It wasn't that he didn't want a wife and family someday, but he was still trying to find his bearings leading the kingdom. There was already too much pressure on his shoulders trying to find a way to push back the darkness and stop the decay. Every day, death spread faster and faster. Many villages had lost their farmlands. How could he put himself before his people? It didn't seem right.

"You deserve to be happy, Finn." Kaitlin reached out and squeezed his arm. "It's almost been four years. Don't you think our parents would want to see you settled?"

"You never give up, do you?"

Kaitlin grinned ear from ear. "It's not in my nature, brother."

"Are you two going to whisper all day?" Everly called up to them from her chair, binoculars in hand. "I think we are going to lose contestant number two. She's holding onto the edge though."

Finn stepped closer to the rail to get a better look. "Wow. She's trying to pull herself back up over the edge."

"Do you think anyone will help pull her up?" Everly asked, her voice hopeful.

"Everyone's on their own in the arena."

Shock filled Everly's voice. "They aren't allowed to help each other?"

"It's not against the rules ..." Kaitlin interjected. "But it is rare."

"Maybe someone will surprise you."

Finn clutched the rail, almost hoping someone would step up and prove Everly correct. Ugh. Kaitlin got under his skin with all that marriage talk. He couldn't afford any distractions right now. Not during the most important event of the year. Maybe the most crucial Royale ever. He couldn't afford to let this beautiful stranger distract him from his purpose. There would always be time for happiness later.

After the land thrived once more.

SEVEN

THERE WASN'T a single moment when Everly was alone. She would spend the days watching the battles with Finn and Kaitlin, then the evenings were spent in the dining hall and ballroom, eating and conversing with the courtiers.

She had only made it back to monolith once, and it proved just as fruitless as the first time. Everly feared she would be stuck on this side of the monolith. Four days away from home, but in some ways, she didn't miss it. She didn't miss the endless amounts of studying and sleep deprivation. The constant worry over her grades slipping and losing her scholarship. If that happened, what would her parents think? Letting them down was not an option. They'd been through enough heartbreak for a lifetime. Everly couldn't let any more disappointment come their way.

Her roommate had always said she was too focused, that she didn't have enough fun. Well, how was dressing up in fine gowns and spending her days with a king? Would her roommate find that fun enough?

Everly was determined to corner Kaitlin and talk to her

privately. She didn't know how much longer she could pretend with Finn. The longer the charade continued, the more awful she felt. He had been so kind and welcoming to her, and Everly did not enjoying lying.

But each time she tried to bring it up with Kaitlin, they were interrupted, or the princess made an excuse to leave, promising they would talk later.

"Are you all right?"

Everly nearly dropped her fork onto the crystal plate. She peered up to find a frown on Finn's face. "Of course."

"You've barely touched your food, and they only bring out dessert for happy plates." His teasing smile conjured a deep laugh.

"We can't have that, can we?" She cut into the juicy steak and took a bite, avoiding the snickers and whispers from the courtiers around the table. While Finn and Kaitlin had been welcoming and kind, the same couldn't be said for the others. Most of the girls looked down their noses at her, sending her hateful scowls when they thought she wasn't looking. And the young men, well, they gave her a wide berth. Especially when they noticed Finn standing nearby.

Dessert was a grand affair, and by far, the best part of the evening meal. Servants in black and white outfits and bowties pushed carts out into the dining room. Each dessert plate held a selection of miniature pies, cookies, or cakes.

A teenage girl, with freckles across her nose and black-framed glasses came from behind and gently set a plate in front of Everly before quietly maneuvering out of eyesight. When Everly first arrived, she assumed that she would be just like the other guests, with a different attendant each time. But after the first day, she recognized that particular girl only served her. Finn and Kaitlin also had their own attendants. The girl didn't say a word to her, but every chance she got, Everly would smile at her and whisper *thank you*. At first the girl's cheeks flamed, and she backed away quickly. But now, after a few days, she returned a small smile in response.

"I was thinking we could take that walk tonight, if you would like."

Those seated at the table ceased their conversations and turned their attention to her. She nearly choked on a strawberry. Coughing, she tried her best to swallow and reach for her goblet, but it tipped, soaking her strawberry shortcake. Kaitlin quickly handed over her glass.

"Brother, you nearly killed her." Kaitlin waved to Everly's attendant. "Please get Lady Everly another shortcake."

"Oh, that's okay, Princess Kaitlin. I was almost finished anyway." She picked up the plate to hand to the girl and then realized her mistake.

Luckily, the girl didn't miss a beat as she took the plate from Everly's fingers and backed away. Snickers of laughter filled the air as Everly gulped the water, trying to hide her embarrassment at her *faux pas*. Instead, she turned to Finn. "That would be lovely, Your Highness. I've been looking forward to seeing the daisies."

"Good." He stood to his feet and buttoned his suit jacket. "Shall we?"

She accepted his outstretched hand and grinned, placing her napkin on the table. "Lead the way, Your Highness."

There. Let them stew on that for a while.

It wasn't until they were safely out of prying eyes that Everly could relax. She inhaled the sweet fragrance of the blossoms, enjoying the cool evening air. The climate was much like home, except here, the temperature dropped as soon as the sun set.

"I should have thought to get you a wrap." Finn let go of her arm and started unbuttoning his jacket.

"No, Your Highness, I'm fine."

"I insist." He held open the jacket and helped her slide it on.

"How do I look?" She held up her arms, laughing as the sleeves covered her hands.

Finn took her arm and rolled the sleeve up to her wrist. "It suits you." His eyes met hers, and Everly had to remind herself to breathe. His gaze lowered to her lips, and she couldn't help but lean forward. Except he dropped his hands and stiffened, resolve hardening in his eyes.

"The daisies are this way." Finn took a step backward and walked down the path to their right.

She hesitated, the wind playing with the tendrils of curls at her neck. The rush of the breeze cleared her head of all the thoughts and feelings swarming around unbidden.

She quickly pushed up the sleeve on her other arm and hurried after him. *You do not belong here, Everly.* She had to remember that. No matter how much this place might suit her.

EIGHT

"FINN? ARE YOU IN HERE?"

Finn glanced up from the stack of papers on his desk and checked the time. Two in the morning. What was Kaitlin doing up at this time of night? He opened the door to his study and frowned. Kaitlin stood at his door, her traveling cape in her arms.

"What's going on? Are you all right?"

"Yes, of course." She walked past him into the room, and he closed the door behind her. Worry and panic welling up. There had to be something seriously wrong. Was it Everly?

"Are you traveling somewhere?

"I received notice that one of the contestants has fallen ill."

"Have you fetched the doctor?"

"You don't understand." Kaitlin's eyes narrowed. "There's nothing physically wrong with her."

"I'm not following." He crossed his arms.

"It's her gift." Kaitlin bit her lip and looked away. "It's vanished."

"What do you mean, 'it's vanished'?"

"I mean, it's not there." Kaitlin started pacing. "You remember during the last day of the arena fighting when the girl went over the edge but held on?"

"Yes, of course."

"This girl had the ability to manipulate nature. She can grow vines, help flowers bloom, that sort of thing. She tried coaxing a vine from the cliff to help her climb back up, but she couldn't do it."

"Maybe she was just scared and zapped her energy."

Kaitlin stopped pacing and nodded. "That's what she thought too. She somehow climbed up the cliff and returned to the battle. But nothing she tried after that worked. She hid in one of the buildings and waited the timer out."

Rubbing a hand across his face, Finn sighed. "And she hasn't been able to use it since?"

Kaitlin shook her head. "We've never had this happen before. What are we going to do?"

"We can't let her compete any longer. She will have to be disqualified."

"But what will we tell the people and the other contestants?" Kaitlin pulled out a chair in front of his desk and sat down. "They are going to be scared and ask questions we don't have answers for."

Just when he thought this Royale would be different and that they were on the verge of a winner. Kaitlin was right, the people would be terrified, and rightly so. Never in their history had anyone lost their gift of Lumen. Had they? Finn didn't have the gift, so he didn't have any firsthand experience. His mother on the other hand—she would know. If only she were still alive.

Finn gestured to Kaitlin's coat. "I take it you already have an idea?"

"I will escort the girl back to her home under the guise she is ill."

He shook his head in protest. "No, you can't leave. We are in the middle of the Royale. You're the liaison for the young ladies. They need you."

"I know, but do you have any other suggestion? If we send her alone, they will be suspicious. And the last thing we need is for the others to find out what happened, and it affect their performance."

"I know you're right, but it's your competition. Tradition dictates that you lead the contestants." A thought hit him, but he squashed it down. Unless ... he got to his feet. "What if I go?" It might just be what he needed. A little bit of time and space. Away from Everly and her emerald eyes and kissable lips. "It's only like what, a two-day trip?"

Kaitlin narrowed her eyes at him. "Yes. But you can't go. How would that look for the king to escort a young lady all the way back to her home? It's not proper. Not to mention, running errands is not a part of your job description."

"And you're sure the young lady can't stay here? We could say she's too ill to travel."

"You know as well as I do that the palace can't keep a secret. Just look at you and Everly."

He whirled around to face her. "What about me and Everly?"

"You can't tell me you haven't noticed all the stares and whispers. You escorted her into the dining room, set her at your left side. You even went on a moonlit walk through the gardens which you invited her to in front of the courtiers."

"I'm just being nice—to *your* friend, I might add." He sighed. "You know, the one *you* invited here without even telling me about it first. There's nothing going on with me and Lady Everly."

"You don't mind one bit that I have a friend here, and you know it. You're stalling." Kaitlin stood and crossed over to him, a grin on her face. "You like her. Admit it, brother."

"I will do no such thing, as I do not have any feelings for her."

"Prove it."

He walked back to his desk and started stacking papers. He was growing tired of this game. "I love you, sister, but you can be a little much sometimes."

She waved her hand as if to dismiss him. "We both know you can't refuse a challenge."

"It's getting late, and we both have an early morning."

"Yes, it is. Which brings me back to our problem." She reached for the stacks of papers and pulled them from his hands. "Let Everly take the contestant home."

He had no words. What was she thinking? Everly was a foreigner in their kingdom with no knowledge of the outlying lands. "You're crazy."

"Why? It's not proper for a you to go with the girl, so let Everly go. I can stay here and keep the other contestants on track. The Royale will not have to miss a beat."

He gaped at her, trying to form a well-thought-out rebuttal. "She doesn't know the kingdom, our rules, our way of life, it seems." He grabbed the papers back from his sister and stuffed them in his satchel. "Sometimes she acts like she's not even from this realm, Kaitlin."

His sister paled, but she shook her head and laughed. "She'd have help. Send a few guards with her."

"Absolutely not."

"Why?"

"Because it's not safe!"

"But you'd let me go?"

"That's not what I meant, and you know it." Anger welled

up and he clutched the straps of the satchel, squeezing them until he could calm.

Kaitlin's voice lowered as she placed both hands on the desk and leaned toward him. "You can't hide in these massive stone walls forever. And you certainly can't protect everyone you care about at all times."

His throat grew thick, and speaking was no longer an option. Kaitlin's words hit their intended mark—and it stung.

"I love you, Finn. But I can't stand to see you like this. You can't let the past's tragedies cause you this much worry."

Finn couldn't look at her. Instead, he sat in his chair and placed the satchel back on his desk.

"Just because Mom and Dad died in a trip outside of the capital, doesn't meant that I will. Or Everly."

He raised his gaze to meet her eyes. "Have Reece make the preparations and speak to the contestant and to Everly. I will escort them both to the village."

"Are you sure?"

"No." He cleared his throat, his mind whirling a million different directions. "But you're right. I can't hide here forever, and the girl must go home. Everly can be a chaperone, and of course, we will have a team of guards accompany us."

"I'll wait until breakfast to talk to Everly. I don't wish to disturb her at this hour." Kaitlin turned and walked to the door but paused before twisting the door handle. "I didn't mean to upset you. I just—"

"Goodnight, Kaitlin." He stood, no longer wanting to talk. Tears welled in her eyes, and he tried to soften his tone. It wasn't Kaitlin he was upset with, and she didn't deserve his curt reply. "You're right, you know."

She met his gaze and whispered, "About what?"

"I do care for Everly. But I refuse to be distracted right now. There's too much at stake."

"Oh, Finn." Pity laced every word. "You take one step forward and five steps back." She opened the door. "If you sacrifice everything in your life for everyone else, what will that leave you with in the end?"

"I don't know."

"Don't let her disappear without telling her how you feel. She deserves to know, and more importantly, what if she cares about you too?"

The door closed softly behind his sister, the finality of the movement seemed to make the unanswered question linger in the air.

NINE

THE TRAIN DEPOT bustled with activity, and Everly let out a sigh of relief that they weren't taking the car. She didn't know if she could ever get used to a car driving at neck-breaking speeds without a driver.

Surely the train wouldn't do the same. Would it?

"Thank you for agreeing to accompany me on this trip." Finn sat beside her in the royal car, decked out in a black suit and jacket. His leather satchel sat in his lap.

"I'm glad I could be of help."

The train doors opened, and a security guard stepped off and walked over to the car, opening their door. "It's all clear Your Majesty."

"Thank you, Gerald."

Finn slid out, and another guard opened Everly's door and escorted her to the train along with the contestant from another vehicle behind theirs. She gave the girl an encouraging smile as she drew closer, but she just pulled her coat tighter around her body and looked away.

"Don't stop, Lady Everly." The guard gently grabbed her elbow, steering her toward the waiting train.

"Sorry—" She tried to search for a name tag, but of course, there wasn't one. "What is your name?" She whispered under her breath, not wanting to break royal etiquette once more.

A dimple formed in his cheeks at her question. "Duncan, my lady."

"It's nice to meet you, Duncan."

The man nodded, ushering her to enter once Finn was onboard. She climbed the stairs and took a moment to soak in the grandeur of the sitting area. What appeared like a train on the outside, was anything but on the inside. Would she ever get used to their strange transportation methods?

"This is the main sitting area, and your chambers are the second door down the hall."

"Chambers?"

Duncan raised his eyebrow. "For sleeping, my lady. King Finn does not like to stay at inns while he's traveling, for security reasons."

"Of course."

"I'm sorry to say you will have to share with our contestant. We only have two rooms aboard this train."

"Oh, don't worry at all. It's not a problem."

Duncan pulled a bracelet out of his pocket and asked for her arm. "If you need anything at all or feel like you are in danger, don't hesitate to push this button." He clasped the silver bracelet and let go of her hand. "I will be there in seconds."

A trickle of fear traveled up her spine. "Is it ... dangerous where we are going?"

"King Finn has strict rules while out of the capital."

Everly tried her best to reason out the meaning behind his

words. He didn't say there was anything dangerous, but he didn't disqualify it either.

"Lady Everly, I trust you are all set for our journey?" Finn came out of one of the doors down the hall.

"Yes, Your Majesty." She turned to gesture to Duncan, but he was gone. She glanced around the sitting area but didn't see him.

"I was told that our contestant, Ava, requested to retire to the chamber car to rest."

"How is she feeling?"

Finn gestured to a row of cushioned seats to their right. "We should probably buckle up. We should be leaving soon."

Buckle up? So, it was going to be fast speeds yet again? She should have known. "Okay ..."

Finn was already in his seat, the click of the belt locking into place. She sat across from him in the booth and reached for the belt, which looked more like a harness.

"Let me help." He unbuckled his, and leaned over, grabbing both straps at her shoulders and crisscrossing in front of her. "Now, latch them on both sides of your seat."

She did as he instructed and took in a deep breath, trying to calm her nerves. "Please tell me someone is driving the train."

Finn raised an eyebrow, the corners of his mouth twitching into a smile. "Of course. What would take three days in a car, will only take one on the rails.

One day? Just how fast would they go?

"Don't worry. It's only the take off and stopping that lurch you around. That's why we have the seatbelts."

"I'm not worried." She didn't even try to make her lie believable.

Finn let out a belly laugh, one that made a few of the security guards glance their way from the hallway. "I'll pretend like I believe you."

"Your Majesty, are you ready?" His guard stepped out from the hall.

"We are all ready here. Is Ava secured in the seat in the bedroom?"

"Yes, Your Majesty." The guard bowed. "I will alert the driver."

"Thank you, Gerald."

Everly waited until the guard left before bringing up the topic of the contestant again. "Do you have any idea what is wrong with Ava?"

Finn stiffened before answering. "No, but I wish I did."

"Well, I'm sure you will be able to figure it out."

"Thank you for the vote of confidence but ..." He didn't get a chance to elaborate because the train car lunged with such a ferocity that Everly plunged forward, her harness not restricting her as it was supposed to. A scream ripped through her throat as her belt detached from her seat, sending her flying from the bench.

"Everly!"

Finn's panicked voice was the last thing she heard before her head smacked the wall and the room swam in darkness.

TEN

FINN SCRAMBLED to unlatch his harness, his heart racing so loud it pulsated in his ears.

"Don't move, Your Majesty." Gerald's voice roared through the intercom, but he ignored it. There wasn't any way he was going to wait until the car was at a safe speed before helping Everly.

Lumen, help him! He couldn't get the buckle undone. He forced himself to stop, to take a breath and try again.

"Everly!" He threw off the harness and sank to the floor, trying to crawl toward her. There was no way he could stand without being knocked over himself.

She didn't move, but he heard Gerald let out a curse at his refusal to wait. It didn't matter. He couldn't live with himself if something happened to her.

"Please be okay." He whispered, gently moving the hair back from her face and searching for wounds. A knot already formed on her head, bruising the right side of her forehead. A small trickle of blood oozed from a cut, but it didn't appear to be too deep.

"Everly?" He tried again, forcing the panic to stay away.

Her eyelids fluttered, and she groaned. "Finn?"

"I'm here." He reached for her hand. "Does anything hurt?"

"My head." She tried to set up, but he stopped her.

"Don't move until we can get help."

"What happened?"

He turned back to the seat. He had no idea why the restraint did not work. He was the one who tightened the strap. "I don't know, but I promise you I'm going to find out."

"Your Majesty!" Gerald raced down the hall and knelt beside him. "What were you thinking?"

"Everly is hurt."

"Are you all right?"

"I'm fine, it's Everly that I'm worried about."

His guard gently examined Everly's head. She groaned in protest when his fingers neared the knot. "Are you dizzy at all? Headache?"

"My head hurts."

"We are about an hour and half away from the next town. We will stop, and I will have a physician board and check her out, but it doesn't appear that anything is broken."

"Help me get her to the chair, and then if you would please find her some medicine."

"Of course."

Between the two of them, they got Everly settled in one of the booths with a glass of water, medicine, and ice pack. He motioned for Gerald to follow him a few feet away from her. "Why would her seatbelt break like that? I checked it myself before we took off."

"I don't know Your Majesty, as soon as we took off from the platform, the land changed."

"What do you mean?"

Gerald cleared his throat and lowered his gaze. "The darkness has reached our border."

From the last report, the darkness was still a good twenty miles away. His team of scholars and students of Lumen believed they would have time to get through the Royale before it neared their borders.

"How did this happen so soon?"

The guard just shook his head. No doubt a loss for words, just like Finn.

"Thank you, Gerald."

"I'll let you know when we get close to the next town."

Finn dismissed the guard and joined Everly on the bench. "How are you feeling?"

"Sore." She lowered the icepack and gave him a goofy grin. "How do I look?"

The bruise was already spreading down to her eye. "Beautiful." He rubbed his sweaty palms on his dress pants. "I'm just glad that you weren't seriously injured." Wasn't he just telling Kaitlin that he refused to get distracted by Everly? And here he was telling her she was beautiful. He needed to keep a better guard on his heart and his tongue.

"I know you can't be serious right now, Your Highness."

"I think we are past this 'Your Highness' stuff by now, don't you think?"

"So, someone has to be wounded to call you by your first name?" Everly teased, but Finn couldn't help but flinch.

"Well, let's just hope that's all that happens on this trip."

Everly placed the icepack back on her forehead. "You're worried about the darkness?"

Finn leaned back in his seat. "You heard that, huh?"

"I'm sorry—I wasn't trying to eavesdrop."

"It's fine. It's not like it's a big secret. The darkness has intruded for years now. It's just no matter what we do, it won't stop."

"Is that why Ava's sick?"

"She's not ill in the physical sense." Finn leaned closer so he could lower his voice. "She's lost her gifting."

Everly dropped her ice pack. "Has that ever happened before?"

"No. Not that I know of."

"So, that's why you wanted to escort her home?"

"Partly. I didn't want rumors to spread, and if she stayed at the castle, the truth would no doubt spread faster than it should. Kaitlin and I didn't want to the other contestants to be scared and alter their performances in the Royale."

"Makes sense." She reached for her water bottle and took a drink. "What happens if the Royale doesn't work?"

"That's not going to happen." He shook his head, pushing back his irritation. Failing wasn't an option. Not again. Not this year. "I'm going to go ask Gerald how close we are to stopping for the doctor."

"Finn, I feel fine, it's just a headache."

"I'm not taking a chance, Everly." He got to his feet. "Please just humor me." He didn't wait to hear her response.

ELEVEN

11

HER HEAD WAS FINE, just like she said it was. The doctor Finn brought aboard the train had some sort of portable CT scan machine that fit in his briefcase. Everly did her best not to appear too shocked when he held the small medical device up to her temple and took pictures. It sent them directly to some sort of tablet that he held up for them to see.

Once Finn was satisfied she was all right and the rest of the cushions were checked for faulty seatbelts, they were off again. Everly dozed off and on, and each time she woke, Finn was still by her side, either reading a book or working from a stack of folders he had in his satchel. He didn't say much, instead concentrating on whatever it was he was studying. If he was annoyed at her for her questions earlier, he didn't show it, but he did seem more withdrawn than before.

Each time she thought they were becoming friends—or possibly more—he shut down. It was just like at the garden the other night when she thought he would kiss her and instead walked away and pretended nothing happened.

He hardly looked up when she told him she was going to

bed. He just mumbled a 'goodnight' and then went back to his books.

She tossed and turned all night, even though her roommate, Ava, softly snored from her side of the room. Finally, when she couldn't handle it any longer, she dressed and made her way to the dining car.

"Good morning, Duncan. How did you sleep?"

"I got a nap ..." He stumbled over his words, and Everly realized she messed up again. She overstepped her place. Ugh. She would never get used to this, no matter how long she ended up staying in the kingdom. Her hand froze on the bagel in front of her. Did she really just think in terms of staying? Wasn't going home her main priority?

"Do you need some help, Lady Everly?" Duncan's voice interrupted her thoughts, and she quickly placed the bread on her plate.

"No, thank you, Duncan. I can manage to get my own breakfast."

"Of course, Miss."

"I did not mean for that to sound rude." She reached for what she thought was strawberry cream cheese. Hopefully they had that in the Kingdom of Lux. "I'm afraid I'm a little cranky when I don't sleep."

"No need to apologize." Duncan filled his plate with some sort of pastry and fruit. "You're not the only one." He gestured to Gerald, who sat at a nearby table staring at a mug of coffee.

"Everly, what are you doing back here?" Finn's voice came from behind her, startling and nearly causing her to spill a container of orange juice.

"I'm getting breakfast, Your Highness."

"Our dinning car is in the other direction."

Other direction? Oh. She glanced down at her plate and then at Duncan, whose face was apologetic. No wonder he asked if she needed any help. "Oh. Well. They had bagels." She picked up her plate and gave Duncan a grin as she passed.

"I thought I told you to call me Finn." He whispered as they headed down the hallway to the other dinning car.

"Haven't you noticed that I'm notorious for not doing the proper thing?"

"That's one of things that I find so interesting about you." He opened the dining car door for her. "I'm going to grab something really quick and then I think it's time to strap back in. We are almost there."

She finished off her orange juice and threw away her Styrofoam cup. "Wonderful." She shuddered, thinking about how the harness didn't hold her in last time.

"Don't worry. I had Gerald double check every other chair in the train."

"I know."

"Come on." Finn led the way back to the seats, and Everly strapped in, giving him a small smile as the car came to a stop.

This time the straps worked.

"Piece of cake."

"Maybe for you." Everly freed herself from the harness and followed Gerald, Duncan, and Finn out the door and onto the platform of the train station. It was far less glamorous than the one in the capital, but Everly could hear voices and city sounds coming outside of the station.

"I'm going to go check with the attendants here and see if the girl's parents have arrived." Gerald nodded to Duncan to take watch and then he disappeared out into the street.

"There are several artisan shops that I think you would like, Everly." Finn said, as Ava joined them on the platform. "Maybe we can spend a little bit of time sightseeing before we have to head back."

"I would like that." She turned to the girl. "Do you have a favorite shop that I should visit?"

The girl gaped at her in shock. Clearly, she wasn't used to people addressing her. "My favorite is the book shop. It has homemade candles and soaps as well."

"That sounds wonderful, doesn't it Finn?"

The girl's eyes widened at her use of his first name, but Finn didn't seem to notice. "Yes, it does."

"Get back in the train!"

"What in the world?" Everly turned to see Gerald running full speed toward them, but Duncan was already pulling Finn toward the door. "Lady Everly, come on!"

Everly forced her feet to move, and she made it up the stairs before she realized that Ava was still standing on the platform, her eyes filled with fright.

"Ava!" She called down to the girl, but she didn't answer. Everly ran back down the stairs and grabbed the girl's arm. "Come on, we have to go."

Ava cried out as a mob of people stormed through the doors of the depot behind Gerald who waved frantically for her to go. She tugged on the girls arm once more but she wouldn't move.

Before she could beg the girl to come on, Duncan lifted her off her feet and tossed her over his shoulder. "Wait, we can't leave her!" Tears flooded her eyes and she blinked them away. "Duncan, please!"

"Gerald will get her." He sat her down in the seat beside Finn, who was already reaching for her harness. "My priority is the King, and then you."

Her hands shook, but somehow she managed to lock her seatbelt into place. Finally, Gerald burst through the door, but he was alone.

"Gerald ..."

He shook his head and took a seat next to them. "She ran away before I could get to her."

Everly closed her eyes and let the tears fall. The train lunged forward.

"What happened, Gerald?"

"The people are protesting your arrival."

"What? Why?"

Gerald's jaws clenched, and he took his time to answer. "They think you're not doing enough to protect them."

"That's absurd!"

Everly flinched at Finn's outburst, but she couldn't blame him. From the moment she met him, he seemed to carry the weight of everyone on his shoulders. She could see it in eyes when he talked about the Royale. He worried for his people.

"What do we do now? What about Ava?" Everly spoke up. Whether she should or not, she didn't know.

"We go back to the castle. Once we are there, I will inquire about the girl. But it's her hometown—I'm sure she will be fine."

"There's one more thing you should know, Your Majesty."

"What is it?"

When I went outside the train depot ... it was pitch black. The trees were bare, and there wasn't a single flower in sight. Everything was dead."

TWELVE

1

"THANK Lumen you are both all right!" Kaitlin burst through the doors of the private sitting room, and Finn nearly toppled over at her embrace.

She clung to him, and Finn hugged her tighter. "Yes, we are both okay." She finally relinquished her hold and moved on to Everly, her eyes widening when she noticed her face.

"I thought you said you were both okay. Did someone attack you?"

"There was a little mishap with the harness in the train. It decided to sling me into the wall."

"You got her to a doctor, didn't you brother?"

He suppressed the urge to roll his eyes at Katlin. Didn't she know him at all? "Yes, we had a doctor brought on board and he did a scan. She is perfectly fine—except for the bruise."

"I'm more worried about what has happened while we were gone." Everly pulled Kaitlin to the couch and sat down. "How is the Royale? How many contestants are left? What kind of trial is next?"

"One question at a time." Kaitlin folded her hands in her

lap. "Everything has progressed just as it should. We have eight contestants left, and today they will go through a series of mental tests."

"What kind of mental tests?"

Finn joined the pair, taking one of the oversized armchairs, taken aback by Everly's enthusiasm over the Royale. After everything they'd been through the last two days, he would have thought she would be ready to run from the palace—and him—without another look back. But here she sat with the two of them as if she'd always been here.

"They are Finn's favorite part of the Royale."

Both girls stared at him expectantly, but he was lost in his thoughts and clueless to what they were talking about. "I'm sorry, what was the question."

"It wasn't a question as much as a statement." His sister frowned, no doubt picking up on the worry behind his words. She knew him—and his moments when his worried thoughts blocked out others around him—better than anyone. No doubt she would question him later.

"I was telling Everly about the mental tests."

"Oh." He sat up a little straighter. "The contestants are placed in a room with a series of scenarios that they must work through to be able to move on. Each decision determines what their next scenarios will be, and each consequence effects what supplies they will have to advance to the next apparatus."

"That sounds extremely complicated."

"You'll see once we get in there." The grandfather clock chimed half past eight. "Looks like we made it just in time. We should go get our seats."

"Oh my. I'm late to meet the contestants this morning. I was so wrapped up in seeing you both arrive. I'll meet you there in a little while, but Finn, don't you dare think we aren't going to talk more about what happened."

He stood, buttoning his jacket. "I wouldn't expect anything less."

He watched his sister practically run out the door, her heels clicking down the hall. That girl had one speed—full throttle.

"Kaitlin sure is feisty." Everly joined him in the hallway, pulling hair down over the corner of her eye.

"If you're not up to going today, it's perfectly fine. If anyone has earned a day of rest, it's you."

"No, I don't want to miss it. It sounds fascinating."

Finn didn't reply, not wanting to press the issue, but by the time they entered the theater, he wished he had. Every time they passed someone in the hallway, they would bow to him, and then look at Everly, their faces a mixture of shock and curiosity. Everly handled the stares better than he probably would have. The rumors that were soon to spread all throughout the castle—that could be a different story. He could count on his staff being kind and discreet, but the courtiers? No one could keep gossip out of their mouths. Which was another reason why he didn't pursue any courtship with the women Kaitlin had tried to set him up with. He needed someone he could trust.

Like Everly.

He gave himself a mental shake and tried to focus on the opening remarks by the Royale host. He had the crowd laughing and eating out his palm. Even Everly chuckled beside him. He glanced over at her, and she gave him a big smile. A man could get lost in that smile.

But no matter how much he wished it could be different—he couldn't be that man.

THIRTEEN

1

THE THEATER LIGHTS FADED, and the curtain pulled back from the stage, revealing small rooms—each decked out in a different theme. They were laid out across the vast stage, almost like cubicles. The crowd seemed surprised as well, as people pointed and murmured to whoever was sitting beside them. Everly tried to look at each one, but she wasn't quite sure where to look first.

Each cube held a different contestant.

"They have to navigate through every cube?" She asked, not even bothering to pull her eyes from the stage.

"Yes, they have to solve the riddle in each room while overcoming the environmental challenges."

"They are like mice in a maze."

"I suppose so. I've never thought of it like that before."

Numbers one, three, four, eight, nine, eleven, thirteen, and sixteen were still in the competition, but Everly only remembered one of their names. Angeline, number four, remained in the running. Along with the girl who used the water to spray Ava over the edge.

On both sides of the stage were two large monitors with each girl's number and their riddle so the crowd could follow along.

"I can't even imagine the amount of focus they need to do this."

"It is rather remarkable."

Angeline was in some sort of jungle room. Everly shuddered at the thought of what could lurk in that space. She stood on a rock, surveying the layout of her cube, while contestant number three, the water girl, was in a cluttered room with no lights or doors visible. Instead, ticking clocks hung on every surface of the room. Number one had a murky pond and nothing else. She was forced to dive into the water for her clues.

"What if you can't swim?" Everly glanced over to Finn, who shrugged his shoulders.

"I guess you have to learn really fast."

"I would be out of the competition right there."

"You can't swim?"

"I can—I just hate going under the water. It sort of freaks me out. I'd much rather float around."

"I wouldn't know."

Everly sat back in her chair. "Wait—you've never been swimming?"

"I don't have much free time, and well, we don't have a pool." He laughed. "It's not like I can go swimming just anywhere."

"I can't believe you don't have a pool." She gestured to the stage. "You have theaters and arenas and can create the most elaborate stage sets I've ever seen. But you don't have a pool?"

"How many stage sets have you been around?"

Should she be honest? Did they act out plays here? Have movies? Everly was so tired of constantly trying to fit in and hide who she was. "I've been in several plays."

Finn's face lit up. "You're an actress? That's amazing."

"Not really." Everly fiddled with her dress sleeves, uneasy with his praise. What would he think if he realized she used those acting skills to fool him? "I studied drama at school."

"Once the Royale is over, and things go back to what they once were, we should go see a play."

Everly focused her attention back to the stage, her throat thick. Finn talked about the future like she would still be here. But she didn't know what the future held for her. What if she could never get home?

"Or not." He cleared his throat. "I'm sorry, Everly, I wasn't trying to assume that you would still be here. I'm sure you're anxious to get home. I bet your family is ready to have you back."

"I'm sure they are." She waved her hand to appear like it wasn't a big deal. But in truth, her heart ached at the idea of her parents worrying about where she was. "We still have a Royale to finish."

Finn continued to look at her for a moment, before finally giving her a small smile. "We do indeed."

"Look! Angeline is out of her room!" Everly stood up, grabbing the binoculars off the table in front of them. The girl was climbing through an opening that appeared in the top of her cube, but it was the bottom of the cube of the cluttered and dark room.

"Now it will get interesting."

"Wait, the girl in the dark room hasn't left yet."

"Nope." Finn grinned.

Everly lowered the binoculars. "So now, Angeline becomes a consequence to the girl in the other room."

"Pretty cool, huh?"

"Very." Everly stole a glance over her shoulder at Finn

before turning back to Angeline. How could she ever go back to her boring life?

FOURTEEN

1

FINN STRUMMED his fingers on his desk, trying to listen to the report Reece just brought him. He would have to be updated on the situation at the train depot, but he just wasn't ready to face it. He'd spent an enjoyable day with Everly, only to have it come crashing to an end at dinner.

Just as he predicted, the rumor mill was in full swing. Courtiers couldn't keep their eyes off the two of them. Everly held her head high all through dinner, laughing and talking with Kaitlin, but he could feel trouble brewing.

If they weren't gossiping about their quick trip to the villages, they were talking about her black eye. Finn nearly jumped up from his desk and threw his chair when Reece said they blamed him for her accident.

"I would never lay a hand on Everly—or anyone for that matter."

"I do not think they meant *you,* Your Majesty, as much as they are saying you failed to protect her."

"It was an accident. No one could have anticipated that the harness was faulty."

"Of course, Your Highness. But you must remember that there is already unrest in the villages. Rumors have spread among the merchants, and the courtiers have overhead the grumblings. They think she got hurt from the crowd and ..."

"And what?"

Reece uncomfortably shifted in his chair. "That you knowingly took her there."

"I have half a mind to close the court for the season and send everyone home."

"I do not think that would help but further spread more rumors. Wouldn't you have to send Everly home as well then?"

Finn lowered his head into his hands. How did everything get so sideways so quickly? Reece was right. Sending the courtiers home wouldn't stop the rumors. He just hated that Everly had to be the subject of such gossip. "So, what do you suggest, Reece?"

"The truth also comes out into the light." Reece sighed. "Eventually."

"How can I help my people when they no longer trust me?" He couldn't stand it any longer. He had to move to think. He pushed away from his desk and crossed the room to the fireplace.

"There has been talk, Your Majesty, amongst the council." Reece hesitated.

"Surely by now, you know you can speak freely. Out with it." Finn leaned against the mantle. "Forgive me. I should not have snapped at you."

"There's nothing to forgive, Your Highness. I'm just hesitant to tell you."

"Okay, now you have me really worried."

"In an effort to show goodwill to the people, you marry the winner of the Royale."

"Absolutely not!"

"You said it yourself. They do not trust you. Show a little goodwill and marry one of their contestants. One of your people from the villages."

"I do not wish to marry, Reece, and you surely know that."

"You may not have a choice in the matter. The council is threatening to hand over the crown to Kaitlin if you do not marry and produce an heir."

"They do not have the power to do such a thing!" How dare the council even suggest such a preposterous idea. He loved his sister dearly, but Kaitlin had no desire to lead the kingdom. She'd told him that numerous times. He wouldn't force such a burden onto her. He couldn't do it.

But could he marry someone he didn't love?

"I'm sorry, Your Majesty, but they do have the power to call it to a vote. All they need is enough of a case to put it into question."

"My parents chose me to be king. They understood that Kaitlin had no desire for the throne."

Reece stood and moved in front of him, placing his hands on Finn's shoulders. His eyes were full of sympathy and understanding. "Finn, I've stood by your father's side since the day he became King. And I have stood by your side since the day that he died."

Finn couldn't speak even if he wanted to.

"I know you were placed on the throne for a reason. One that you can't even see right now. I also know you carry such a weight from your parents' deaths that you can't move past it. You have to accept that you aren't made to carry this alone. Let Lumen in. Let the light do what it is meant to do."

Finn stared at his oldest and longest steward, letting his words sink in. The cost was too high. He couldn't do what Reece and the council wanted of him. "I cannot marry someone I do not love. Especially when my heart belongs to another."

Reece dropped his hands from his shoulders. Understanding dawning on his face at the truth behind Finn's words. "You're speaking of Everly."

"I won't do that to her. To myself. It isn't right."

"I know." Reece sighed. "I know, Your Highness."

FIFTEEN

1

"I CANNOT MARRY *someone I do not love."* Everly nearly dropped the tray of hot chocolate and strawberry shortcake as Finn's shocking announcement came through the door. Gripping the wooden tray, she leaned in, holding her breath. Seconds later, another voice mentioned her name.

"I won't do that to her. To myself. It isn't right."

As if she wanted to marry him anyway. She was still in college and had her whole life ahead of her. Plans were already made. Strict plans that she could not afford to deviate from. Her parents depended on her. They'd already lost one child, one perfect daughter, with the perfect career. One that they could be proud of. A doctor.

She worked tirelessly to keep her scholarship and perfect grades so they would be proud of her as well. There was no time to fall in love with a king from some distant world.

Everly placed the tray on the ground next to the door and backed away. Ignored the sting of the tears threatening to spill over. What did she care if he didn't want to marry her? She was supposed to go home anyway.

Right?

Clasping sections of her dress, she lifted the hem and ran. Down the hallway of the private quarters, down the flights of stairs, and across the castle to the garden doors. Servants startled and moved out of her way, and a few called out to her to ask if she was all right, but she kept running.

Thank goodness Kaitlin loved ballet flats or she would have abandoned her shoes at the first staircase. The moon was almost full, cascading more light than normal across the walkway to the monolith.

She had to go home. She couldn't stay here another moment. What was she thinking before? She treated her time at the Kingdom of Lux as a vacation, a sabbatical from her life. And for what? To develop feelings for someone who didn't—wouldn't love her back?

Everly blindly ran for the monolith, not even caring that rose bushes caught and snagged her dress. She pressed her hand against the stone, willing it to send her back.

"I just want to go home." Desperation clung to her words, as she walked around the monolith, touching different spots, standing in different areas, but it remained silent.

No bright lights like before. No strange writing appearing at the top of the structure.

Nothing but silence.

Just like all the other times she tried to go back home.

And each time that happened, she told herself it would work the next time she tried. And if didn't, well, she would just keep trying. And trying. Then one day, if she was patient, it would happen.

But what if it never worked? What if she really was stuck here? What would she do? Where would she go? Staying at the castle was not an option. Not now. Not when there wasn't any option for a future with Finn.

The pain of that realization hurt worse than she was prepared for.

"No!" Everly sank to the ground, letting her tears come out in waves. This couldn't be the way this ended.

"Everly?"

She looked up to find Kaitlin standing beside her. Wiping the tears away the best she could she got to her feet, trying to smooth out her tattered dress. "Your Highness."

"What are you doing out here at this hour?"

"I could ask you the same."

If Kaitlin was angry for her snappy reply, she didn't act like it. Instead, her gaze softened. "Are you trying to go home?"

"Yes." There was no reason to pretend otherwise. "I've tried several times, but it doesn't work."

"Would it be selfish of me to say that I'm glad?" Kaitlin took a step closer and gave her a sad smile. "I've really enjoyed having you here. I can't explain it, really, but you're a breath of fresh air."

"I've enjoyed being here as well, but Kaitlin, you know I don't belong. I'm not royalty, I'm not a courtier, I'm not even 'Lady Everly.'"

"You are more of a lady than anyone else I know, even if you wear strange clothes and shoes."

Everly laughed, and it felt nice to finally be able to talk freely with Kaitlin. "I've tried so many times to talk to you about all of this, but you always avoided me."

Kaitlin nodded. "I know. I'm sorry. I shouldn't have."

"Then why did you? You had to know I was going crazy trying to figure this all out." Everly sighed. "Trying to hide who I am from Finn."

"I know. Again, I'm so sorry. I noticed how good you are for Finn. How you've drawn him out of his shell." She crossed her arms. "He's actually smiling now."

Ugh. Could it hurt any more? Kaitlin might as well have stepped all over her heart. "I have to go home, Kaitlin. My parents—they must be besides themselves."

"Couldn't you make a home here as well?"

"I don't think it works that way."

"Why not?"

"Because he doesn't love me!" The words shot out of her mouth before she could censor them.

"Oh, Everly."

"I'm sorry. I shouldn't have said anything. Forgive me, Your Highness, but I'm going to go back to my cell." She rushed past Kaitlin, horrified at her behavior and her words. Kaitlin had been so kind to her and didn't deserve her childish outburst. She did ignore the reason why she came, but she had also saved Everly from having to compete in the Royale. How bad would it have been for her if she got outed for competing when she had no abilities? Inevitably, they would have kicked her out of the palace, and she would be on her own. With no access to the monolith, no roof over her head. She would have been utterly alone.

Everly shut her bedroom door and leaned against it. Her heart raced from her sprint back to the castle. What was she going to do? How could she face Kaitlin tomorrow? And how was she going to look at Finn and know he'd talked about her to someone? Confided in that someone that he could never love her?

Maybe she should just come clean to Finn anyway. Tell him all about how she stumbled into his kingdom. Maybe he would do what she didn't have the courage to do. Maybe he would send her away.

SIXTEEN

"WHERE'S EVERLY?" Finn scooped a helping of jam and spread it across a piece of bread. He elected to take breakfast in the sitting room of their private quarters, and Kaitlin joined him. "Did she go down to the dining room this morning?"

"I'm not sure."

Finn ran the words back through his mind. She used her tone that she reserved for when she had some secret she couldn't share.

"You haven't talked to her?"

"I saw her last night."

He dropped his bread to his plate. *Last night?* "How late?"

Kaitlin reached for her juice and took a sip. "I don't know. Before I went to bed."

"You are terrible at keeping secrets, sister."

Her brows furrowed. "I could say the same to you."

Ouch. He didn't like keeping secrets from his sister. She was the only family he had left, and he told her everything. Except what he learned last night. He had yet to bring up what

Reece confided to him. Finn didn't have the stomach to tell her she might just become queen. But no, he couldn't do that to her. Not when she'd confided in him of her dream to have a family and not be hindered by the weight of running the kingdom. She wanted to travel. To see lands she'd never been to before.

No, she deserved the truth, no matter how much he wished he didn't have to burden her with it. "Reece stopped my study last night."

"What did he want?"

"He said that there were rumors at court that Everly was hurt because of me, and that I put her in harm's way."

"But that's ridiculous!"

"You know that, and I know that. But the council fears the people will not be able to set aside their mistrust until I marry someone." He paused, watching her process his words. "They want me to marry the winner of the Royale, to appease the villages."

Kaitlin slammed her silverware onto her plate. "They cannot force you to wed."

He wanted to laugh. Didn't he say the same to Reece? "In fact, they can."

"I don't believe it." Kaitlin got to her feet. "There has to be something we can do." She studied the clock and then turned back to him. "We have a little bit of time before the start of the Royale. We will go talk to the council members and put an end to this right now."

"It won't work."

"It will. We will go as a united front." She nearly rolled her eyes. "You're the King!"

"Yes, and they are the council put into place to intervene if it's been brought to a vote."

"They voted on this?" Her voice turned cold.

"Yes." He cleared his throat. Lumen help him, he didn't want to tell her what they would do if he refused. "If I refuse to wed the winner, they will pass the crown to you."

Disbelief crossed her face before it changed to anger. "No. They can't do that!"

Finn stood and wrapped her in a hug. "Don't worry, I'm not going to let that happen."

She pulled away. "You can't seriously be thinking about marrying one of the village girls."

"I don't have a choice, Kaitlin."

"Mom and Dad always said we could marry for love. They would never force an arranged marriage on either of us."

"They are not here."

"I need a minute." She walked over to the door and touched the handle, turning to face him. "I've got to get ready for today's event. We're supposed to crown a winner today."

Finn put his hands in suit pockets and stared at the ground. "I know."

"You need more time to decide—"

"I've already made my decision."

"What about Everly?"

Finn flinched. He couldn't think about her right now. Not when he had to do the right thing for his kingdom, for his people. "She's not from Under the Stars, Kaitlin."

From Under the Stars. How that phrase had always haunted him. Taunted him. Hung over his reign like a gloomy cloud. The one who would heal the kingdom would come from Under the Stars. The castle and the kingdom villages couldn't ever see the stars. They were situated too low in the valley. But the other lands? They were spread far and wide. Under the canopy of stars.

"I can't even look at you right now." Kaitlin pulled the door open. "You have to stand up to the council and find another way. You can't let her go, Finn."

She slammed the door before he could reply. But even if he could, there was nothing he could say that could make everything right.

SEVENTEEN

1

EVERLY CLIMBED the stairs to the royal box at the outside arena, Duncan following closely behind. She was getting used to his quiet presence. In a way, it was comforting. Like she really was a part of the royal family. What would happen to him once they all found out the truth and sent her on her way? Would he get assigned to someone else?

Would he eventually become the future queen's guard?

She couldn't think about that. Instead, she squared her shoulders, held her head high and entered the booth as if she wasn't wearing her broken heart on her sleeve.

Today was the last day of the Royale. Three girls were left. One, three, and four. Five girls were taken out during the last match—the one with the rooms and obstacles. Angeline, a crowd favorite, was still in the running. People chanted her name as soon as she entered the arena.

Everly scanned the box seats quickly, looking for Kaitlin, and was pleasantly surprised to see her sitting in her seat. Usually, she had to join them later, after she talked with the remaining contestants.

Whatever the reason for her arrival now, she was grateful. Everly hurried across the room and took a seat on Kaitlin's left, leaving the middle seat empty beside Finn.

"Lady Everly, I was afraid you were ill or something." Kaitlin squeezed her arm. "I'm glad you made it."

"I wouldn't be anywhere else." *More like she couldn't go anywhere else.* She caught Finn turning to wave to her, but she turned away. She had to get ahold of her emotions before she could talk to him.

"Did you eat breakfast in the dining room?" Kaitlin asked, curiosity in her eyes.

"No. I had some toast and oatmeal in my room."

"Oh." The disappointment was evident in her voice, but Everly kept talking, more nervous than usual.

"Tell me about today's event."

The princess's eyes lit up. "Well, you watched the physical matches, and the mental trials, now we are on to my favorite, the Battle of Growth."

"Battle of Growth?"

"Each gift of Lumen is different, of course. While some may have the same gift, there's always something unique to how they approach that gift. Some variation that fits their personalities and strengths."

"That makes sense." In her world, talents worked the same. There were so many different talents, but each person made those talents distinctive.

"Well, for this challenge, they have to use their gift and make something grow."

"You mean like make a plant bloom or something?"

Kaitlin tilted her head to the side, considering her words. "In a sense. But it doesn't have to be exactly that."

"I'm confused."

"Lumen is the source of light. When he gives gifts, they are gifts of peace, light, healing, and growth. Maybe it's coaxing a flower to bloom or illuminating a dark room. Or maybe, it's simply letting the light in to change you. To make you grow as a person, to cancel out the darkness around you to fill you with hope."

Tears pricked her eyes, and Everly risked taking a glance at Finn. He was watching her, clearly moved by Kaitlin's words. "That's beautiful."

Kaitlin beamed. "I think so too."

Everly turned away and quickly wiped her eyes. "So, how does all of that translate into the Royale?"

"That's a good question. We can't obviously test some of these aspects. They are personal and how could you even measure something like that?" She sighed. "So, we have to focus more on how their gifts help others, or our surroundings."

"Like how the villages are covered in darkness?"

"Yes, like that." Kaitlin sighed. "But you must remember, it's more than just darkness plaguing the lands. They're also dying. The darkness is corrupting everything it touches."

"But I still don't understand how you can test this. The darkness isn't here at the capital."

"It's at the borders now, which is far closer than it's ever been. Usually we set up an arena with decaying plants and trees. Dry and scorched land. Dried up ponds. That sort of thing. But this time, they are at the border. They are going to test on the real thing."

"Wow."

"It's starting." Finn's quiet voice interrupted their conversation, and Everly watched the giant screens unveiled from the arena floor. The host entered, explaining to the crowd the change in location. Murmurs ricocheted through the stadium and Everly peeked at Finn, trying to gauge his expression at their unrest.

"The Council of the Kingdom wishes for me to make an announcement before we begin." The crowd hushed, everyone intent on the hosts words. "The kingdom is pleased to announce that King Finn will wed this year's winner of the Royale!"

The crowd erupted in cheers and whistles.

"King Finn, please rise and give us a bow."

Everly watched in horror as Finn got to his feet and waved to the crowd.

EIGHTEEN

1

HOW DARE they stoop so low? Finn had no choice but to stand and wave to the crowd, plaster on a smile, and bow. He couldn't even bring himself to look at his sister, at Everly. To see their shocked and horrified expressions.

Oh, how Everly must hate him. He put the pieces of his conversation with Kaitlin together and realized that she had to have run into Everly last night. Which meant Everly was the one to leave the tray of Marsh Cocoa and the strawberry dessert. Of course it was her. He should have recognized that right away.

When he picked up the tray, the pot of Marsh Cocoa was still hot. Which meant she must have overheard his conversation with Reece. Did she think he wanted to marry the winner of the Royale? Is that why she left without speaking to him and why she hadn't even looked at him all morning?

What must she think of him now?

Finn took his seat and tried to focus on the Royale, but there was no use. The closer they came to a winner, they more anxiety plagued him. He couldn't watch the screens. After number three was eliminated, Finn had to force back the temptation to pace. He couldn't risk the people seeing him. With the announcement from the host, they had more cameras than ever pointed at the royal box.

The council was wrong. How dare they go behind his back and announce such a thing to *his* people? Especially when he wasn't even sure of his decision. After his talk with his sister, his resolve wavered. He doubted he could go through with it. And after realizing it must have been Everly at his door last night, that maybe she loved him back?

He couldn't marry the winner. He had to find a way to get the council to see reason. Once the winner was able to beat back the darkness, then the people's faith in him would be restored. They would know that he came through on his promise. There would be no reason to go through with a sham of a marriage.

Sweat dripped down his neck, and his hands shook. All he wanted to do was talk to Everly and clear this whole thing up. Surely, she would understand he was doing everything in his power to make things right. That he had to weigh all his options. That once he was able to save the kingdom, then maybe they could find some way to convince the council to allow him to marry whomever he wanted. He owed her a conversation and an explanation.

"Angeline's going to be the last one standing." Kaitlin's voice broke through his thoughts. How had he missed the whole thing? The girl with the lightning had somehow managed to outshine the other two contestants.

Oh, no.

He was out of time.

"We have a winner!" The host yelled, trying to be louder than the roar of the crowd. "And we have a royal engagement!"

"Lady Everly ... wait!"

Finn turned around to see Everly leaving the royal box, a confused Duncan quick on her heels.

"I'm sorry, Your Highness, I don't believe that I'm feeling well after all." She curtsied, something Finn had not seen her do since she first arrived. "If you'll excuse me."

"Look at what you've done!" Kaitlin hissed under her breath at him.

"What I've done?" He faked a smile in case the cameras were pointed toward the box. "I had nothing to do with that announcement."

"Well, now, how are you going to fix it?"

"I'm still trying to figure that one out."

NINETEEN

1

HOW MUCH MORE COULD SHE take? Everly picked up her fork and tried to eat but ended up pushing the food around on her plate. She tried to get out of dinner, but Kaitlin begged her to come, and she had already caused a stink earlier by leaving right after the winner was announced.

Courtiers no longer pretended to lower their voices while she was around—they were flat out talking about her being jilted by the king. And to add to her shame, Angeline sat beside him at the dining room table, in *her* spot.

She had to go back to the monolith tonight. After dinner. She would try one more time, and if she couldn't go through, well, she would leave the castle. Her stomach churned at the thought. She had no idea where she could go, or how she would support herself once she got there, but surely she could figure it out.

Everly peeked over at Finn and wished she hadn't. He stared at her. Openly stared directly at her. She blinked and forced her gaze away, focusing on her uneaten food.

"Lady Everly, I was wondering if you would like to

accompany me to the celebration after dinner. I would be honored if you would save me a dance."

She dropped her fork and turned toward the courtier on her left. A tall, lanky young man, with disheveled blond hair and beady eyes. "Dance?"

"Yes, my lady." He gaped at her like she had suddenly grown a second head. "The dance in honor of the Royal Engagement."

"Oh, I'm sorry—"

"Sir Bernard." He gave her a crooked smile.

"I'm sorry, Sir Bernard, but I think I'm going to retire early tonight."

"Oh." His face fell, and she turned back to her plate and picked up her fork. She scooped up a bite of grilled fish, praying everyone would look away from her embarrassment.

"But surely you are free now to court whomever you'd like."

The fish lodged in her throat. She sputtered and coughed, trying to dislodge the chunk of meat.

"Everly?" Kaitlin reached for her, and Everly gestured to her goblet for more water. The stubborn piece of fish was not moving. Panic set in, and she stood, unsure of what to do.

"Move out the way!" Strong arms wrapped around her, and she was pulled backward. But the food continued to be stuck.

"Come on!" Another push to her abdomen, and another, and finally the chunk of fish flew out of her mouth onto the floor.

"Thank Lumen!" Another arm wrapped around her, and Kaitlin's tear-streaked face came into view as she hugged her. Everly returned the embrace, looking over Kaitlin's shoulder into Finn's haggard expression. She mouthed *thank you* to him, and he bowed his head to her.

"Come on. Let's go get you cleaned up before the dance."

Kaitlin was already pulling her toward a small powder room, so she had no choice but to follow.

"I'm okay, Kaitlin, really."

"I've never seen anyone more prone to accidents."

"I know. It's a gift. What can I say?" Everly tried to laugh, but it fell flat. She collapsed onto a settee as Kaitlin locked the door.

"I'm sorry about Sir Bernard. He was way out of line."

"I was more surprised than anything." She rubbed her forehead. "I'm so embarrassed. Tell me, just how bad was that? Did everyone see what happened?"

"I could lie and say *no*."

"Great. Now I really am the laughingstock of the court."

Kaitlin waved her hand in the air and Everly noticed her palm was bandaged. "Nah, they will laugh at someone else tomorrow."

"What happened to your hand?"

She hid her hand in the folds of her dress and shrugged. "Oh, I don't know. It's nothing."

"It's not nothing." Everly reached over and gently turned Kaitlin's hand over. "That's a big bandage for nothing."

"I cut it on some rose bushes when I was pruning."

"What were you doing pruning roses?" She narrowed her eyes at Kaitlin. "Don't you have gardeners to take care of that for you?"

"Ugh. Okay, fine. I was going to tell you anyway, because this whole situation has gotten so out of hand."

"What?"

"Just a second." Kaitlin got up and crossed over the sink, turning on the faucet at wide as it would go. "I have the gift of Lumen."

"What?" Everly's mind raced. "That's amazing!"

"No. You don't understand. No one can know."

"But why not?"

"Because it's outlawed for anyone to practice it within the capital. The Villages of the Stars can use their gifts, but not the citizens of the Kingdom of Lux."

"Wait, what?" How could that be? Weren't they just doing the Royale because they wanted someone to use the gift of Lumen to heal the darkness?

"Come on, I will show you." She turned off the water and reached for her arm. "But do not speak a word about it until we get outside."

Kaitlin looped her arm through Everly's and led her out into the dining room, which was now empty. Music and laughter floated from the ballroom. Eyes followed them as they made their way on the outskirts of the dance floor to the garden doors. Everly ignored them but couldn't help but search for a particular pair of hazel eyes.

Finn took a step in her direction, but someone dressed in a fancy suit and hat stopped him. Kaitlin dragged her down the walkway and to the monolith.

"Read it."

Was she serious? "I have no idea what that says, and you know it."

"Really? You can't read that?"

"No."

"Fine. It says, '*She will come from Under the Stars, during the seventeenth moon. The one with the power to illuminate the kingdom from the darkness.*'"

Everly nodded confused. "Yes, I know. Finn told me."

"When the darkness came along with the prophecy, this monument was built, and the scholars of Lumen debated for months on what it meant." She shivered. "They decided that since the girl would come from under the stars, then all the funding and resources would go to the outlying villages, and since they funneled everything there, then there wasn't any reason to help the people who lived in the castle and the Kingdom of Lux to further their gifts."

Kaitlin's eyes filled. "A few years later, the king at the time, decreed that no one in the castle or the capital could use their gifts—because theirs were no longer needed."

"Oh, Kaitlin. That's horrible." Everly couldn't imagine being told that she could no longer do something she loved.

"But I still practice. In secret." Kaitlin wiped her eyes. "I was helping a new rose bush grow and tripped. When I fell, my hand landed on some thorns."

"So, Finn doesn't know about your gift?"

"No."

"I still don't understand what this has to do with me, though. Why did the monolith bring me here?"

"I brought you here."

Everly took a step backward, trying to make sense of everything that Kaitlin was telling her. "You?"

"Why do you think the garden is so alive?" Kaitlin gestured around her. "Why it's blooming and full of life but our borders are covered in the darkness?"

"Because you've been using your gift here in the garden."

Kaitlin nodded. "This is the one place that I don't have to hide. I was out here the day you arrived. I was practicing and thinking about the Royale, and then the monument lit up, and then you were there." She let out a small chuckle. "The blast knocked me on my back."

"Me too." Everly sighed. That day seemed like so long ago. "So, you think I'm the answer to the prophecy."

"Yes."

"That's crazy!" Everly shook her head, already formulating a rebuttal.

"You come from another world, right?" Everly nodded, too

numb to speak. "And you can see stars from your world?"

"Of course. But I'm not seventeen, so it can't be me."

"Neither are the girls who compete."

"The prophecy says *seventeen,* though." Everly massaged her temples. She was getting a headache.

"When we have children, we don't start counting their moons until their second birthday."

All the breath left Everly's lungs. Of all the silly rules. Everly paced the small opening in front of the monolith. It couldn't be true. It just couldn't. How could she save an entire kingdom? It was comical.

"Everly ..." Kaitlin whispered.

"The contestants are really nineteen years old." She laughed out loud. A deep belly laugh. "I'm nineteen." She could barely get the words out.

"Everly!"

"I know, I know. We need to tell Finn, but I'm still trying to wrap my head around this first."

"No—Everly, look!"

Everly stopped and turned to where Kaitlin pointed. The monolith. It was lit up.

No.

No. No. No.

She needed more time. She wasn't ready to leave. Not when she needed to explain to Finn the real prophecy.

"Everly? What's going on?" Finn's voice drew her gaze from the monolith. He had just rounded the last corner before the walkway went straight to the structure.

"Everly, run!" Kaitlin's frantic cries urged her feet to move, but it was too late.

The sonic blast radiated from the monolith and sent her spiraling once more onto the ground. Away from Kaitlin, away from the Kingdom of Lux, and away from Finn.

TWENTY 1

THE POOFY TULLE of her dress twisted all around Everly's legs. She tried to sit up, but her head spun, probably from the blast that knocked her several feet away from the monolith.

The kingdom. The prophecy. Finn!

"Finn?" Everly propped up on her elbows, taking in the surroundings. But it wasn't the castle, and Finn and Kaitlin were nowhere in sight. Tears sprang to her eyes when she realized what had happened.

The monolith had brought her home.

And yet, she didn't feel at home at all.

"Everly?"

"Carter? Is that you?" She glanced over to her right where a startled Carter stood, his equipment still in his hands as if she'd never left.

"Where did you go? Where is Ned? And Tyler?"

"Wait—they aren't here?" She struggled to get to her feet. "A little help, please?"

"Oh! Sorry." He slung his camera strap over his shoulder

and pulled her up. He let out a long whistle. "Umm, did you go to a ball?"

"You have no idea." Everly grinned. "Hey, do you know where my backpack is?"

He pointed to the other side of the monolith. "Yeah, it's over there."

She hurried to it, unbuckling the pack, and shifting through the contents until she found her phone. What are the odds that it would still be charged?

Fifty percent.

Weird. She held it up to her face to unlock it and then checked her messages. Nothing from her parents or her friends.

It was like she'd never left at all.

"Carter? How long have I been gone?"

"I'm not sure. I just got back from going to the car, and you guys were gone. I didn't know what to do. I kind of freaked out, ya know?"

"Yeah, I totally understand that."

"Anyway, I waited a few minutes, and it started lighting up again, and then *whoosh*, you fell to the ground." He rubbed the back of his neck. "Are you going to explain where you went?"

"It was a magical place called the Kingdom of Lux. A princess found me, and then I met her brother—the king. Except their kingdom is dying from some type of mysterious darkness, and they were holding a Royale to find a girl from Under the Stars to save them."

"Whoa—Everly, you're not making any sense."

"I know! It's all so crazy." Everly gestured to the monolith. "That thing dropped me into a magical world. And I'm the one who's supposed to fulfill the prophecy."

"Are you feeling okay?" Carter reached out to feel her forehead. She swatted his hand away.

"No, actually I'm heartbroken." Her voice cracked at

admitting it out loud. "I was about to tell Finn that I figured out the prophecy and that I love him—when the monolith sent me back here."

"How long were you there?" Carter asked, his eyes wide, curiosity seeming to override his speculation.

"A little over a week."

"Wow."

"I know." She looked at her phone and then back to the monolith. "It can't be."

"What?"

Everly reached out and grabbed the front of Carter's shirt. "Tell me that I'm not seeing things. It's glowing, isn't it?"

Carter raised an eyebrow but turned back toward the monolith. "Oh, you're right."

"Then I can go back!"

"Are you serious?" Carter grabbed her arm to stop her. "You can't do that!"

"Carter, I have to. I have to go back and help Finn."

"Everly this is crazy. What about your parents?"

A stab of guilt stopped her from running straight for the monolith. He was right. How could she walk away from her family? But the truth was, they raised her to always strive to do the right thing. How could she leave Finn and Kaitlin and a whole kingdom of people to suffer when she had the ability to prevent it? No, her parents wouldn't want her to squander her abilities and purpose.

"I don't have much time. Do you have your phone?"

"Of course. Why?"

"I want you to record a message for my parents and give it to them. And hopefully, I will be able to come back to them after this is all over."

"I don't know ..." He hesitated, holding his phone in his hand but not moving to video her.

"Please, Carter. I can't leave again and not at least tell them why."

"Okay." He nodded and held up his phone. "Go ahead."

Everly stumbled through the beginning of her message. How was she supposed to say goodbye to someone she loved? Especially when she wasn't sure she could ever come back? But by the end of the message, she grew more confident. They would be proud of her. And she didn't have to be her sister for that to happen. She tried to end her recording with the hope that she would do her best to one day come back home.

"Done."

She texted Carter her parents' contact information and then slipped her phone back into her bag. "Thank you, Carter."

"Do you think Tyler and Ned will come back?"

"I don't know."

"Will you try to come back?" He kicked a loose stone on the ground. "What if this king guy—Finn or whatever—what if it doesn't work out with him?"

"Well, it brought me home once before, didn't it?"

"Seems like a lot of risk for no guarantee."

"Isn't anything in life that's important like that?" She smiled. "I mean, we discovered a magical monolith!"

He stood a little taller. "That's right, we did."

"You'd better video this so everyone will believe you."

Carter laughed and readied his camera. "Good luck!"

Everly waved and then walked toward the structure. She couldn't explain it, but this time, she felt like it was waiting for her. She paused, turned back to Carter, and then ran to give him a hug.

"Thank you, Carter, for the best first date I've ever had."

TWENTY-ONE

"FINN, don't you think it's time to come back inside?" Kaitlin's worried voice called from behind him, but he didn't even bother to turn around. For almost a day, she'd begged him to leave the monolith. But how could he when Everly disappeared before he could even tell her how he felt?

"She's going to come back, Kaitlin."

His sister sighed and sat on the blanket beside him, wrapping her arm around his shoulder. "I know. I can feel it too."

"I'm sorry, Kaitlin."

"For what?"

"Not realizing you had a gift. For not championing that gift and overturning a silly rule made such a long time ago."

"How were you supposed to know?"

He gazed up at the starless sky and sighed. "Mom had the Gift of Lumen."

"What?" Kaitlin leaned away from him. "How do you know that?"

"I found one of her journals after she died."

"I don't even know what to say."

"I used to think that if only she were still alive she would know what to do about the darkness." He gently nudged her shoulder with his. "But now I know I should have been asking you."

She wiped her cheek with her fingertips. "Well, I've been trying. But we know it's Everly who's supposed to heal the land. I just don't understand how."

"I know you've explained everything about how she got here, but how did I not put it all together?"

"You can't blame yourself. None of us realized until ..."

"It was too late."

His sister shook her head. "No. I refuse to believe that's it's too late. And you don't either because you're still sitting out here."

"There's something else I need to apologize for. And I didn't realize it until you were explaining to Everly about the Battle of Growing." He rubbed his tired eyes. "I let the death of our parents stop me from growing."

"Oh, Finn." Kaitlin reached for his hand. "I've wished I could take that burden from you long ago, but you always carried it alone."

Is that what he did? Carry it all alone? He didn't mean for his worry to become a burden for his sister and his people to shoulder. All this time he thought he was doing the right thing. Being strong for everyone and taking the brunt of the responsibility. Wasn't that what a king did?

But now, sitting with his sister, waiting for Everly to come back, he knew he was wrong. Letting someone else help ease the burden wasn't a weakness but a strength.

He may have not brought the darkness to the land, but he didn't do his part to expel it. Instead, he let it linger. He let his grief and pride fester until the darkness shut out the light within him. He only started to realize it when Everly fell into his life.

"It's all my fault." His throat tightened. "I shouldn't have carried it alone, but I did. I forgot that even though I don't have a Gift of Lumen that everyone else can see, I still have the gift of light in me. I silenced that light, and in turn, it kept the darkness here."

"You can't blame yourself for what is happening across the kingdom, Finn."

"I know, but I let my own darkness creep in." He reached for his sister's hand as everything clicked into place in his mind. "The prophecy never meant that one single girl would heal the land." Finn laughed, relief flooding him at finally figuring it out. "Everly fulfilled the prophecy because getting to know her, falling in love with her, it reignited the light in me."

Kaitlin didn't say anything, so he continued. "Don't you see? Now we can reverse that silly rule and invite the light back in."

"I don't know what to say, brother." Kaitlin's eyes filled.

"Thank you for bringing Everly here to guide me back to the light and for never giving up on me."

"Well, if I did, I would have to be queen." She giggled, wiping away her tears. "And I really don't want to be queen."

He laughed with her, and it felt good. Freeing. "Oh, I haven't had the chance to tell you, but I told Angeline that I wouldn't marry her."

"You did? When?"

"After the Royale. Before dinner." He sighed. "They already had her place set when I arrived, and I tried to get Everly's attention all evening, but I kept getting pulled away. I wanted to explain to her that I was going to fight the council, and that I loved her."

"I'm proud of you, brother."

Finn let the conversation fade to silence. There really wasn't anything else to say. All he could do is wait. After a while, Kaitlin got to her feet and squeezed his shoulder. "I'm going to turn in."

"Goodnight, Kaitlin."

"Goodnight."

"Kaitlin, wait." He froze, staring at the now lit up monolith. "Something's happening."

"Get back! You don't want to be close when the blast goes off." She frantically waved him toward her, and he sprang to his feet, hurrying to Kaitlin's side just as a pulsating white light flashed around them.

"Yeah, that blast is no joke."

Everly.

His breath caught in his throat, and he couldn't move. She got to her feet and tossed some sort of strange looking bag on the ground before giving them both a big grin. Dirt smudged her cheeks, and she was wearing the same gown she'd worn to dinner the night before, but it was ripped in places. Strawberry blonde curls fell around her face, and her emerald eyes glistened in the moonlight.

She'd never been more beautiful.

"Everly, you're back."

"I am." Her grin faltered. "Finn there's so much I need to tell you—the prophecy—"

"I know. You're the girl from Under the Stars."

"I don't understand it at all, but I think we were supposed to meet." Her voice broke. "Before you, I thought I had to be the perfect daughter to make up for my sister's death. I got so wrapped up in who I thought I was supposed to be that I forgot to be ... me."

"And I forgot how to let the light guide me. I was drowning

in my own darkness and didn't realize it until you fell through the monolith and disrupted my entire life."

Kaitlin nudged him forward, and he stumbled to get his feet to work correctly. "One clumsy accident after another."

Everly closed the distance between them. "I certainly do know how to make an entrance."

"I wouldn't have it any other way." He reached out and pulled her to him, this time not hesitating to kiss her. A long and deep kiss that chased every lingering doubt and shadow away.

He pulled back but lowered his forehead to touch hers. "I love you, Everly."

She grinned, before leaning in and claiming his lips again. He didn't mind one bit. The girl from under stars was back in his arms.

"Guys, look!" Kaitlin squealed, pointing up to the sky.

Thousands of stars twinkled overhead, the darkness blown away by the light radiating from within him.

Everly laced her fingers through his. "I love you too, Finn."

The End

THE EYE OF THE BEHOLDER

C. KEVIN THOMPSON

ONE

1

DISILLUSIONED

NEVILLE EDWARD DANSBURY BENT OVER, holding his mid-section. The gut-punch feeling of a wrecking ball smashing into him engulfed his entire torso. His head throbbed, and a queasiness rose up to meet it.

He grabbed his forehead with his right hand and steadied himself just as a red beam of light streaked across the sky. An explosion, two hundred yards from his position, blinded him for a moment. Debris flew in all directions, and dust and smoke billowed toward the darkening sky.

Ned staggered away from the blast and immediately backed into a stone wall. He turned and looked straight up at a massive structure. Its wall rose at least thirty yards into the air, maybe more. As far as he could see in the dusk-like conditions, its length went in both directions.

Across a road of some sort stood another structure. Smaller in height and width, and appearing to be made of the same stone, it was older and in a state of disrepair, compared to the wall behind him. Strangely shaped trees with purplish leaves protruded from cracks, running their boney limbs across the face of it. It reminded him of pictures he'd seen in a magazine of stone wall trees in Hong Kong.

These look creepier, though.

The sky grew darker by the second as something big cast an enormous shadow. He couldn't tell if it was a natural phenomenon or a result of smoke from the nearby skirmish. A blueish hue, easing in intensity, radiated down from an oddly shaped astronomical body. The body's spray of light mixed with the smoke and dust, gave the entire scene an eerie, shadowy feel.

However, there were no stars. None at all. Ned stepped away from the taller wall and walked into the middle of the road, scanning the heavens.

Maybe they're just not visible yet ...

Suddenly, an acrid odor drifted in his direction. He covered and uncovered his nose to try and locate its origin. He turned the opposite direction, but the smell, burning tires mixed with the odor of a mildew-covered skunk, pierced his nostrils.

The dusty road veered to his right, and it led in the direction of the recent explosion before disappearing around a bend. To his left, it traveled over a rise and out of sight.

Ned took ten steps and stopped. In the distance, coming up from behind him, a rumbling noise grew in intensity. Something flying. Something mechanical. But unlike anything on Earth. He spun around, looking up. The racket grew louder, and the ground shook.

He faced the towering wall, when a red beam of light ripped through the sky above his head. It struck the decrepit wall now behind him with force, and the explosion sent searing heat in his direction. A section covered by the creepy trees with purple leaves disintegrated before his eyes. The red beam dissolved it into non-existence. The force of the blast sent surrounding stone tumbling down into the road as smoke rose from the now gaping hole.

Ned pressed up against the taller wall just as movement caught his eye. Rounding the bend, a group of beings ran toward him. They darted side to side, avoiding weapons-fire. Yet, to Ned, they didn't look scared. They looked tired.

Are they a family, perhaps? There was a smaller being in the arms of a larger one, and two of the taller specimens carried something resembling short swords.

Another red beam of light zapped the ground with wicked force. A large hole instantly formed near the fleeing group, who jumped around and over it with relative ease.

A third beam of light slammed into the towering wall near Ned, knocking him off his feet. He rose to one knee, shook the cobwebs from his mind, and opened his eyes. The energy of the blast sizzled through his extremities, yet he marveled at how the stone structure remained unscathed, unlike its counterpart across the road.

Another beam struck the ground and exploded between him and the small group still running in his direction.

"Hey!" he said, waving his arms. "We need to get inside! The gun blasts don't have any effect on this build—" Ned's lips and tongue froze mid-sentence, swollen and unable to move. His throat constricted, and he couldn't make any sound. He could barely breathe.

A shearing pain stabbed him in the back, and he staggered to his right and tried to regain his balance just before everything went dark.

TWO

1

DISCOMBOBULATED

NED OPENED HIS EYES. Puffy white clouds drifted past him in the bright afternoon sky. A soft breeze brushed against his face, and the warmth of the sun calmed him.

He tried to sit up, but something heavy pressed down on his shoulders, urging him to remain flat on his back and relax. He did so, and the weight dissipated.

Birds sang in the distance. He closed his eyes and listened.

Mockingbird. Cardinals. A hawk.

He could tell the difference. He'd learned the sounds years ago while traipsing through the woods with his father, looking for animal life to study.

Reaching out to his side, grass tickled his forearms. Three to four inches tall ... mixed with dandelions. He picked one and held it up, peering at it. He blew, and the seeds pulled away and floated on the breeze, destined to find a home and start the cycle of life all over again.

He dropped his arms to the ground, and at once, the grass no longer caressed his arms, soft and inviting. Instead, it transformed into pebbles ...

No. Rocks.

Small, sharp rocks.

Each one a scalpel, poking him in the back.

And it wasn't even his entire back. Only the upper part.

As he tried to process this weird cauldron of feelings, the jabbing, almost cutting sensation now covered both shoulders, his arms, and his neck.

He touched his face. "What is happening?"

The pain slowly decreased, and he tried to sit up again, but the heavy hands forced him down this time.

"Ned? Ned? Where are you?"

Angela?

Why would his annoying sister be looking for him in this meadow?

"Dad's looking for you. You better get home before he loses it."

It was strange. His sister was fourteen years old ... again.

I've been here before. 'Dad's in Europe. On assignment with the British biology team. Don't you remember, Angela?'

"No. I don't. But are you surprised? Why would I remember? Like you tell me all the time, I care way too much about makeup and clothes and my smartphone to pay attention to such things."

The pain continued to subside as Ned struggled to process the conversation. "Wait. Those are my lines. That's what I said when—" Ned grimaced as a bout of cold sweats morphed into a wave of nausea.

"Ned, you're going into shock."

'Angela, how would you know what shock looks like?'

"I'm not kidding. You need a doctor."

No, I need to sleep. I'm tired. Been burning the candle at both ends. Just need sleep ... just ... sleep...

"Hey, are you all right?"

'Haven't you heard a word I've said?'

A hand pressed on his shoulder. Another touched his forehead, then his cheek, before brushing through his hair.

'Angela, don't touch me like that. That's not cool.'

He suddenly smelled something warm and inviting ... molasses, perhaps?

No, vanilla ... I think it's van—

His eyes fluttered open, and his breathing intensified.

There, inches away from him, was a being.

He sucked in a deep breath and let out a gasp. He attempted to sit up, trying to push the creature away from him at the same time, but he couldn't.

"Are you all right?" The being spoke with an accent he didn't recognize.

Ned eyes darted left and right, but he couldn't turn his head. "Where's Angela?"

"I do not know what an 'An-ge-la' is," the being said. Bright green with a strong tint of blue mixed in, its facial features were soft. Eyes that matched its skin gave the creature an effervescence. Dark, flowing hair came down from the top of its head and gently draped over its shoulders. It floated, as if the being were underwater.

Ned strained to look down. The being wore an intricate robe made of a silk-like material and in a pattern he had never seen.

"Are you all right?" the being said again.

"I'm not sure." Ned winced. Three simple words caused his forehead to ache and his head to spin. "Where am I?"

"We are on the outer ridge. Just a little farther, and we will be out of the reach of their interceptors."

"No, no, no. I mean, *where* am I? I was in Nevada a few minutes ago. With my friends? Tyler? Everly? Carter?" Ned strained to look past the being. "But this isn't Nevada."

Another explosion occurred off in the distance. The being jerked in fear and used its body to cover Ned as best it could. "We must leave this place. It is not safe here. That interceptor will be back."

"Where is here? And who are you?"

"My name is Hadar. And you are on my home planet, Sonarou."

One of the other beings, standing off to the side, motioned with its hand. "Hadar, we must go. Now!"

Ned groaned as he struggled to move. "I can't sit up. I can't move anything but my eyes."

Hadar stood and reached out her hand. "We must leave now. We do not have time for deception."

"Deception? Who's the one playing some weird prank?"

Another explosion hit just over the rise.

"Please," Hadar said. "We must leave now, before we are captured."

Ned studied the being's frame. There was a strength about it he admired, even if it was part of an extravagant hoax.

Hadar grabbed him by the arm and pulled.

"Ouch!" Ned grit his teeth in agony.

Hadar released his hand. "You are hurt."

"It's my back. I can feel pain, but I don't feel anything below the waist."

Hadar stepped over his body to get a better look.

"Hadar!" yelled the being holding the smaller, child-like one. "I hear foot soldiers. They are drawing near. We must leave."

"He's wounded, Sorietah." Hadar knelt down and rolled Ned to his side.

At once, she covered her mouth. "You have been shot with a nodek, and the end of it has broken off."

Sorietah scanned their immediate surroundings. "That means Solobaid's army *is* close."

Hadar peered at her friends. "We must not dislodge it. It is acting like a plug. He will bleed to death if we do."

"Then," Sorietah said, "you must get him to the healer."

Ned coughed and shook, fearing his lungs were filling with fluid. "What is a *nodek*?"

"It is a dreadful weapon." Hadar shook her head with disdain. "The tip of it is dipped in the poison of a Redda. One drop of poison can kill a Sonarouan in a matter of hours."

"Then, you're right. We don't have any time to lose." Ned drew in a deep breath. "I can get up."

"No!" Hadar stepped forward and draped herself over Ned. "I will take you to the healer now."

A soft snapping sound gave way to two enormous wings spreading out above Ned. Each wing's pattern matched the one on Hadar's garment.

Hadar nodded at her friends. "Soriateh, we are ready."

The tallest one pointed at the only being left not carrying somebody. "I will take the lead. Rena, you protect our flank."

Rena nodded, and their wings spread out.

"Can you hold on to me?" Hadar said to Ned.

"I know this may be an odd time to ask, but are you male or female?"

"I am not familiar with your words."

"Boy or girl? Man or woman? *X* chromosome? *Y* chromosome?"

"Hadar!" Soriateh said. "We must leave now!"

Hadar gave a quick glance over her shoulder. "I am a young-bearer, if that is what you are asking."

Ned smiled. "We call those females on my planet."

"Then, I am a female." Hadar positioned herself to help Ned up. "Are you a female too?"

"No. I am a male. One that is very adamant about who touches me. I'm not big on affection. But I do want to get out of harm's way."

Ned wanted to wrap his arms around her neck, but they weren't responding to his brain's commands. "But I can't move."

Without a word, Hadar wrapped her arms around Ned's chest and her legs around his. With considerable ease, they both lifted off the ground and followed Soriateh.

"I'm not a fan of heights, either, just so you know." Ned's eyes widened as they crested the ridge and ascended into the darkening sky. All he could see for miles was destruction. A village of considerable size off to his right glowed as the embers of what remained danced in the distance.

"What is going on here?"

"We do not have time for questions now."

"But everything is being destroyed. Why are you—"

A red beam whizzed past them, coming from above and striking the ground below.

Hadar clutched Ned tighter, twisted her wings, and glided around the blast.

Smaller, more numerous red beams rose from the ground, converging on their position.

Hadar yanked Ned to the left, then to the right. She suddenly pulled her wings in, close to her body, and they rocketed toward the ground like a missile.

"What are you doing?" Ned said.

Hadar expanded her wings and caught a gust of air rushing upward from the growing canyon beneath. "I am trying to live."

Soriateh glided closer to the group. "It will be better if we split up. I will head to the north and try to draw their fire. Rena, head south and do the same. Hadar, you stay on course, take the rest with you, and get that creature to the healer."

All three nodded without a word.

Ned admired how calm they seemed. So matter-of-fact. It was how he pictured the Navy Seals or Black Ops responding back home.

They were on a mission.

"I'm not feeling too well ..." Ned's voice was weak. "I think I'm gonna throw up."

Hadar whipped them to the left and flapped furiously over the top of a small mountain until a cool breeze met them on top of the outer ridge. She continued her ascent until they were high above the mountaintop.

One last red beam shot toward them, but she saw it coming and easily angled to her left out of its path.

Hadar stopped flapping her wings and soared away from the battle. "What does that mean? 'Throw up'?"

But Ned said nothing.

"Are you okay?"

She pulled him close and shook him, but Ned's eyes were closed. He felt her rotate him in her arms and examine his back.

"Oh, no. The *nodek* is gone."

THREE

1

SPEECHLESS

NED'S EYES fluttered and fought to focus on the images around him. Weak and extremely sleepy, he attempted to move, but nothing responded. His brain ordered his hands to his face, but they remained at his side.

Only able to move his eyes, he strained to peer down at his extremities, worried that he was restrained, a prisoner of his greenish-blue abductor with the wings.

He tried to speak, but all he could do was blow small bursts of air out past his lips, making a faint, burping sound.

"Hadar, I believe our guest is waking," came a voice from behind him.

Another voice sounded from a distance. "Soriateh, did you say something?"

"Yes. You need to come in here."

From Ned's right, Hadar's face came into view. "Soriateh said you had awakened. You have been asleep a long time."

Ned tried to respond, but his lips would not cooperate.

"Do not try to speak. The healer gave you Ayngua. It makes

us relax so the body can repair itself. It will eventually pass." She patted him on the arm and smiled.

Ned eyed her, trying so hard to communicate, but all he could do was stare at Hadar.

There was something about her ... something that made him curious ... besides the obvious strangeness of her looks and the utter fascination of the entire situation in which he found himself.

It was her facial expressions that made her different than anyone he'd ever met. Sincerity flowed from her words. True concern motivated her actions.

Something "else" radiated from her, though. Some other quality Ned had difficulty singling out in his drug-addled state. One he'd never experienced before, and for a scientist, having no point of reference, no baseline, and no set of parameters to measure made the "problem" intriguing and frustrating all at the same time.

Ned's inner reckoning led his eyes from her face ... to her expressions ... to her eyes ...

"You have stopped bleeding." Hadar glanced at his torso. Her eyes slanted into what Ned interpreted as an inquisitive look. "Did you know you are red on the inside?"

Ned wanted to respond, but his mind, still fuzzy and unable to do two things at the same time, centered on her eyes. The pupils, actually. How they differed from his. Ovals instead of circles, and how they dipped down toward her nose.

"Are all your species that way?"

Ned tried to speak again, but all that came out was a soft whimper.

"Are you sure he cannot talk?" Soriateh said. "We need to know who he is."

"Are you worried he is a spy? And if he was, why would they try to kill their own spy?" Hadar laughed at the thought and gazed at Ned. "Does he look like one of Solobaid's men? Or any of us?"

"No, but—"

"Then, you have nothing to worry about, Soriateh. He is in no condition to do us harm right now."

Soriateh harrumphed. "Very well." He marched toward the door. "I need to get an update from Rena."

Hadar reached up and stroked Ned's forehead, running her fingers through his hair, tracing his hairline and circling his left ear. "I will keep an eye on our guest."

"I will be back soon."

Ned tried to stop Hadar from touching him, but all he could muster was a rapid breathing pattern.

"Do not be afraid," she said. "Sorietah means no harm. He just worries too much. And I will not ask any more questions. You cannot speak yet. We can discuss these things later."

Ned took a quick breath and continued to stare at Hadar. He suddenly realized what the "something else" was...

Her beauty ... not just outer ... although that, too, is intriguing ... but inside ... what makes her who she is ... where the sincerity comes from ...

He admitted he'd never been one for that sort of thing. Just ask Koki. The Asian woman Tyler and Carter had reminded him about just earlier that day. Koki was nice. And pretty. She, too, acted sincere in her efforts to get to know Ned.

"However, relationships take time," Ned reasoned in those days. "Time away from the task at hand. Valuable time that could, and should, be spent unraveling the mysteries of nature, the mysteries of the universe."

Ned's mind recalled those very words, spoken in front of his bathroom mirror as he prepared for his classes that day. He had always been able to shun amorous feelings, quite easily, for the sake of the mission at hand. And the mirror always agreed and supported his resolve.

Human entanglements, revolving around the complicated formula of what humans called "love," repelled him. He'd seen too many of his friends, both in high school and now in college, become infatuated with a member of the opposite sex. It was often to the point of ridiculousness and utter madness. Grades, jobs, and long-standing relationships with friends would be abandoned in favor of a fanciful quest for affection.

Ned always likened "love" to seeing a Christmas present under the tree for the first time. The girlfriend or boyfriend looked so joyous, so sparkly, so promising, and ultimately exciting. The problem was, he reasoned, that they were already infatuated with the present *before* they ever opened it to see what was on the inside. And more times than not, when they finally took the time to open the present, they were disappointed because it wasn't what they thought it was. The wrappings, the anticipation, and the hype were better than the actual gift.

That's why Ned shunned relationships. They were okay for his parents, his sister Angela, and his friends. They could do whatever they wanted. All he asked was for them to stop playing matchmaker, thinking he was somehow lonely and in need of companionship. His work was his companion. The mysteries he surveilled, studied, and attempted to solve, provided all the excitement he needed.

Science had always been "his girl."

However, as he lay on his back, struggling to keep his eyes open and unable to speak, he realized that there was something unique about Hadar. It was in her gaze. It was the way she looked at Ned ...

It's like she truly cares ... and not just about my physical state ...

He couldn't explain it. He just knew it to be true.

And yet, she didn't even know him.

She's never unwrapped the present...

But she loves it, nevertheless...

And not in a giddy way either. This was more mature. Real.

He tried one last time to speak, but she placed her hand over his mouth and said, "Shhh. Go back to sleep. We are safe here. Allow the Ayngua to work. We can talk later."

With those words, Ned's eyes closed again, but the image of Hadar touching his hair, with her concerned expressions, filled his consciousness until it drifted away into deep slumber.

FOUR

1

INTERNAL AFFAIRS

SEVERAL HOURS PASSED before Ned sat up and stretched. His muscles ached, so much so that he imagined that was how someone felt after being beaten by a thousand baseball bats. The middle of his back stung, too, and was tight.

"How do you feel?" Hadar's voice lilted from across the room.

Ned continued to stretch. "I feel okay ... I guess. But it's weird. It's like my brain says, 'Move your arm upward and stretch,' but the message gets delayed before my arm can finally respond. I can talk, and that's a good sign, but that message is also delayed." He stretched his legs. "And my back, man, it's really tight. Like I've got ... stitches or something."

"I am not sure what 'stit-ches' are, but I believe you speak of the covering." Hadar stepped closer and knelt down next to him. "We may be able to remove it and replace it with something less restrictive. Let me check it."

Ned turned so that his back faced Hadar.

Gently, Hadar peeled it from his skin until she held it in her hand.

"Can I see it?" Ned gently twisted in her direction and immediately grimaced. "Whoa. That's a lot of blood. Am I still bleeding?"

Hadar took one last look at his back and shook her head. "We will need to cover that up, though. The healer must continue his work."

"Which is?"

"To heal you, of course." Hadar smiled. The answer was in the phrase.

"So, he's a doctor."

"I do not understand. What is a 'doctor'?"

"That is what we call healers on my planet." Ned scanned the room. A window of sorts to his left gave him a limited view of the sky outside. "And that brings me to my next question. What is the name of this planet?"

Hadar's eyes squinted a little. "I am not sure what a 'planet' is."

Ned swept his arm around, motioning to the entire room, and then pointed out the window. "This place. Where you live. What is its name?"

"Oh," Hadar said with a sudden look of understanding, "our *kingdom*. It is called Sonarou."

"Say that again."

"So-nah-roo," Hadar emphasized the second syllable.

Ned used his hands to cover his ears. What Hadar said and how her lips didn't match the words troubled him.

He then found a small device, similar to a hearing aid, in each ear. He grabbed one of them with his fingers.

"No!" Hadar said. "Do not pull on those."

Ned stopped and lifted his hands in the air in surrender.

"If you do," she continued, "you will do damage to yourself." She tapped her ears. "They are listening orbs. They help you understand what we are saying. See," she said, turning her head so Ned could see her ear. "We wear them as well. It helps us understand what you are saying."

"So, it's some kind of universal translator?" Ned used his index fingers to feel the devices in his ears.

"They are translators, yes."

"I have to say," Ned said, looking under the makeshift bedsheet, "I've never visited a kingdom before."

"You do not have kingdoms where you live?"

"Well, we do, but we've never called the entire planet a kingdom." Ned continued to search the room. "Have you seen my shirt?"

Hadar offered another puzzled look.

Ned pretended to put one on.

"It is over here." Hadar stood and walked over to a small table covered with some kind of storage units. "It was damaged when you were hit with the nodek." She retrieved it and handed it to her patient.

He scanned it and didn't see any holes. "How was I stabbed in the back without it making a hole in my shirt?"

"There were several holes, actually. But I repaired it. Your people make interesting garments." She pointed at the shirt. "What does that say?"

Ned held the shirt up and chuckled. A picture of beakers sitting on a science table, with each one containing a green liquid that was bubbling over and spewing fumes covered the lower half. He read the caption to her: "*Lab Safety Be Accursed. I Want Superpowers.* It's a little joke. You probably wouldn't understand. My friend Tyler thought it would be funny and bought it for my birthday."

"What are 'superpowers'?"

"Abilities that are not normal to people like me. For example, being able to leap over tall buildings in one jump or fly through the air. That sort of thing."

Hadar glimpsed over her shoulder. She lifted her wings just enough to make them visible. "Do I have superpowers?"

"Technically, no. Although, your wings *are* amazing. However, I am assuming you were born that way. Superpowers are also things you can do that others of your kind cannot."

"I see." She tucked her wings back into their normal station. "Are there many people on your ... planet ... who have these superpowers?"

Ned smiled at the absurdity of the question. "Well, actually, only fictional characters have superpowers. No real person has them."

Hadar's perplexed expression made Ned laugh.

"Yeah, we humans are a piece of work." Ned gingerly slipped his arms into the shirt. "Probably best that you not get too attached to me."

Hadar held up her hands. "You must wait until the healer arrives. He will be here soon. If you put that on now, it may stick to your skin."

Ned strained to see over his shoulder. "Is it that bad?"

"I have seen much worse. However, I do not know how your kind handles such injuries. All I do know, is that the healer had to repair your structure. There are rigid but fragile white things inside of you. Did you know that?"

"My *structure*? You mean my *bones*? My *skeleton*?" Ned stood, attempting to feel his back. The stiffness was real, and the injury was dead center. "What did he do to me? I need to see it."

Hadar took him by the hand. "Come with me."

"Okay." Ned tossed his shirt on the bed and followed.

She led him into the next room, where strange-looking, grey furniture, made from some kind of stone, lined one wall off to the left. Funky chairs and small couches sat behind tables, made from the same kind of stone. Ned thought the entire space was a Sonarouan student union. All it was missing was a coffee bar in the corner and the students with their noses in their books or their eyes glued to their phones.

In the middle of the room, something akin to a mirror stood disconnected from everything else. Hadar stopped in front of it and tapped the upper right corner. A screen, displaying writing similar to what Ned had witnessed on the top of the monolith, appeared. She tapped several symbols until the screen vanished. She gently took Ned by the shoulders and stood him directly in front of the device.

Instantly, the "mirror" became an X-ray machine. He could see all the bones. He lifted his arm, and the bones and muscles moved with incredible detail. "This is like an MRI on my planet, but way better. What kind of technology is this?"

Hadar squinted. "I do not understand the question."

"How did you make this machine?"

"I do not know. You would have to ask the healer."

Ned turned, and there, in the middle of his back, was something foreign. "What is that?"

"That is the work of the healer."

"Yes, I understand that." Ned reached out and tapped the device with his right finger. "But what is that thing attached to my spine?"

"Oh. That is a Pougantoh. It will die and dissolve with time."

"Die?" Ned faced Hadar with a slight look of horror. "You mean to tell me that the healer put something *alive* in my body?

"Yes. We use Pougantohs all the time. It feeds off your body and holds the structure together until the broken pieces heal. Once the structure heals, the Pougantoh dies."

Ned spun around and examined the foreign entity in his back. "I want it removed. Immediately."

"We cannot do that. If the healer removes it, you will be not be able to move."

"Is that because you put it in there?" Ned pointed at his back displayed on the device. "What has it done? Grafted itself into me with its tentacles? Injected me with some nerve agent? Or is it the kind of parasite that secretes a toxin, if it is removed?"

"The Pougantoh does not harm. It only heals."

Ned stepped closer to Hadar. She was a foot taller than him, but he didn't care. "Then, why will I become paralyzed if you remove it? If it's only meant to heal, that doesn't make sense?"

"When I brought you here, the nodek that was in your back had fallen out. Your wound was deep, and the weapon had already left behind its poison, which spread throughout your body. In addition, the nodek had damaged the structure in your back." Hadar leaned over and pointed at a specific area on the device. "These."

"My spine."

"That is what you call these things piled on top of one another?"

"Yes."

Hadar moved closer to the device and then placed her finger on it. "These two here. They have something connecting them together."

"Yes. We call them nerves, and they are tied to the spinal cord. It is here."

Hadar stood erect and faced Ned. "Your nerves connecting those two had been cut. The healer said that was why you could not move when we brought you here. He also said you would not be able to move ever again, if we did not reconnect the ... *nerves*. So, he did, and then placed the Pougantoh there to finish the work."

Ned's head swirled as he processed her words.

I must have been paralyzed when they brought me here ...

And she said the weapon severed my spinal column ...

It's a wonder I didn't asphyxiate ...

On Earth, he would have been a paraplegic, at a minimum. Wheelchair-bound for the rest of his life, for healers with this particular skillset and technological advances did not exist on Earth. Neither did Pougantohs.

Ned staggered backward until he slammed his shoulder into the wall behind him. Pain radiated across his back, but he gave no indication to Hadar.

"Are you okay?" Hadar rushed to aid him.

Ned collapsed until he sat flat on the floor. He gritted his teeth and just stared at the device, which now was blank.

"I think you need to go back into the other room and lie down," Hadar said. "You have lost your reddish color."

Ned closed his eyes, leaned his head back against the wall, and laughed to himself.

Hadar took Ned by the hands. "Let me help you stand. Maybe that will help your color return."

He waved her off. "Can that device see more than just my bones?"

"Yes. It can see anything."

"I need to see my circulatory system. Where the blood is."

"You also need nourishment. I noticed your readings when you stood by the examiner. They have dropped since you arrived."

"Well, first things first." Ned gripped her hands and stood up slowly. He was amazed at Hadar's strength, and how easy it was for him to get to his feet. He walked over to the device and stood in front of it again. His bones reappeared.

"And that reminds me of my earlier question," Hadar said. "Did you know you are red inside?"

"You're talking about my blood?"

"I assume so."

"Well, it is red when it has oxygen in it. It turns a dark red or purple when there is no oxygen left."

"You are very different from us." Hadar touched the device again in the upper corner. Within seconds, the bones morphed into thousands upon thousands of veins and arteries.

"What color is your blood, Hadar?"

"Ours is green, when it is in our bodies. It becomes blue when it leaks out." She shrugged and pursed her lips. "Therefore, I guess that although we are different on the inside, we are more alike than either of us would have believed."

Ned stepped closer to the device. "It appears so." He pointed at a specific place on the screen. "Can you enlarge the section were the Pougantoh is?"

Hadar nodded and used what Ned perceived as her two index fingers. With a slow, deliberate motion, she slid her fingers away from each other. The device zoomed in until the area of the T-4 through T-7 vertebrae crystallized into a stunning image.

Ned monitored the blood as it coursed through the arteries and veins. He became fascinated by the detail. He could see the Pougantoh, with small tentacles wrapped around something circular, which he knew were the vertebrae. Similar appendages encircled the nearest artery, and small protrusions, similar to syringes, impaled the wall of the artery. Blood corpuscles, one at a time, rose up the "syringe" and eventually entered the tentacle.

Hadar said it fed off its host until the work was done ...

Ned shivered.

"Are you cold?" Hadar said. "I have a covering you can use until the healer arrives."

"No, it's not that." Ned stared at the screen. "I was just

thinking about a movie on my planet." He bent over slightly and checked his stomach. "Never mind."

Hadar took Ned by the shoulders and turned him slowly to face her. "You are upset with us. You fear we have done something to you that will prove harmful."

Ned peered into Hadar's eyes. "I don't know what I think right now, to be totally honest."

"I assure you, we have nothing but good intentions."

Ned laughed in a somewhat relieved manner. "On my planet, many *bad things* started with good intentions."

"I fully understand your skepticism. I, too, would be doubtful, if our situations were reversed. Your planet sounds very hostile as well."

Ned smirked, and a slight smile emerged. "Does that ever make you angry? Upset?"

"I am not understanding—"

"The violence. One minute, I was standing in a peaceful part of my planet. I was surrounded by woods and birds. A slight breeze blew through the trees. I was with my friends. We were simply examining something interesting, and then ... *Bam*! I was in the middle of a war zone, attacked by people I didn't even know existed."

Hadar removed her hands from Ned's shoulders and allowed them to fall to her side. "Yes. I abhor the violence. Especially when I see King Solobaid take people captive. For when they fall captive to him, very, very few ever escape. And the stories told by those who have survived are enough to freeze your soul."

"Who's Han Solo—whatever-his-name-is?"

"King So-lo-baid. He is the ruler of Anneheg. He is a cruel leader and a cunning warrior."

"I take it those ships with the red, Star Trek phasers were his soldiers?"

Hadar tapped the device in the upper corner, and it converted into a map of Hadar's solar system. She used her fingers to zoom in on two worlds, close in proximity to one another. One was a distinct, aqua blue. The other was a blazing fire red.

"There are only two worlds in our system that can sustain life. This is our kingdom. Sonarou." She pointed at the blue planet. "And this one is Anneheg. There was a time, long before The Great Dispersion, where both planets were blue and full of life."

"So, what happened? How did Anneheg become red? And what are those red spots on your home world?"

"All the red places are where King Solobaid reigns now."

FIVE

1

PEERING ACROSS THE DIVIDE

HADAR TOOK Ned by the hand and led him into an adjoining room, where one end appeared to be made of glass. It overlooked a mountain of sorts. Off to the right, just within view, a waterfall cascaded down, disappearing into a chasm. Steam rose from it, making him wonder if the water was hot or if the air outside was cold. Either way, he concluded that the scientific law of condensation and evaporation worked on this planet too.

On the far end of the room, lined up in front of the glass wall, were circular items, two feet or so in height and approximately eighteen inches in diameter. Hadar stood next to one of them and patted it with her hand. "Sit."

Ned did so, gazing out into a Sonarouan forest.

"My people are called 'The Leiponta,'" Hadar walked over to a container protruding from the wall. "We are a people who travel from one region to another. We never stay in one place forever."

"So, you're nomadic." Ned continued to peer into the forest.

"If 'no-ma-dic' means we move around, then yes." Hadar's back was to Ned. She stopped what she was doing and looked out at the forest as well. "It was not always this way, though. At least, that is what I have been told. The older ones know of a day long ago when our entire kingdom was as it is here, only safer. More peaceful. No war. No battles. They tell of a time when King Solobaid was small and had little power over the people of Anneheg. They were not like Sonarouans, but they were not like they are now either. They have become much more ... 'self-serving,' as one of the older ones puts it."

"Is that bad?" Ned said. "Being self-serving? I know a lot of people on my planet who fit that description. Some of my friends even say *I'm* self-serving."

Hadar finished her task and walked over to Ned. "Here. Partake of this. It will restore your strength and reddish color." She opened it, handed it to him, and sat next to him with her hands in her lap.

"Thank you," Ned said. He took a sip. "It's good."

"You will feel better soon, once you drink it all."

Ned took another sip as he gazed outside. "Tell me about your kingdom. I want to know why both planets are no longer blue."

"I was not born yet in those days. The changing of Anneheg happened many, many times ago. The older ones have told us about how it was once a relatively barren place. I mean, it had many of the things Sonarou had—food, water, calm skies, a comfortable climate, but hardly anyone lived there because very few *wanted* to live there. Everyone wished to be a Sonarouan and follow the ways of Ahsay."

"And who is Ahsay?"

"He was the king of Sonarou."

"*Was*?"

"It is a lengthy story. I may tell you it one day, but all you need to know right now is that He was good. Always good. Ahsay never made any decisions that harmed his people, unlike King Solobaid."

Ned took another sip, finding it hard to believe anyone could be good all the time. "Okay, then. So, if everything was so *perfect*, what happened?"

"One day, some of the older ones questioned Ahsay. They suddenly believed Ahsay was not telling us the truth. Of course, the remaining older ones wondered how this could be. No one had ever questioned Ahsay before. Not that his ways had never been discussed ... even argued at times. However, the arguments were never done in a spirit other than to understand his ways more. To be a better Sonarouan than before. To better serve one another. To live like Ahsay taught us to live. To honor Ahsay with our lives. Our lives were to be so others would honor Ahsay, too, regardless whether that individual was a believer or not.

"Of course, the thought of unbelievers living among us was utterly ridiculous to many. They would continually ask, 'Who would ever wish to defy Ahsay? He is the giver of life. Who wishes to not live?'" Hadar frowned. "Yet, some did. Some eventually were persuaded that the ways of Ahsay were not true. They believed Ahsay lied to us. Thus, they chose to leave Sonarou and start a new kingdom on Anneheg.

"Shortly after this, a name began to emerge. A whisper at first. A whisper that grew into a name. A name that grew into a person."

"Solobaid," Ned said on cue.

Hadar's eyes slowly moved from the forest outside to Ned. "Yes. It was Solobaid. At first, no one understood why anyone would reject the ways of Ahsay. However, as the name of Solobaid emerged, so did his teachings. And when his teachings reached the ears of the older ones, then they knew who had started the exodus to Anneheg."

Ned finished his drink and set the cup down. "Let me guess. Solobaid infiltrated your people and turned them. He got them to believe his way of thinking. Right?"

Hadar nodded. "Those who believed in Solobaid changed their way of life, yes. And they opposed the ways of Ahsay. Instead of being good and doing good, according to the ways of Ahsay, they became the opposite, even though they believed their new way of life was good."

She stood and stepped closer to the glass wall. "I was told a story recently. The son of one of the older ones named Cilegna grew up and was taught the ways of Ahsay. One day, when he was a fledgling, he desired to have something that was not his, so he took it. When this act was discovered, it was brought before the older ones. When they questioned Cilegna about why he took the item, he said he was told that Ahsay was selfish and wanted to keep all things for himself. He claimed Ahsay was using the Sonarouans to make himself rich and powerful. Therefore, Cilegna reasoned, if that is the way of Ahsay, then he was not only following it, he was embracing it as truth.

"The older ones asked Cilegna where he had heard such things, and he said—"

"Solobaid taught him these things."

Hadar spun around on her heels and paused before answering. "That is right." She squinted slightly. "How did you know? Were you here when this happened?" She stepped closer to Ned. "You do not look like us, nor do you look like those of Anneheg. But, how do you know of this conflict? I did not even know until I was of an age of understanding. And even then, I did not fully understand why Ahsay left, why Solobaid's armies were growing, or why Anneheg has become so powerful while our kingdom has dwindled." Hadar came within a couple of feet of Ned. "Yet, you seem to understand a great deal."

Ned lifted his hands in surrender as her blue-ish green skin and furtive eyes had an entirely different vibe now. "You think I'm some sort of spy? Sent here by Solobaid to send information back to him?"

Hadar's eyes narrowed. She held up her right arm and extended her fingers.

Ned thought she was going to zap him with some kind of electrical current, Emperor Palpatine-style. However, a strange but alarming appendage protruded out of each finger. It worked like a cat's claw but looked like a deformed eagle's talon.

"It would not be the first time Solobaid has done this," Hadar said. "He has used others."

Ned kept his hands up. "But did he ever use somebody who looks like me?"

"No. They have always been Sonarouan."

"I'm not a Sonarouan. And I'm not from Anneheg. I'm a human. From the planet called Earth. From a country called America. From a state called California. From a college in Camino." Ned held out his arms and laughed. "I could not look any different from your people than this." Ned dropped his arms to his side. "And besides, all your talk about 'the ways of Ahsay' sounds very similar to a religion we have on Earth."

Hadar's demeanor didn't change. "Does it?"

Ned zeroed in on Hadar's claws. "Yeah. They didn't have claws, though. Instead, some of them had swords. Others had bows and arrows. Later, they carried guns. So, same difference, I guess."

Hadar examined her hand and retracted the claws. "They are for our protection. Not for harm."

"Could have fooled me."

"They put our enemies to sleep, but they never kill. It gives us time to get away without causing harm. We were all born this way." She studied her hands. "I have never had to use mine ... yet."

Ned cleared his throat. "Well, thank you for not making me your first victim."

Just then, a whooshing sound and a latching sound emanated from one of the other rooms.

They both stood, but Hadar held out her arm and stopped Ned from proceeding. "Stay behind me."

She walked into the room containing the bed just as another Sonarouan stepped inside. She raised her hand and the claws reappeared.

The other Sonarouan stopped. His eyes widened in mild shock. "It is me, Hadar. I have come to check on our guest."

Hadar inhaled, half-relieved and fully frustrated. She closed her eyes and retracted the claws simultaneously. "Meno, I apologize. It seems our tense discussion has possessed me more than I care to admit."

"It must have been some discussion." Meno closed the door behind him. "One I must hear."

Hadar lifted her arm, motioning toward the bed. "Ned, sit down and tell us about this ... 're-li-gion' of your planet you mentioned. Meno is the healer. He can examine you while you explain it to us."

Meno bowed and nodded in Ned's direction. "We have already met, but you probably do not remember."

"Right. So, you're the one responsible for putting this thing in my back?" Ned squinted and turned to Hadar. "What did you call it?"

"Are you talking about the Pougantoh?"

"Yes, that's it."

Meno lifted what amounted to be an eyebrow. "I did. It is

what is making it possible for you to do anything right now while you heal. The Pougantoh creates the necessary connections to make movement, speech, breathing ... all of it possible. Without it, you would still be on the bed, unable to move. And probably, if I understand your body's inner workings correctly, you would never move again, unless your kind has internal healing powers we are not aware of." He motioned toward the bed. "Shall we?"

Ned sat down on the bed and switched his gaze from Meno to Hadar and back again. "Our bodies can heal themselves of some things, but not everything. And definitely not spinal cord injuries."

Meno's interest peaked. "That is what you call the stacking in the middle of your body?"

"The spinal column, yes."

Meno nodded, content with the answer. "Turn and face that way so I can see your back. And while I examine your wounds, do continue the explanation I interrupted."

Ned adjusted his position to the foot of the bed. "Your people said Ahsay was the giver of life?" He pointed at Hadar. "You mentioned his 'ways.' And all I was saying was that it sounds a lot like Ahsay is some kind of supernatural being. On my planet, some people would call such a person God, or a god."

Meno glanced at Ned out of the corner of his eye. "Describe this 'God' of yours?"

Ned let out a deep sigh. "He's supposed to be this all-knowing, all-loving, all-everything spirit or something. There are people on my planet, who believe the universe, which includes my home world, was created by this God. Everything was allegedly perfect in a garden called Eden until a person similar to your Solobaid showed up. His name was Satan. He messed things up too. Got the two people in the garden to disobey God.

"Many, many years later, in an effort to fix things, God came down to Earth in the form of a baby—uh, a small human being—and grew up, lived an allegedly perfect, sinless life, and then was put to death so that we all could live *forever* ... whatever that means ... in a place called heaven." He scoffed. "Just a bunch of feel-good nonsense, if you ask me."

Hadar's expression of angst had morphed into one of inquiry. "I am intrigued. Can you tell me more about this 'God'? He and Ahsay are very similar it seems."

Ned sighed. "Look, I'm no expert."

"Just tell us what you know."

Ned shook his head, wondering how he got into this mess. "The people who are followers of Jesus call themselves Christians. And they are still waiting for Jesus to return. At least, when I was taken from my planet and plopped down in the middle of your little war, they were still waiting." He looked at his wrist and pretended to be wearing a watch. "But because I don't know what year it is here right now, I have no idea if that event has taken place or not. I'm just guessing it hasn't ... although I don't think it ever will." Ned paused and looked around the room. "Which reminds me ... where is my backpack?"

"We found nothing with you," Hadar said.

"I had it on me when ..." Ned's thoughts trailed off into—

"Why do you say that?"

"Say what? My backpack was—"

"No, I mean, you said you did not think it would ever happen. The return of ... what was his name again?"

"Jesus."

"Yes. That person. Why do you believe it might not happen?"

Ned pursed his lips and scratched his ear lobe. His "little signal," his mother used to call it, when he was made to talk about uncomfortable things. "Because, it's all a bunch of hocus pocus to me. Fairy tales. Make believe stories to help some people feel better about their troubles."

"I take it then that you are not a follower of this Jesus of whom you speak," Meno said.

"You take it right."

Hadar had circled the room, listening to Ned describe it all. When he finished, she stopped, but her eyes were still aimed at the floor, still pondering his words. "Your Jesus sounds so much like our Ahsay."

"Well, he's not *my* Jesus."

Hadar flashed a puzzled look at Ned. "I am confused. Why would he not be? What on your Earth could be more wonderful than your Jesus?"

"Oh, that's a simple answer. Science."

SIX

1

DREAD

NED WINCED as Meno poked his back with something sharp. However, the momentary pain didn't distract his awareness of Hadar's expression. Her perplexed look became more and more bewildered as she stared at the floor. She was rubbing her head with her finger. Her eyes were shut, and she had a weariness about her.

Ned craned his neck to look at Meno. "What's wrong with her?"

"You are sounding more and more like an Annehegan. And I am guessing she had higher hopes for you than that."

"Look," Ned said, "on my home world, we study everything about it. We study the atmosphere, which is the air we breathe. We study the oceans, which are huge areas of water. We study all the animals, all the plants, all the insects. We study the ground and all the things underneath it. We even study ourselves. We learn how it all works together ... and sometimes doesn't work together, so that we can make life on our planet better." Ned chuckled to himself. "And we sometimes study weird occurrences, like a creature named Tessie, which was what we were doing in the woods when we found the monolith."

Hadar's eyes squinted even more, and it made Ned chuckle inside. By her expression, Ned believed she thought he had admitted, happily, to being entirely moronic.

"Tessie? The monolith?" Hadar finally said. "I do not know these things of which you speak."

Ned groaned at the pain that suddenly shot through his torso. "What are you doing back there, Doc?"

"I am not sure what 'Doc' means," Meno said without pausing, "but I am cleaning the wound. Then I will place a new patch over it so it can heal completely." He glanced up at Ned. "Please. Continue. Your world sounds very strange to me. I wish to hear more."

Ned returned his gaze to Hadar. The look of compassion and care he'd seen earlier had faded away.

"My friends and I were at Lake Tahoe, searching for an alleged dinosaur that was supposed to be extinct ...uh ... which means no longer alive. All their kind don't exist anymore. That's what makes studying things like Tessie so intriguing. If they do still exist, we'd call that a monumental, scientific discovery."

Hadar and Meno glanced at each other, and it made Ned feel uneasy.

Great. They think I belong in a mental institution. He shrugged. "I told you the story was weird."

"I want to hear more about this 'mo-no-lith.'" Hadar said.

Ned grunted again as Meno touched a tender spot. "While we were on our way to the lake to see if we could find Tessie, I witnessed something shiny in the woods. It stood about ten feet tall, had three sides, and each side had a different kind of writing on it.

"I faced one side, while two of my friends took the other

two sides. One second, we were explaining what we saw to each other ... describing the different languages on each side ... then the next second, *Bam!* I was here." Ned shrugged and lifted his hands. "Which, by the way, you haven't found anybody else from my home world here, have you? Another guy, like me, and a girl? Their names were Tyler and Everly. And possibly another guy named Carter?"

Hadar frowned. "No one has told me, if they have."

Meno shook his head as he put the finishing touches on Ned's back. "If others like you had been found, I would know about it. I have to examine all peoples, especially those who are not Sonarouan. It is part of the healer's job."

"Right."

Hadar walked over to Ned, sat down beside him, and took his hands in hers. "We can look for them. I can tell my people to do so."

"You must think I'm hallucinating or something ... 'He's lost too much blood, and now he's speaking gibberish.'"

"If your friends are here, and they are within reach, my people will find them."

"What do you mean within reach?"

Meno stood and packed up his little bag. "You may put your garment on now. And I will leave you two alone. However, before I depart, I must warn you both. If your friends are indeed here on Sonarou, and they are not in our safe haven beyond the ridge, then it is imperative that neither of you go and try to find them."

"But if they're here, I must find them."

"But how do you know? They could be anywhere. Even back on your home world." Meno took a couple of steps toward the door and stopped. "Before I depart ... tell me again. What language did you see on this 'mo-no-lith' you examined? Had you ever seen it before?"

"No. Not before that time. But I did see it again." Ned pointed into the other room. "In there. On the big screen TV-looking thing you have in the other room."

Meno knit his brow together, forming a deep furrow. "Our language? That is what you saw on this 'mo-no-lith'?"

Ned nodded. "I'm pretty sure."

Meno set his bag down on the bed and motioned for Hadar and Ned to follow him into the next room. He activated the screen, and immediately what Ned estimated to be the Sonarouan alphabet appeared, forming lines from top to bottom and left to right until almost the entire screen filled with the images.

"These are all the letters of our language. Do you recognize any of them?"

Ned studied the screen for several seconds. "What I saw on the monolith had eight characters. I'm not sure which eight it was, though ... but I know the first two were these," he said, pointing at two on the far left of the screen. "I think the third one was this one," pointing to a character in the middle.

Meno shot Hadar a look of concern. "Are you sure?"

Ned peered at the alphabet for a few seconds more. "I'm pretty sure. Definitely so on the first two. Oh, and the last one was this one." He tapped on the screen to the far right. "I remember this one at the end because of the uh, squiggle? The curly tail of the design inside the circle. There aren't any others up here like that one, so that has to be it."

Ned exhaled, feeling confident in his recollection. He turned to see Meno and Hadar eyeing each other with scowls. "What is it?"

Hadar took a step back, allowing the elder Sonarouan to take the lead.

Meno stepped forward and manipulated the screen again. The alphabet started moving around. Some characters disappeared, while others completed several arrangements. Each alignment of symbols had the first two characters and the last one designated by Ned contained in its formation.

"These are the only words in our language that have those three distinct letters in those specific locations. As you can see, there are seven words. Do any of these look familiar?"

It didn't take Ned long to narrow it down. "This one," he said, pointing at the third one from the bottom.

"Are you sure?" Meno said.

Ned peered at the words again. "Yeah. I mean, that one, and the one at the top, are similar, but I don't remember seeing these two letters." He pointed at the middle of the word on the top. He thought for a few more seconds before shaking his finger at the fifth word down the list. "Yeah, that's the one. That's what was written across the top of the monolith on my side." He faced Meno. "What is it?"

Meno's eyes turned dreadful. "It is the word *sotehtap*."

"What does it mean?"

"It is an ancient word. One we do not use much in our time. We have other words for it now." Meno took one last, concerned look at Hadar. "It means 'to experience pain; to suffer; doom.'"

SEVEN

WARNING

MENO MANIPULATED the screen again and displayed the writings of Ahsay. "*Sotehtap* is used *only* to describe those who ignore or reject the words of Ahsay."

He touched the screen and turned a section of the writings a different color. Immediately, the words grew in size, and the sections before and after that section faded into the background.

"It says, 'For those people, they will see, only too late, the error of their decisions. And when they cry out for mercy, none will be given. For they will cry out in anguish, not because they now understand fully their choices—choices to follow Solobaid, choices to follow their own whims—but because they only wish to be saved from the *sotehtap*,' which means 'the pain, the suffering, the doom.'"

Ned wrinkled his brow as Meno read. "Why would such a message—in your language, no less—appear on a monolith on my home world of all places? And with two other distinct but different languages on the other two sides? That makes no sense."

"How do you know the other languages were different?" Meno said.

"Tyler and Everly described them to me. We were each standing in front of one of the sides and comparing them when the light at the top appeared."

"Do you remember how the other languages were depicted?" Hadar said.

"One was made up of squares, and the squares had dashes and dots. The other one seemed more random. Tyler said one letter reminded him of one of the United States, Michigan, to be exact. But you have no idea what the shape of Michigan is." Ned paused, realizing how absurd his descriptions must sound to Hadar and Meno. "And he said another letter looked like a fried egg."

Meno twisted his face into a bewildered expression. "You speak such difficult words."

"And who says language arts is an unimportant class in high school?" Ned huffed in frustration and motioned with his hands. "Do you have something I can use to write it all down? Then, you may recognize it."

"Just a moment," Hadar said, rushing into the other room. A minute later, she reappeared with a special kind of pen and an advanced version of an electronic tablet. She showed Ned how it worked and then handed it to him.

Ned drew the first set of characters Everly had described to him. Once he finished, he held up the tablet for them to see. "I'm not sure if I did these letters justice, but that is how she described them."

Hadar held out her hand. "May I?"

"Sure." Ned handed her the tablet and watched as Hadar swiped her finger across the face of the tablet in the direction of the big display, standing next to them. The image jumped from the tablet to the larger screen.

"This does not look familiar to me," Meno said. "It is definitely not Sonarouan, and it is not Annehegan either."

Hadar handed the tablet back to Ned. "Draw for us the other language."

Ned did so, and this time, he swiped the screen and transferred the images to the larger screen himself.

"That one does not look familiar to me either," Meno said.

"Are they some kind of ancient Sonarouan dialect, perhaps?"

Meno shook his head. "No. We have some ancient languages, variations of our present language, but they are nothing like this."

"Why would our language be linked with these other two?" Hadar took the tablet from Ned along with the pen. She peered at the smaller screen. "If they are not from our kingdom or any kingdom nearby, who could possibly know our words to use them this way? And why?"

"I have a more important question that needs to be answered." Ned asked Meno to go back the word he saw on the monolith. Once Meno did, Ned pointed at it. "Why this word? Why not one of these others? Why not a different word altogether? Why not the word for 'Welcome'? Or the word for 'Hello'? Why the word for 'gloom, doom, and despair'? And what were the other words Tyler and Everly saw? Did those words mean the same thing in other languages, or did they mean something entirely different?"

Meno stared at the screen. "My guess? Someone is trying to warn you ... and possibly your friends. We can only assume their words, in the languages they witnessed, also conveyed a similar meaning. Having three random messages leading to three different experiences does not make sense. If that was the case, then it would mean someone is conducting a celestial experiment. However, if the messages all meant the same thing, then the meaning of the monolith and its purpose are clear."

"But why use foreign languages at all?" Ned said. "If I was to be warned, and if Tyler and Everly were to be warned as well, why not use our own language?"

Hadar's eyes lit up. "Could it be that you have already heard this kind of message in your own language? And you still chose not to believe it?"

EIGHT

1

TURMOIL

NED PACED BACK and forth across the room while Hadar and Meno conversed in hushed tones. With each trip across the floor, his frustration and anger intensified. He was a scientist. He was the one who was to conduct the experiments. Being the lab rat was uncharted territory and uncomfortable. He wasn't a fan. He despised it.

And who is doing all this? And why are they doing it to me?

He replayed Hadar's words over and over again. She believed Ned may have been sent to Sonarou to learn a lesson, or better yet, "get saved," as his mother and grandmother would say. The entire experience added the layer of humiliation to his angst and anger. Hand-in-hand those two emotions grew exponentially and raced down a road Ned knew didn't lead to happiness or joy or redemption.

However, as he paced, he worked at retuning those feelings, a technique he had used so many times in the past. He spent the next five minutes convincing himself he was content to travel that road. He had found in his short life that indignation was a great motivator, if controlled. He'd accomplished some of his best work when he was frustrated or unsatisfied with the results. It would drive him harder. Make him more determined and focused.

Of course, it was in those times when people, like his friends, Tyler, Everly, and Carter, or the Asian girl from UC-Davis, Koki, became collateral damage in his assault on and acquisition of knowledge. Even his relationship with his family had become an on-again, off-again, strained, but pragmatic arrangement throughout his last few years at home.

Knowledge is power.

Ned said it to himself as part of his mantra, and he believed it. For him, knowledge was the truest form of existence. Studying biology and chemistry was the clearest path to accomplishing his goal of examining everything, knowing everything, and understanding it all.

"You must study the concrete, the testable, the material things in this universe, to find the real answers," he told one of his professors just a week ago. "Looking at hypotheticals in areas like quantum physics or philosophy are ultimately a waste of time, unless they can be somehow tied to what already exists and help explain it."

Yet, as he walked back and forth, those beliefs—the ones he had banked his entire life upon—were being challenged. Shredded, actually. Just the presence of Hadar and Meno in the same building served as the equivalent of shock treatment. All of his biology and chemistry, all of his science, all of his knowledge and power, had been stood on its head.

Then, it got driven into the ground with a cosmic sledgehammer.

And all that this scientific chaos did was cause the exasperation and fury to nudge Ned closer and closer to the boiling point.

Meno and Hadar had stepped into the other room to

discuss all that had occurred. Ned could hear them talking, but he could not make out the majority of the conversation.

Finally, it struck him, Ned spun around in a pivot. He marched into the other room and blocked the doorway. "I must go look for my friends. If they are here, we can compare our experiences, and that may provide the answers we are looking for."

Meno stopped talking and faced Ned. "Our people are looking already. If your friends are here, they will be found."

"I can't sit here and just wait." Ned straightened his stance. "But I understand if you do not wish to go."

"It is not that we do not want to help," Hadar said. "We are helping. Our people are good at what they do. They found you, did they not?"

Ned pinched his brow together and shook his head in protest. "No. You were running from something when you found me. I couldn't have been there more than a couple of minutes before that. So, there is no way you 'found' me in such a short period of time."

"You are correct. We were running from something. King Solobaid's army." Hadar spoke softly. Her words weren't defensive. They, instead, seemed incredibly calm, and they became warm when she took him by the hands. "However, we were running in a different direction when we were alerted to your presence. That is when we changed our route and came to you."

Ned's angst and pent-up hostility with the entire situation incrementally dissipated, like a slow leak of air in a balloon. The heat from the fever rising inside him was being replaced with a different kind of warmth. The kind he felt when he was lying on the bed earlier, awakening from the coma he had experienced when he first arrived.

It's her eyes...

When he gazed into Hadar's eyes, they conveyed something he could not explain. The science he relied on, to understand everything he had learned so far, had no answers. Yes, he understood the chemistry of what the greeting card companies called "love." He knew about endorphins, the adrenaline, the dilating of the pupils, the quickening of the pulse, and such. He knew the physiological signs... and how they affected the body and the mind.

The eyes are the window into the soul...

That was something his mother had taught him when he was about ten years old. "What the eyes see enters the soul, Neville. Therefore, you must be careful about what you put in front of them. You must guard them. Whether it be images or words on a page. Once they enter the soul, they never truly leave. They are never lost completely. They become part of you, which can be good or bad, depending on what you have seen. You may think you have forgotten about it, until something crosses your path. A song. A smell. A word spoken by someone. The memory of that song, that smell, that word steps out from behind the curtain and dances front of the camera of your mind, just as vivid and real as when you first saw it." Then, his mother would tap him on the chest. "Just remember, my son, science cannot fathom the power of the heart and the soul. There's nothing to measure, but they become the measure of that person. There's nothing to quantify, but there is little in this world weightier than the heart and soul in the matters of life and death."

Ned stood there, holding Hadar's hands. Peering into her eyes, his mother's words danced before him like never before. They helped him understand, be it ever-so-poorly, the feelings he was experiencing at that very moment.

"Are you okay?"

"I was just remembering something I heard a long time ago. That's all."

"Then it is agreed. You will remain here while our people look for your friends," Meno said.

His words snapped Ned out of his daydream. "I can't just sit here and do nothing."

"You won't be," Meno said. "You will be healing, which is very important. You must understand. If something happens to you, and the Pougantoh is not able to complete its work, then you will be unable to move. And at that point, I am not sure we will be able to correct the problem—"

A sudden knock at the door, almost a banging, occurred, startling the three of them simultaneously.

Meno motioned with his hands for Hadar and Ned to remain silent. He walked over to the door and listened.

Another forceful knock sounded. "Meno! Let us in. It's me, Ohcert. Otpurkopa is with me."

Meno quickly opened the door and allowed the two visitors inside. He then peeked outside to make sure they were not followed. "What are you doing here?"

"Soriateh sent us. Our position has been overrun," Ohcert said. "The ridge no longer is the barrier is once was. Solobaid's army has figured out a way around it."

NINE

BELIEF

MENO GLANCED at Hadar with a grave look. "How long ago was this?"

"Before the rising."

"What's going on?" Ned said.

"We have less time to stay here than we believed. We must prepare to move to the caves." Meno placed his hands on the shoulders of Ohcert and Otpurkopa. "Tell the group we leave tonight. At the falling. And only take what they can carry. We will not be able to stay ahead of Solobaid's army if we haul too many additional provisions."

Ohcert and Otpurkopa nodded, patted Meno on the shoulder, and waved at Hadar before leaving.

"When exactly is 'at the falling'?" Ned said.

"When our khammah falls below the sky and darkness follows."

"You mean your sun? The bright light in the sky? You're talking about sunset?"

Meno nodded. "Is that what you call them on your home world?"

"Yes."

"We had two khammahs in the heavens before The Great Dispersion. After it, the smaller of the two died. It did not explode, thankfully, or else our kingdom and Anneheg would have been decimated. Instead, it simply stopped giving its light. When that happened, it altered our calendar. The days are much shorter now, and the food supply has diminished as well. We also fear that the course of our kingdom in the heavens as we travel around the khammah has been forever changed."

"That, of course, is of no consequence," Hadar said, "if Ahsay returns before anything catastrophic occurs."

Meno nodded. "A good reminder, to be sure."

"So, you're running and hiding from Solobaid and his army? Defeat and retreat?" Ned eyed Hadar, then shrugged at Meno. "That's all you do? While you wait for this Ahsay to return?"

"We rescue those who disavow allegiance to Solobaid and wish to follow Ahsay."

"But those escape routes were cut off now, correct?"

Meno waved his arm in the direction of the door. "According to Ohcert, yes."

Ned felt a little woozy and sat on the bed. He wasn't sure if it was his physical state causing the issue or his growing agitation with Hadar and Meno and their reticence against fighting back. To think that Hadar was some kind of Sonarouan pacifist was disheartening. "Okay ... so let me get this straight." He placed his elbows on his knees and held his face in the palm of his hands. "The one thing you were doing, besides existing, was helping people escape Anneheg. But now that the escape routes are no longer safe, you can't even do that, so your answer is to hide in some caves?"

"Yes, if we wish to remain safe," Meno said.

"We will try and develop new escape routes, if we can,"

Hadar said. "But that takes time. Those routes—the ones Ohcert just reported were compromised, were not part of the first passageways. There have been many since the beginning. This one was just another in a series of secret paths we have developed and lost. And we will create more, if Ahsay delays his return.

"However, it will be more difficult this time because we will have to operate from the caves. It puts an added distance that gives Solobaid and his armies more opportunities to intercept and capture the escapees as well as us."

Ned inhaled deeply, trying to keep the intensifying urge to vomit from actually happening. "So, he's cornering you. It's a game of chess. Check. Check. Check. Soon, it will be checkmate."

Meno wrinkled his brow. "I am not familiar with those terms."

"It's a game we play on my planet. If one player gets checkmate, then it's game over. The other player has no moves left. They're trapped."

Hadar shook her head. "No, no, no. We will never be hunted down and captured ... or worse. Ahsay will come before that happens. Being captured by Solobaid's armies is not to be tolerated."

Ned lifted his head slowly. "What happens if you *are* captured?"

Hadar sat down next to Ned. "Do you remember the pictures of Sonarou and Anneheg I showed you earlier?"

"Yes."

"The blue regions were the areas within reach? The red ones were not? Remember that?"

"Yes, but are you telling me you can't go into the red areas?"

"No. I mean, *we can*," Hadar said, pointing back and forth

between herself and Meno, "but it is highly discouraged, even for us."

"Why?"

"Because those who do rarely return."

Ned sat up slowly and faced Hadar. "But I thought you said you wouldn't get captured?"

"Not if we are living according to the ways of Ahsay." Hadar gently took Ned's hands in hers. "However, if we venture into the red areas for the purpose of rescuing those who finally see the errors of their ways in following Solobaid, and we are captured in the process, then we are protected. Even if Solobaid kills us, we are still free."

Ned inhaled again, believing the nauseated feeling stemmed from some kind of deficiency. Iron, perhaps? *Too much blood loss* ... He closed his eyes. "I don't understand. How can you be *free* if you're captured? Or dead?"

Hadar squeezed Ned's hands.

The warmth soothed his battle against the nausea.

"When you are part of Ahsay's kingdom, you are always free."

"That's as clear as mud."

Hadar's gaze moved from Ned to the floor, like she was recalling a bad dream. "Remember how I told you about King Solobaid? How he convinced his first followers to deny the ways of Ahsay and proclaim Ahsay to be a liar? And then they fled to Anneheg?"

"Yes."

"Not too long after that, King Solobaid sent spies into our land to see how we were doing after the first group left. The spies would go back and report to him, and then he would send others here, disguised as Sonarouans, to continue his work. They secretly spread lies, changing the way some of my people thought about Ahsay and his ways. It started problems. Ones that lasted for many, many times."

"Times? You used that word before. Do you mean days? Months? Years?"

"I am not familiar with your words. But in our kingdom, a time can be short and only involve one rising or falling. Or it can be long and cover many risings and fallings."

"I get it now. You're talking about days, then. Maybe even months."

Hadar gripped his hands a little tighter.

Ned squeezed hers in return. "Continue."

"The people who were tricked into believing the spies questioned Ahsay and rejected his ways, just like the first group. They finally became so powerful, they changed the minds of many Sonarouans, leading them into a full-fledged revolt. They even rewrote the ways of Ahsay, creating a different version, altering the meaning and leading even more people astray.

"This ... *issue* ... lasted for a long time until those who were in positions of leadership finally rejected Ahsay altogether and clamored for another leader."

"Let me guess. King Solobaid."

"Yes. Some suggested that he should become our new leader. That recommendation was met with swift opposition, I am told. Therefore, as a compromise, some suggested other candidates. Unfortunately, they were secretly loyal to Solobaid." Hadar smiled in a triumphant manner. "But Ahsay predicted this would happen, and those still loyal to him were not surprised when it did."

"So, who became the new leader?"

"Nobody. The older ones rejected it all. They handed down a different ruling instead—to exile the followers of King Solobaid to Anneheg, including those on the ruling council who no longer followed the ways of Ahsay. The council said that if they wanted to follow Solobaid, then he already had a home for them. They were to go there."

"However," Meno said, "the older ones were not able to remove all the spies because they didn't know who all of them were."

Ned faced Meno. "So, all that did was leave behind spies who could start the entire process over again."

Meno nodded. "Yes. And as Hadar said, it did. Over and over again. Many times."

Ned turned back to Hadar. "What happened to Ahsay? You speak of him as if he died."

"After many, many times, the number of followers of Ahsay dwindled. Ahsay was eventually rejected as leader. That is when he said he was leaving Sonarou. But he promised he would come back, and when he did, he would bring an army and defeat King Solobaid once and for all."

"So, he just *left*?"

"As it has been told to us, yes," Meno said. "We learned later that this wasn't the first time Solobaid rebelled against Ahsay. Apparently, long before Sonarou and Anneheg existed, Solobaid was part of Ahsay's kingdom. He was a powerful ally."

Ned sat in mild disbelief. "So, you're telling me Ahsay abandoned you here to fight against Solobaid and his army all by yourselves? Knowing their history? Knowing how powerful Solobaid is?"

"No," Meno said. "What Hadar describes has been called The Great Dispersion."

Hadar faced Ned a little more squarely. "When Ahsay left, he took with him all who believed and followed his ways. Those who were left behind didn't follow him at all and would not have wanted to go with Ahsay, even if he offered. They believed the lies of Solobaid. All of them relocated on Anneheg because they wanted to be closer to the Solobaid's palace." Hadar stopped and studied Ned's eyes. "I was very little when this happened."

Ned lifted his chin and his mouth fell agape. "Your parents were followers of Solobaid?"

Hadar nodded as tears formed in the corners of her eyes.

"And when Ahsay left and took his followers with him, life on Sonarou became quiet and empty." Meno stepped to the window and peered outside. "There was a calming presence here once, according to the older ones. Our kingdom was much different then. What you see now is not how it was meant to be. When Ahsay left, so did The Presence. And that is when the smaller khammah gave up its light as well."

Hadar frowned. "It is true. That is why my family left and traveled to Anneheg. They believed the lies of Solobaid and believed life there would be better."

"I take it that wasn't the case?"

Hadar's eyes became pools. "I witnessed things I cannot erase from my memory."

A sudden swell of emotion rose within him. He gripped Hadar's hands as he listened to her speak.

"I saw a father kill his very own son," Hadar continued, unfazed by Ned's response, "because his son adored a female ... which was not allowed unless the parents approved. The father was afraid they would try to join under the beliefs of Ahsay and as Sonarouans, and if they did, their offspring would be a humiliation to the father's family. Annehegans do not join because they care about one another. They do so to use each other. They create offspring in vile ways and for sordid purposes."

"Are you saying they do not commit to one another in what my people would call a bond of love? Where two people make vows to love, honor, and cherish each other for the rest of their lives?"

Hadar scoffed. "Annehegans teach that the thing you call 'love' is a lie. They believe there is no such thing because Ahsay taught it was so."

Ned scratched his temple. Trying to make sense of this world was just as hard as figuring out the logic of his home world. "But the Annehegans do understand that they still love something, right? In their case, it sounds like they love themselves. Nobody can go through life not loving anything or anyone. It is a philosophical impossibility."

"That is not how they understand it," Meno said, still staring out the window.

"What Meno says is true." Hadar closed her eyes for just a moment. "I overheard the argument between the father and his son. The father said it would be better if his son was dead than to join with a young-bearer in the traditional Sonarouan way." The tears streamed down Hadar's cheeks now. "The young one's name was Hirach. He pleaded for his life and vowed to end the relationship, but the father called him a liar. He told Hirach that he saw the eyes of his son ... how he looked at the female ... how he cherished her. And he saw how she looked at his son too.

"Hirach's father became furious. He blamed Hirach for trying to bring the ways of Ahsay to Anneheg. He said those feelings had no place there and would get them all killed." Hadar opened her eyes and shifted her gaze to meet Ned's. "Before Hirach could respond, the father pulled out a suxo and plunged it into Hirach's stomach."

"A *suxo*?" Ned pulled his hands away and made a thrusting motion with his hand. "Like a sword or a knife?"

"They are this long." Meno never turned to face Ned. Instead, he held his hands apart about a foot so Ned could see.

"Very light. Very sharp. And they are often coated with the poison of a Redda, so that if you cannot kill your adversary, all you have to do is cut them with it. The poison will finish the job within a few hours."

Ned inhaled deeply, holding his emotions in check. "I wish I could say all this sounded foreign to me, but we have very similar problems on my home world."

"I am not so sure." Hadar wiped the tears from her face. "I cannot believe such cruelty exists anywhere else but amongst the people of Anneheg."

Meno continued to look out the window. "She is right. I, too, witnessed things I cannot forget. I was younger than Hadar when The Great Dispersion occurred. My parents had fallen prey to Solobaid's lies, and they were making preparations to leave Sonarou and move to Anneheg when it happened." Meno's shoulders slumped, as if the memories became a great weight upon him. "Stories emerged about groups of former male Sonaroueons—people with whom I grew up—terrorizing villages. They allegedly took the young females from their families and dragged them to the breeding grounds that existed on the other side of the kingdom's boundaries." He shuddered. "It is said that after taking the young women away, they would kill the older men and women who tried to protect their offspring by locking them inside buildings and then burning the entire village to the ground."

Ned coughed a bile rose in his throat.

"Preventing your children from being used in whatever way Solobaid's people saw fit was not allowed. Parents were supposed to offer their children freely to Solobaid. If they refused, they were slaughtered, and their bones were crafted into weapons." Meno paused with a sigh. "A not-so-subtle reminder to other parents of the fate that awaits those who reject Solobaid's demands."

"And for the young men, they, too, had to be offered to Solobaid, if he wished it," Hadar continued. "They were either made into soldiers for Solobaid's army or used as warnings against rejecting Solobaid's wishes."

"Warnings?"

"Army leaders would kill them and hang their bodies from the corner of the palace walls as warnings against defying the king."

Ned's head swam as this alien history unfolded before him. He gripped Hadar's hands tighter. "How did you and Meno manage to escape?"

"My mother hid me away for several times. I lived in a hole under our home on Anneheg. Then, as some of the Sonarouans began to understand the errors of their ways and long for Ahsay, they escaped and came back here to start a new life and wait for Ahsay's return. My family was part of the third group to utilize the escape routes." She paused. Ned wondered if she suddenly recalled a moment long forgotten. "That's when I overheard the argument between Hirach and his father. I was hiding in a bastalaga, waiting for the Sonarouans to arrive and help my family to safety, when it occurred."

Ned's eyebrows knit together. "You were hiding in a what?"

"A *bastalaga*. It is a device the Annehegans use to carry off all the things they do not use any longer. Those things are taken to the fire pit outside the city and burned."

Ned's expression softened a little. "Sounds like a garbage truck to me."

"If 'garbage' is something on your planet you throw away because nobody wants it anymore," Meno said, with little emotion, "then yes. We call it *bast*. The device it is carried upon is called an *alaga*. Many of our people were referred to as *bastalaga* by the Annehegans, simply because we chose to follow Ahsay. They said we were throwing away our lives by doing so.

"But we accept that name, if it means we will be reunited with Ahsay one day." Hadar said.

"We do indeed. But sooner than later," Meno said, turning from the window, "Solobaid and his armies will find us, if Ahsay does not return in time. We all agreed that we could remain here, so long as the ridge remained unbreached."

"But now that it has been?" Ned's face was stoic.

"We hide in the caves of Mount Sonarou until new escape routes can be forged."

"We must start packing, Meno," Hadar said. "We have little time before the falling."

TEN

1

DECISIONS

MENO AND HADAR pulled out large boxes from a closet of sorts, discussing what should be taken and left behind.

Ned watched and listened until something occurred to him. It was the way Meno walked. He pointed at the healer. "You. It was you."

Meno turned and scowled. "What are you talking about?"

"You were helping others escape when they found me. You were lagging behind. You had your back to me until the very end, right before Hadar picked me up. That's when I saw your face."

Meno shrugged. "Yes. I was there. My job was to protect the others." Meno took a few steps closer to Ned and placed his hand on Hadar's shoulder. "However, besides you, we were also able to save the little one Rena was holding in her arms."

"Yes." Hadar's voice sounded melancholy. "Her father and mother were killed right in front of her. She, too, will now have to live with those memories."

Ned sat tense for several moments, attempting to process all the information being thrown at him. "That means you know how to get back and forth between here and Anneheg without being detected?"

"No." Meno became firm. "Those routes have been compromised. As more and more Sonarouans left Anneheg, word got back to King Solobaid. That's when the attacks here began."

"That is how the blue areas on Sonarou turned red," Hadar said.

"When we found you," Meno continued, "the attacks had spread to that region. It was the largest advance King Solobaid's armies had made in many times. It appears now that his people have determined where the escape routes lead."

Hadar pushed an item down into the box. "It also means there are no longer any escape routes left. The one being used when we found you was the last one."

Meno opened a door and removed some fabric. "If there are any remaining believers left on Anneheg, they are trapped. Even if they somehow escaped, once they landed on Sonarou, they would be captured and tortured for information."

Ned peered back and forth between Meno and Hadar. "There's got to be a way. There's always a way."

"Only if you wish to get captured," Hadar said.

Meno grabbed some sort of chair and moved it out of the way. "I am not sure how the people on your home world capture others, but King Solobaid does so here by promising complete freedom. To do whatever you want, whenever you want, with very few rules or laws to restrict you. This was how he lured many of my people.

"Solobaid convinced them that Ahsay was trying to keep them from a life of liberty and joy with all of his laws and restrictions. However, they were deceived. The exact opposite was the truth." He tossed an item into the box. "But they believed Solobaid's lies anyway. From that moment on, they were *enslaved.*

And to change their minds meant certain death. If they ever tried to argue with Solobaid's orders, they were killed. They could only survive by becoming more and more like Solobaid himself."

"I don't understand. How can the kind of freedom you describe be a bad thing in your kingdom?" Ned offered Hadar a puzzled look. "That's exactly what my countr—uh, kingdom, believes in. We fight to keep others from destroying or removing our liberty. Our entire political structure is founded on the principles of sovereignty."

Hadar stood in silence and listened to Meno and Ned speak. She finally zeroed in on Ned. She walked over, sat down, and placed her hand on his shoulder. "Can I ask a question?"

Her hand sent a pulse through his torso. A sudden, short burst of arrhythmia caused him to take a deep breath and shiver. "Certainly."

"You said earlier that on your planet, you studied everything about it, correct?"

Ned scratched the back of his head. "Yeah. We call that science."

Hadar smiled politely. "And you said you studied everything so you can make life on your planet better, correct?"

"Yes. The more we know about our environment and everything about it, the better informed we are to tackle issues that arise."

"Has your 'science' helped?"

"Uh, yeah. I think so."

"So, your home world must be wonderful."

"It is, but—"

Hadar patted Ned's shoulder. "But—?"

Ned blinked.

What's happening?

Hadar rubbed his arm gently. "I mean, is your planet a better place to live than it was before you started using your science to study it? If so, maybe we could learn from you."

Ned chuckled nervously as the sensation of her hand on his arm sent chills throughout his body. "Well, um, we have made some improvements, I think." He placed his hand on hers and held it still. "For example, there are animals that would no longer be around, if we had not created laws to protect them. We also have ways of digging wells and purifying water for people who do not have such amenities. Technology has made life easier for thousands, and the advent of electricity totally changed how we live."

"So, where you live is becoming more and more like a paradise then?"

Ned laughed. "That's probably a stretch." He peeled her hand off his shoulder and held it. "Some people would say they live in paradise because of *where* they live. Others would heartily disagree because of where *they* live."

"I do not understand."

"I do not understand either," Meno said, grabbing something off the windowsill.

Ned chuckled, but this time, in frustration. "On my planet, better is a bit of a relative term."

Hadar squinted and shook her head.

Ned sighed and pulled his arm away before standing up. "People on my planet are fickle. Someone can live in Hawaii and believe it is a paradise. Another person can do the same thing and say it's not. Their determination of paradise is based on their own personal likes and dislikes."

Hadar folded her arms. "That actually sounds very similar to Solobaid's planet. His followers determine what's best for them. They can even take the belongings of others, use others, even kill them. They can do whatever pleases them, even if it does not make the other person happy."

"But how can a society survive without any rules or laws? We call that anarchy where I come from."

Hadar shrugged. The answer was obvious to her. "It all depends on who is more powerful at that moment in time. If you are stronger than the person from whom you wish to steal, then you get to take the other person's possessions, which could even be family members."

"That sounds like a bunch of bullying and thugs to me. My world's history is fraught with dictators who did exactly what you are describing. Nazi Germany being a recent, comprehensive example, but there have been plenty of others."

"Did those who called themselves 'Na-zi-Ger-man-y' take things from others?"

"Yes. Ironically, they invaded their own kingdom first and enslaved people of their own kind. Then, their brand of hatred spread to other kingdoms as they swept across an area known as Europe."

"Did they have soldiers who helped carry out these plans?"

"Yes."

"Did the soldiers take things from people too?"

"Yes."

"Did they ever have to answer to anyone? Or were they allowed to do whatever they wanted all the time?"

"They had superiors they had to obey, or they would be punished. Ultimately, they answered to one man—Adolf Hitler."

Hadar's eyes turned sorrowful. "Ned, you just described the kingdom of King Solobaid. His soldiers have the freedom to take what they wish, unless it conflicts with what Solobaid wants. When that happens, then they have to acquiesce to what he desires."

Ned cringed at the thought of Earth being more like Anneheg than Sonarou.

Hadar stood and walked over to the box. "Ahsay left his teachings behind for us to read. We found that what he taught was true, and that our ancestors were following the lies of King Solobaid.

"We believe that freedom without rules and laws is *lawlessness*. It is the opposite of freedom, actually. This is what Ahsay teaches. And when lawlessness reigns, like it does on Anneheg, then those in power make the rules and laws. And the followers of Solobaid are the only ones benefit who benefit."

"So, what are your people doing to stop Solobaid?"

Hadar released a heavy sigh and repacked the items in the box. "There is nothing we can do when it gets to that point."

"If you truly believe Ahsay is a liar," Meno said, "and you truly believe Solobaid is telling the truth, then there is no hope for you. Your fate is sealed."

A smug look slowly emerged on Ned's face. "Oh, I get it. You get one chance at believing in this Ahsay character, and if you blow it, there's no second chance. One and done, as we would say on my planet?"

"No, no, no," Hadar said with a troubled look on her face. "Ahsay gave people many, many chances to believe. He has given them this world. He has given them life. All the good things in this life—family, children, food, our beautiful world—all of it comes from Ahsay. However, if someone finally comes to the conclusion that all of Ahsay's teachings are a lie, or at least, a hoax, what other hope is there? In whom else does one believe? What do they trust? For as you said, everyone believes in something. No one can go through life doubting everything."

"However," Meno said, retrieving some kind of weapon

from the other room, "belief must be in the right thing and in the right way as well. That involves trusting unequivocally."

"He is right. There is living proof back on Anneheg of fellow Sonarouans who believed wrongly," Hadar said, taking the weapon from Meno.

"Meaning?" Ned said.

"There are not only those who have rejected the ways of Ahsay completely. There are others who got captured by Solobaid's soldiers, who heard Ahsay's teachings and believed *some of it*, but they did not commit their existence to Ahsay.

"Therefore, they became vulnerable because they did not choose to live in the blue areas. They desired to live in the areas where Solobaid reigns. It was when they traveled away from here and into Solobaid's red areas when they got captured and were promised so many lies. As a result, they thought they could be followers of Ahsay but still 'enjoy the freedom' of Solobaid's lawlessness."

"Unfortunately," Meno said, "they were deceived in the process, thus believing wrongly. You cannot be Sonarouan and Annehegan."

Ned rubbed his forehead. The discussion reminded him of the arguments his mother and his uncles always had at every holiday get-together. She was always trying to get them to "see the light," while they refuted her "misguided beliefs" with scientific fact or political and philosophical counterarguments. He'd sit there as a young teenager on his smartphone, trying to ignore the banter, but no matter how many games he played, listening to the heated discussions always made him wish he could drive himself to the get-togethers so he could leave. And this was how he felt now. "When a person gets captured by Solobaid, what makes that a bad thing?"

Hadar frowned with a mild look of shock mixed into her

wrinkled brow. "Death. Both for life on Anneheg or here on Sonarou, and for life in the times beyond."

"Ah," Ned chuckled in derision. "You have one of those here too? A life after death?"

"Do you not have times beyond on your home world?"

"Depends on who you ask."

"I do not understand."

"He is saying everyone on his home world does not believe in a times beyond." Meno tossed a few more items into the box. "Is this correct?"

"Yes. And those who do believe in such a thing have many different ideas of what it is comprised of." Ned jeered. "Like this place, for example. You believe in some version of life after death, because of what Ahsay teaches. Yet, he's gone, and you're here getting ready to move into caves? Why doesn't he just come now and rescue you?"

"He will return," Hadar said with force. "He promised. However, he said The Purging must happen first."

"Yes. The Purging is the last sign." Meno pointed out the window. "What you witnessed when you arrived in our kingdom ... that is the beginning of The Purging. Those of us who were left here, who have now accepted the teachings of Ahsay after The Great Dispersion, must endure The Purging."

"The purging of what exactly?"

"Those who refused to believe Ahsay." Meno's face became downtrodden. "You asked why it was such a big deal to be captured by Solobaid. It is The Purging. That is what makes it so important. Every individual who rejects Ahsay and aligns with Solobaid will be purged."

"How? What does Solobaid do to them?"

"Ahsay teaches that there will come a time, when Solobaid becomes so hungry for power, that he will break all of his alliances. He will then start destroying everyone, even those who claim loyalty to him. However, their loyalty will not be enough to save them. In the end, his plan has been—from the beginning of his revolt against Ahsay—to kill everyone, including Ahsay."

"Well, that's not going to happen to me," Ned said, standing up straight as he did. "I'm getting out of here before his goons overrun this place."

Hadar blocked the doorway leading outside. "You cannot leave. You will never survive."

"She is correct," Meno said. "One strike to your back, and you will never walk again."

"I'll take my chances."

"I cannot allow it." Hadar held out her hands.

Ned expected the claws to reappear. "Look, I appreciate your concern. But if that monolith says my future is nothing but doom and gloom anyway, why stay here with you, or move to the caves, and prolong the inevitable?"

"Because you still can be—"

Ned jammed his finger in Hadar's face. "Don't say it!"

"Say what?" Meno said.

"Saved by Jesus. Rescued by Ahsay. Or whatever you people call it." Ned jerked his hand away. "I don't need saving. I just need to get back to Earth."

Hadar didn't flinch. "And how do you propose to do this?"

"There was a building close to where you found me. It was a tall building. At least three stories high. Solobaid's weapons had no effect on it. If I can get inside, then maybe I can hide until I figure out where the portal to the monolith is."

Meno shook his head and laughed. "He is speaking of the E'duth."

Hadar nodded, agreeing with her friend.

"What is the E'duth?"

"It is the central location for the worship of Solobaid here on Sonarou. Whenever Solobaid captures a region, he creates a place of worship there."

"Oh, so it's his version of a holy place? That sort of thing?"

"Do not make light of what you do not understand," Hadar said with a little agitation in her voice. "It is the one place Solobaid has promised never to touch, never to destroy. Those who worship there are protected from his armies and his weapons. That is why you cannot go there. If you do, your life will forever serve Solobaid."

Ned stood for several awkward moments, looking back and forth between Hadar and Meno. "I appreciate all you have done for me. I really do, but I don't belong here." He held out his arms and scanned his own body. "I'm not supposed to be here. Somehow, I got tossed across light years from Earth and hopped over and under galaxies until I landed on your doorstep, so to speak. Now, I just want to get home. Can you understand that?"

"We can." Hadar placed her hands on Ned's shoulders. "And we do. I just do not wish to see you fall into the wrong hands for the times beyond. It lasts forever."

That strange warmness returned and enveloped Ned's mid-section. Goosebumps crisscrossed his chest, his back, and both arms. He reached up and placed his hands on Hadar's arms. "I'll remember what you taught me."

Hadar smiled and observed Meno, standing in front of the box, holding a garment of clothing.

Meno shrugged and then motioned for her to proceed.

She patted Ned on the shoulders before leaning over and brushing her right cheek against his. She then stood up straight and wiped a tear from her eye. "That is how we show affection for one another on Sonarou." She stepped to one side of the doorway and waved her hand for Ned to leave.

Ned, feeling customary, motioned for Hadar to lean toward

him enough so that he could give her a little peck on the cheek. She did so, and he kissed her. His heart fluttered for a brief second before returning to its normal rhythm. "That is one way we greet each other and say goodbye on my home world."

Hadar placed her hand over her cheek. "I like your way too," she said. "Maybe someday, you can return and tell me more about your home. Maybe, you could even take me to your plan-et."

Ned grinned. "You'd definitely be the talk of the town."

"Here," Meno said. He held out a suxo. "You may need this."

"But what if I cut myself with it?"

"This one has not been coated with poison. So, you are safe, unless you stab yourself."

All three of them chuckled as the realization of Ned's departure filled the room.

Ned took the knife and held it up. "Thank you."

Meno opened the door and made sure the way was clear. He stepped outside and Ned followed. He led the trio away from the building about twenty feet and stopped. "See that path? The one leading through that field?"

"Yes."

"Take that path and stay on it until you come to a large tree. The path splits there. The one that heads to your right goes back to where we found you."

"Where does the other one go?"

"To the ridge where Ohcert and his group were positioned. If you go that way, Ohcert and the rest will turn you away."

"Well," Ned said, swallowing hard, "we don't want that." He reached out his hand.

Meno stared at his hand and then lifted his eyes to meet Ned's.

Ned grabbed Meno's right hand and began the motion of a

customary handshake. "This is another way we say 'Hello' and 'Goodbye' to our friends on Earth."

Meno shook Ned's hand and gawked at Hadar. "You do not wish to place your mouth on my cheek, like you did with her?"

Ned stopped shaking Meno's hand and closed his eyes. He laughed out loud, and Meno pulled his hand away. "Meno, the greeting I gave Hadar is customary more so for a male and female who kind of ... you know .... admire each other?"

Meno's eyes opened wide. "I understand now."

Ned eyed Hadar and waited for her reaction.

She smiled, walked over to him, and gave him a peck on the cheek, before pulling away slowly and gazing into his eyes. "Did I do the customary greeting correctly?"

Ned cleared his throat as he waited for the goosebumps to finish their courses. "Uh, yeah. You're a quick learner."

"Goodbye, Ned. I hope you find your way back home."

Meno reached out his hand and shook Ned's again. "I wish you the same."

"Thank you. For everything." It was Ned's turn to wipe his eyes. He took a few steps backward, thanking them again for all their help, but his eyes were mostly aimed in Hadar's direction. Finally, with a deep breath and a sense of purpose, he took the path through the field, waving at Hadar until she was out of sight.

ELEVEN

1

MISTAKE

NED PASSED the fork in the road, at the big tree, several hours earlier. Although, it wasn't close to any tree he'd ever seen before. It was more like a cactus, with bunches of grapes hanging from branches that grew together into an intricate lattice. Ned examined it for several minutes before moving on, wishing he'd had his smartphone to take pictures.

Where did my phone go? I had it in my pocket when the monolith zapped us...

Ned wondered if it was lying in the middle of that road where Hadar and her group found him.

'Cuz no one is going to believe me without proof...

He noticed that as he ventured farther and farther away from his newfound friends, the skies grew darker. He thought at first it might just be their version of night. However, as he crested the latest knoll, the smoke rising into the sky told a different story.

He recalled Ohcert's words, of how Solobaid's armies had advanced upon them. "They had found their way around the ridge." Implication? They found the escape routes. Which meant they were looking for them.

Hadar and Meno had said Solobaid was upset because people were "finding religion" and leaving Anneheg.

That would grind a petty dictator's gears.

Especially if the dictator thinks he's some kind of deity.

Ned didn't know how far the caves of Mount Sonarou were from the building where he'd stayed. However, with Solobaid's armies this close to that building, and with those armies literally burning and pillaging everything in their path, it wouldn't be long before they reached Hadar and Meno.

As Ned scanned the destruction ahead, memories of Hadar flooded his mind. The ones where she held his hands and brushed his arm had a particular effect. And definitely the one where she brushed his cheek with hers ... and when he kissed her cheek ... and she kissed his.

He'd never experienced anything close to that before, and he wasn't sure how to process those feelings. Were they physiological only? Just simple biology taking its course? Or were they something beyond the physical?

It's hard to determine the difference when you're new at the game.

Ned finally surmised that either way, he'd probably never see her again, so he'd never truly know. Although something was definitely different. He'd always been able to shut down amorous emotions in the name of scientific ambition. "Working for the greater good always involves sacrifice," he told one of his classes during a presentation during his freshman year. And watching his classmates turn that phrase on its head for the sake of "relationships" made zero sense to him.

But seeing evil advance, firsthand, on a people who just wanted to do what they believed was right made Ned suddenly realize that he may have stumbled across the answer to the struggle he's been feeling inside.

Ned spun around and gazed at the path behind him.

Hadar...

Should he go back? Would he be of any help? He literally didn't know the lay of the land. Just the little path.

However, as he stood on the ridge, Ned's next move crystallized in his mind. He reasoned that he may not know much about Sonarouans and Annehegans, nor how their world's work, but he knew a thing or two about science.

And it seems the law of physics applies here as well.

He knew he couldn't outmuscle Solobaid and his army, but he could outsmart them. Beat them at their own game. And maybe, just maybe, he could help Hadar and her people by stalling Solobaid's advances, if nothing else.

He would be a "freedom fighter."

It's time to bring the old-school Earth militia to Sonarou. Science-style.

NED TREKKED in the direction he thought would lead him back to where the monolith deposited him. In the middle of the road.

Beside that tall building that couldn't be damaged. And next to the other wall with the creepy-looking trees growing out of it.

He finally made it to the top of the last ridge and surveyed the landscape. In every direction in front of him, war raged. A small village, nestled amongst some trees and beside a winding river, lay at the bottom of the hill. Its outskirts smoldered as the tentacles of war constricted around it. He crouched down as a group of soldiers ran down a road. They were brandishing weapons, playing the part of teenage terrorists blowing through a village in Africa or the Middle East.

They were entering home after home, looting as they went, and throwing their spoils of war onto a large cart pulled by a Sonarouan-version of a beast of burden.

Large machines—tanks on Earth crossed with something out of *War of the Worlds*—rumbled through the streets with a spotlight scanning all the dark areas.

Looking for enemy combatants, no doubt.

Ned lifted his eyes from the village and peered more toward the horizon when he spotted a building. It stood taller than all the others and out of place. He wondered if that was the building the monolith planted him beside the moment he arrived.

I need to find out.

Taking the most secluded route to the bottom of the hill, he inched his way around the outskirts of the village, hoping he was still heading in the direction of the tall building. The odor coming from the fires all around reminded him of the smell he'd experienced when he arrived. Right before he got a nodek in the back.

A sudden feeling of dread washed over him as he ran and hid behind a half-destroyed wall. He flattened his back against it, feeling the stitches and bandage tighten as his breathing escalated.

What were you thinking, Ned? You're not a soldier. You're not some super spy. You're a scientist. You should be in a lab right now.

Working on your superpowers ...

They'd come in handy about—

"Hey!" came a voice from behind the wall.

Ned crouched down and moved to the end of the wall where a small bush stood.

"Over here!"

Another voice came from behind the wall, out of Ned's view.

This is not good!

"What do you have?" Came a third voice, closer to Ned than the others. This one was higher-pitched. Ned couldn't tell it if was a woman or a young soldier. Or both.

"Prints," the first voice said in a low, commanding tone. "In the sand. See?"

"I do." The first person sounded cautious now. "Those are strange. I have never seen prints like those before."

"Neither have I. And they are not an animal's prints."

"Sonarouan?"

"Possibly. We have cut many of them off from their people. Their supplies must be running low. They could be making shoes out of something to protect their feet. That would explain the strange design."

Ned examined at his feet and noticed his shoes. He slumped his shoulders.

They must be my footprints.

"Do you want me to call it in?"

"Not yet. Let us follow the path and see where it leads."

No, no, no. no. no. Ned panicked. If they were this close, they could walk around the wall and find him immediately. And a sudden confrontation with an armed alien, in the dark, would not be good for him. He had to move.

He got down on all fours. Quietly, looking in all directions, he scurried in the one direction he believed gave him the best cover, using a grassy area to mask any additional footprints.

As he got about halfway across the prickly foliage, he noticed their voices got farther away instead of closer. He got to the next batch of brush and circled around it. Flopping down on his belly, he spied in the soldiers' direction.

To his shock, the soldiers were following his footprints all right, but they were following them backward. He watched as they slowly circled the outskirts of the village and tracked the prints up the hill.

Oh, no ...

If they keep following my prints, they figure out the rest of the journey using the path ...

And that would lead them straight to Hadar and Meno.

Ned watched the soldiers reach the top of the hill and stop. He could see them talking and pointing at the ground. They made various hand gestures, but he couldn't determine their meaning.

I've got a bad feeling about this.

What do I do?

I can't let them capture Hadar and Meno.

He witnessed one of the soldiers pull out some kind of food and break it into two pieces. He handed one to the other smaller soldier, and they stood together, eating and talking.

But I need to get back home too.

Ned surveyed his surroundings, and off to his right, the band of young soldiers with the cart come back into view.

The men standing on the hill waited while the young soldiers climbed up to join them, leaving their cart of spoils at the foot of the hill. Once they did, the older one of the original group of soldiers said something to the entire group. Ned figured he was the commander of this little platoon, and he was giving them orders.

From behind him, the sound of machinery approached. The ground shook, and it grew more violent as it closed in on his position.

The older soldier said something into a device on his wrist and then waved something in his direction.

Within seconds, an interceptor flew overhead.

In the direction of Hadar and Meno.

Just as the flying machine cleared the hill and disappeared from sight, the band of now fourteen soldiers, led by the older one, headed single file in the direction of his friends.

Ned's heart pounded inside of him. A cold sweat beaded up on his face.

Unwittingly, in his haste, being the inexperienced field operative he was, he'd led Solobaid's forces straight to Hadar's doorstep.

With something as simple as his own footprints.

And Hadar, Meno, Ohcert, the others weren't heading for the caves until dawn.

That'll be too late.

Ned jumped to his feet. "Hey! I'm over here! I'm over here!" He frantically waved his arms, keeping his eyes on the top of the hill. "You Annehegan morons! You're going the wrong way!"

Ned ran over to the cart of spoils and rummaged through the debris until he found something shaped like a gun. He held it up and pointed it in the direction of the soldiers, who had now vanished from sight.

He pulled the trigger, and a large red glob of something shot out of the end. It struck the side of the hill, and everything the red goo touched disintegrated into dust.

Ned dropped the weapon in fright. He wanted to dig through the cart more and find something a little less "Men in Black," but he didn't have time. He picked up the weapon again and pointed it high. He aimed it in the direction of where he thought the soldiers would be and fired.

Another red glob sailed over the hilltop.

Ned waited.

That should get their attention.

He stood with the weapon pointed at the top of the hill, but he didn't see anyone peek over the rise.

Feeling desperate, he ran back up the hill. "I'm over here! You're going the wrong way!"

He clawed his way up the embankment with his left hand while he held the weapon in his right. Yelling his words over and over, he gasped for air and neared the top just as the sound of a million machine guns being locked and loaded overpowered his raspy voice.

He froze and slowly lifted his vision as an interceptor cleared the edge of the hilltop with a giant spotlight shining in his eyes.

Ned dropped the weapon and lifted his hands in surrender just as one of the younger soldiers shot him with the Annehegans' version of a tranquilizer gun.

It shot out of the end of the barrel, instantly opened, and little claws spread out. The device struck him in the stomach, and Ned shrieked at the large spider-like weapon. It gripped his belly and injected something into him simultaneously.

Within seconds, the ground below Ned became unstable. His knees buckled, and he fell face-first against the dirt before rolling down the hill into a state of unconsciousness.

TWELVE

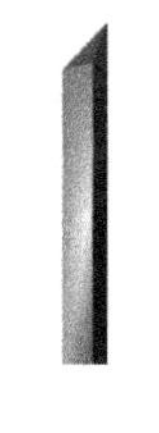

CAPTIVE

NED AWOKE to the sound of machinery. The roar was too low for a truck or a tank. Even an airplane engine's pitch was too high.

He opened his eyes, but everything was blurry. All he could see were blotches of dark colors. Red. Brown. Black.

He reached for his eyes and face, but he couldn't move. It reminded him of when he was first conscious in the presence of Hadar.

But this was different. Ned could feel the metal bands around his wrists as they pinched his skin.

He also wasn't lying down on some bed. He was sitting on a floor. His arms were stretched out beside him, pinned to the wall like some makeshift, medieval torture room.

Across from him, he could make out the silhouette of someone sitting in a chair, but he couldn't tell who the person was.

"King Solobaid," the person sitting across from Ned said, "your prisoner is waking up."

Ned twisted his neck in all directions, but he only saw one person. A soldier, no doubt.

Solobaid is here?

"Very well. Bring him directly to me."

"Who, uh ... who are you?" Ned said.

"I do not believe you are in any position to ask questions," the soldier said. "As a matter of fact, I was going to ask you the same thing."

"I'm from Earth." Ned chuckled at the absurdity of his predicament. "Ever heard of it?"

"No. But that would explain your hideous looks."

Ned chuckled louder and blinked, attempting to clear his eyes and get a better look at his adversary. "That's funny. I thought the same thing about you."

"As I see it, you are the only one on Sonarou who looks the way you do. That makes you the freak. And Solobaid likes freaks. He is fascinated by them. Anything out of the ordinary intrigues him. That is why I am bringing you to him."

Ned listened to the soldier speak, and he recognized the voice. It was the older soldier who led the little platoon over the ridge. "Sorry I had to shoot at your little band of brothers back there. I just needed to get your attention. That's all."

"And why would you do that?"

Ned's eyes cleared some. He could see the form of the soldier in greater detail now. He was very similar to Meno and Hadar. Except, his skin was mottled with red splotches, giving the appearance of some kind of skin disease. *Or they could be scars from battle.* "To get you to do exactly what you are doing now. I wanted a meeting with King Solobaid."

The soldier sat up straight. "Why?"

"I hear he runs things around here."

"He is the king. He rules everything. Sonarou is next."

"Well, if he doesn't rule Sonarou, then he really doesn't rule *everything*, does he?"

The soldier slammed his fist on the table beside him. "Enough! You will remain quiet until we arrive on Anneheg."

Ned felt a sudden rush of adrenaline. "What did you say?"

"We are traveling from Sonarou to Anneheg."

"I thought Solobaid was on Sonarou?"

"Not yet. Therefore, we must take you to him. We will arrive at his palace soon."

His palace? The place where they hang young Sonarouans from the walls as deterrents against insurrection?

The fear and dread Ned felt earlier was miniscule compared to the avalanche cascading upon him now. He had miscalculated something. He was under the impression Solobaid was on Sonarou. It was *his* armies advancing against Hadar and her people.

But why wasn't he leading them in battle?

Ned's heart rate skyrocketed. He knew his blood pressure was probably in the danger zone. The adrenaline coursing through his body made him feel woozy, and he was about to vomit.

However, the cause of all these feelings wasn't just his horrific predicament, as bad as it was. What angered him more was his realization of how inept he was. How unprepared he was. How his "science" had been rendered powerless in the presence of something akin to military strategy and experience. He now had to rely on the science even more. It was his only way to escape.

The door to his left opened, and another Annehegan soldier entered the room. "Diqap, I have orders from Solobaid."

"We already have orders. We are to bring the prisoner to Solobaid's palace."

"Yes, sir." The soldier handed the commander an electronic box. Ned determined it was their version of a tablet.

The commander tapped the top of the small box and stared at it for several awkward moments before lifting his eyes and peering at the soldier. With a glance at Ned, he spoke a different language Ned didn't understand. The soldier nodded, grabbed the box, and exited the room.

"What was all that about?"

"It would appear King Solobaid wants us to prepare you."

"Prepare me? For what?"

Just as the words left Ned's mouth, the door reopened, and four soldiers entered.

The commander simply nodded at the one soldier who had already been in the room.

Instantly, two of the four warriors walked over to Ned, knelt down on either side, and grabbed his arms. They unshackled him, stood, and pulled him up into a standing position.

"Take him to the armory," the first one said.

"No, wait." Ned struggled to get his arms free. "You've got it all wrong. I'm not the enemy here."

"And that is why you shot your weapon at us?" the commander said.

"I was just trying to get your attention. That's all. If I wanted to kill you, I would have climbed all the way to the top of the ridge and shot directly at you."

"It would seem your plan worked. You have our attention." The commander motioned his head. "Take him."

NED WAS LED DOWN A DARK, dungy hallway by the two soldiers holding his arms. Another of the guards led them while the fourth one followed behind.

He had tried to wrestle his arms away when they first accosted him, but their strength was intense. If he made one false move, they'd rip his arms out of the sockets with ease.

They made it to the corner of the hallway and entered a room with a strange-looking chair in the middle. To Ned, it was a barber's chair with wires and straps connected to it.

No ... it's more like an executioner's chair.

"Listen, fellas, I really don't have the stomach for this. I'm not a soldier. I'm not a fighter. I'm a scientist, albeit a young one. I have no idea how I ended up on Sonarou."

The soldiers ignored his pleas as they forced him into the chair and strapped his arms and legs down.

"It's a crazy story, actually. About how I ended up here."

"You have been determined by King Solobaid to be a spy," the first soldier said. "Therefore, we have been directed to treat you as such."

"No, no, no, no, no," Ned said. "I am not a spy. I swear it."

"Did you not mention that you were from a location called Earth?"

"I did. I mean, I am from Earth." Ned wrinkled his brow. "What do you know of my planet?"

"If you are from Earth and you are now here, then you must be a spy. You are here to aid the Sonarouans."

"I didn't even know you people existed until a few hours ago! I was sent here by some monolith-looking thing. All I was doing was examining it, wondering what it was, and then a pulse of light came out of it, and *Bam!* I was here."

The first soldier crossed his arms, and Ned got a closer look at the red splotches of his skin. The jagged, crisscross pattern screamed "Disease!" more than scars. Scalier more than battle-worn. Almost reptilian.

Ned curled his lip in revulsion. "And how do you know about Earth, but we don't know about your planets?"

"We have reports," the soldier said confidently, "of a spy matching your description being shot by one of our soldiers. Then, you were aided by a group of renegade Sonarouans and fled to the hill country." The soldier smiled. "And it would appear, by the tracks you left behind, that you traveled a long distance. We are guessing they will lead us to their hideout. Thus, according to King Solobaid, that makes you a spy and an enemy of the Annehegan Empire."

Ned's beads of sweat returned. "You've got it all wrong. That report you are relying on wasn't about me."

The first soldier pulled the small box from his belt and tapped the top of it. He then held it up for Ned to see.

It was a video, taken from high above. Ned surmised it was from one of those interceptors flying around in the sky. The video showed him standing in the middle of that now infamous road. Five Sonarouans come around the corner. As explosions occur nearby, Ned sees an Annehegan soldier standing on top of the wall with the creepy trees growing out of it. Ned's back was to him when the soldier threw the nodek at him. It struck Ned in the back just as another explosion rocked the area. Hadar and her people then rushed up, grabbed Ned, and flew away as the interceptor chased them.

Ned gulped as he watched the video. "I can explain all that."

"No need," the soldier said. "Not now at least. You will have plenty of time to explain it to King Solobaid."

"But you don't understand," Ned said. "I'm a college student. I'm a scientist. I have no military background. I don't work for the government. I don't—"

"Enough!" The first soldier motioned to himself and his comrades. "You misunderstand us. We do not care about you. We do not care about what happens to you. In all actuality, we look forward to preparing you for what you will experience at the hands of King Solobaid. And beyond."

"And beyond? Beyond what?"

"It is too difficult to explain, and it would make no difference if we did." The soldier pulled a lever and pointed at his comrades to proceed. "We will allow the process to explain it for us."

Ned struggled against restraints, but nothing budged. He mustered every ounce of strength he possessed, but all it did was cause him to growl in anger. That's when another soldier, standing to his left, plunged a weird type of needle into Ned's stomach. A sudden blast of heat enveloped his torso, and he became dizzy again.

"What did you do to me?"

"It is the beginning of the transformation process," the first soldier said. "Soon, you will feel everything, but the glorious part is that you will not be able to die from it."

"I don't understand."

Another soldier hooked metal leads to Ned's feet and hands before pressing a button. Instantly, on a monitor directly in front of Ned, a range of dials sprang to life.

The soldier then grabbed a type of gun off the nearby table and pressed it against Ned's upper arm. He depressed a trigger, and the gun stabbed his arm with some kind of syringe. "Ouch!" Ned witnessed his blood fill a tube located on top of the gun.

The soldier pulled the gun away when the tube was full. He held the device up and pressed a button on the side while shaking it vigorously.

The blood in the tube turned from crimson red to a dark blue.

"What did you do to my blood? It's like you removed the oxygen."

The soldier said nothing while he hooked the end of the gun to some kind of machine. Turning the machine on, it sucked all the blood out of the tube. Immediately, the monitor in front of Ned changed to a different screen, and within seconds, information he could not decipher flashed in several different lines and graphs.

"That is precisely what we did," the soldier said. "I introduced a toxin into your blood sample. When we mixed the two together, it eradicates the oxygen from the blood."

Ned shivered. "Why would you do that?"

"To inflict pain, of course."

"Why would you want to inflict pain on me?"

"Because that is what we do to our enemies."

"That is not entirely true," said another soldier. "We enjoy inflicting pain on just about anybody. Enemy or not."

Ned listened as all the soldiers laughed derisively.

"The toxin percentage is ready," another soldier holding a different gun said.

"Proceed," the commander said.

"No wait!" Ned squirmed, pulling at his restraints. "You can't do this."

The soldier said nothing. He slammed the end of the different gun against Ned's left arm and pulled the trigger. A slight hissing sound escaped from the device until the tube emptied of the fluorescent green liquid.

A sharp pain moved toward his shoulder, slithering inside his veins, trying to get out. His shoulder swelled, and instantly the pain circled his neck and inched down his spine. When it enveloped his torso, whatever was creeping around his back now sat on his chest. He gasped for air, but he might as well have been underwater. The gasping brought no relief. The pain shot down both legs and raced up his right side until his entire body ached for oxygen.

The dials on the monitor went haywire, and even though Ned couldn't read them, he knew what they were probably saying. His heart was about to explode.

Then the pain reached his cranial area, and the worst headache he had ever experienced. A thousand hammers attempted to pound their way out.

Ned gritted his teeth, but he couldn't hold the flood of emotion welling up from inside at bay any longer. He let out a cry, and tears pooled in his eyes as the horrendous pain intensified.

He expected to die. His mind knew his body could not exist much longer without oxygen. And now, with his entire frame wracked with excruciating pain, manifesting itself as a billion cuts from a million knives, he gritted his teeth so hard, he just waited for them to crack.

The soldiers, watching in silence at first, began to laugh and comment on how his body was handling the torture. They spoke of how weak he was, and how little they had to do to get him to this point.

"He is definitely not a Sonarouan!" one of them said.

"If he is from Earth, then they are a weak species," said another soldier.

Ned overheard some of what was said, but the ringing in his ears drowned out much of the conversation.

"Try the nodek," one of the soldiers said. "Cut off each appendage, one at a time."

"No." The commander's words were firm. "Allow the toxin to run its course first. If he is in a great deal of pain, he may not feel the nodek."

"You are correct. We must wait." The first soldier grabbed Ned by the hair and wrenched his head back. He leaned forward until his face was inches from Ned's ear. "We want him to feel death. We want him to beg for it. But he will eventually realize his reality." The soldier pushed Ned's head away with considerable force.

Ned couldn't speak, but his thoughts were surprisingly lucid, despite his oxygen-deprived state. He tried to say something in response, but all he could do was growl in pain.

Just let me die!

Please! Pleas ... Plea ...

The dials on the monitor, fluctuating at first, plummeted until the last one stopped moving.

And so did Ned.

THIRTEEN

1

SUFFERING

WIND RACED past Ned's face. The sound reminded him of the day he jumped from a plane, skydiving with scientific equipment strapped to his arms and legs. But this time, it was different.

I'm falling ...

Falling!

He opened his eyes, but all he could see was darkness. Yet, the farther he plummeted, the darker it got.

And it's getting hotter, but I don't see any flames.

Ned realized he was looking up. Using his arms and legs, he maneuvered his body so he could face down and see what was coming.

In the darkness, seemingly miles away, he could see a small light. It grew bigger as his speed accelerated.

The temperature rose until his skin started to feel hot to the touch.

The light grew brighter, and Ned could make out flames. Their hungry tongues lapped at him.

Then, as his body reached the edge of the flames, the light

went out, the flames disappeared, and Ned struck the bottom of the abyss with horrendous force.

Or so he thought.

Ned opened his eyes just as a soldier slammed his fist down on Ned's chest.

"Stop!" the commander of the soldiers said. "It appears he is alive after all."

THE TOXIC PAIN lingered for several minutes as Ned slowly regained his ability to breathe. Yet, throughout the experience, he couldn't understand how it worked. Scientifically, things didn't compute. He endured discomfort without breathing for what was described to him as almost half an hour, but here he was, still alive. His blood pressure must have been through the roof, and his heartbeat reverberated inside his chest the entire time without fail.

The agony had been so intense at one point, the commander ordered the others to leave him be. "People of this creature's planet are weaker than I thought," the commander said. "And we must have him coherent when he is brought before the King. Therefore, do not administer anything else. We will save the other parts of the procedure for afterward."

A sentiment for which Ned was thankful.

But a sentiment, nevertheless, that still seemed so illogical.

He'd received no trial. No fair hearing. He had been deemed a spy, judged to be guilty, and an attempt at his execution had been administered all at the same time. And he hadn't even seen the king yet. Justice was definitely a foreign concept here.

Or maybe it was reserved only for certain kinds.

Those loyal to Solobaid, no doubt.

THE CRAFT LANDED, and Ned was escorted out of the "Little Shop of Horrors" by the same regiment of soldiers that had taken him inside. His arms were clasped together in front of him with a metallic band that wrapped around his waist.

They exited the spacecraft and walked across a large barren area toward an elaborate structure built on the side of a hill.

King Solobaid's Palace.

He peered off to his right. A tall, billowing tower of smoke rose high above the top of the wall, originating from a location past a small range of hills. The smoke drifted with the stifling breeze in their direction.

The air was dry, and a foul smell grew in intensity as they neared a massive stone gate built into a wall that Ned estimated at least fifty feet tall.

Smells like something died ...

A cart, similar to the one the soldiers used when they were pillaging the small village, was being pulled by a beast unlike anything he'd ever seen.

Shaped like a bear from its front shoulders all the way back to its tail, it stood on feet resembling an elephant's with eagle's talons sticking out of end. It had no fur, and its skin was leathery. It reminded Ned of a rhinoceros. The mottled red color with dark brown stripes running vertically from its neck to its hind quarters gave the animal a prehistoric feel.

The beast was led by another detachment of soldiers, and different body parts hung off the edge of the cart.

Sonarouan body parts.

And the cart was heading toward the tower of billowing, acrid smoke.

A shiver raced through Ned's body when he spotted another beast, similar to the one pulling the cart, standing off in the distance, grazing on a small patch of vegetation by a nearby tree.

One of the soldiers standing beside him let out a yelp, and the beast jerked its head from its meal in their direction. The soldier waved his arms and let out another call, and the animal bolted from its stance and lumbered on all fours toward them.

A soldier pulled something from his pack and fed the beast when it arrived, petting it on the head while it chewed its treat. He then draped a strange, hairy-looking vine around the beast's neck, threaded it between the front legs, and crisscrossed it under the belly of the animal. The vine was then pulled gently until it trailed the beast by at least twenty feet.

The commander slapped his hands together. "Tie him up,"

Two of the soldiers pushed Ned toward the end of the rope.

"No, wait, fellas. I can walk. I'm feeling well enough. I don't need a lift."

They ignored his protestations and forced him to his knees. One soldier held him in place while another threaded the vine around his waist. He then looped it over Ned's left shoulder and back through the metal ring wrapped around his waist. Then, he threaded it over Ned's right shoulder and through the metal ring again.

"Uh, guys, you know how this is gonna work, right?" Ned said, doing the mental calculations in his head. "If this animal pulls me, it's gonna to yank on my hands. When that happens, I will face plant into the dirt because my hands are tied to my waist"

"We are aware," the commander said with a hint of glee. "This method of transportation is used to inflict pain and keep enemies in line. And if there is one thing on Anneheg we enjoy, it is inflicting pain and keep our enemies in line."

"But that's if an enemy is an enemy. And he's being

resistant, right? I'm not your enemy. And I'm not being resistant. Besides, resistance is futile anyway, right? I mean, that's what I've been told," Ned said with a nervous chuckle, "when it comes to alien species."

The commander feigned a smile, took two steps forward, and slapped the animal on the rump.

Instantly, the beast lunged forward and ran toward the other soldiers who had run ahead.

Those soldiers turned, stood, and waited for the right moment before releasing a smaller, energetic animal that had been brought out to them in a small cage. It frittered back and forth and from side to side, anticipating its release.

The rabbit-like animal had large back legs for its size, making its appearance comical.

When the soldiers unlatched the door to the cage, the small animal darted out, almost dancing as it gained its freedom, until it caught a glimpse of the larger beast coming toward it. It let out a shriek, and raced off to the right, toward the tower of smoke.

The beast veered to its right and gained ground on the smaller one.

Ned coughed and sputtered as the larger animal dragged him mercilessly across the dusty, barren, expanse. The rocks lying in his path became sharp, bludgeoning instruments of torture, striking him all over as his body flipped and flopped from side to side.

The smaller animal, seemingly sensing the distance between him and his attacker shortening, stopped on a dime and darted back in the other direction, toward the stone gate.

The beast dragging Ned didn't really slow down. Instead, it made a wide, sweeping turn to the left as its prey zipped toward the walled city for cover.

The centrifugal force caused Ned to barrel roll across the

stony ground until the beast's redirected path jerked his body, almost snapping his neck in two.

The smaller creature reached the wall and scurried under one of the gates.

The lumbering animal, chasing madly after the smaller one and unfazed by the unopened gates, didn't slow down.

One of the soldiers let out a cry, and the gates began to open inward.

The beast hit the gates with force. Only open about two-feet-wide, the four-feet-wide beast blasted through the gate and was immediately met with a mass of people, heading to and fro.

The battering ram of a beast clobbered the people standing in its path before angling to its left. The large animal plowed into a stack of wood and launched Ned sideways, rolling several times before crashing into a stone wall.

Pain radiated everywhere. With his arms still fastened to his waist, he arched his back and rolled onto his back. Groaning from the pain, he opened his eyes.

Inside the wall was a lively, noisy, mass of commotion. It reminded him of a scene from Helm's Deep. The people, who were probably hustling and bustling before he arrived, suddenly stopped what they were doing and gathered around Ned.

Ned didn't move. Instead, he gazed at them, blinking and coughing, attempting to clear the dust from his eyes.

One of the people said something Ned didn't understand, and within seconds, the mob's inquisitive demeanor turned septic. They threw things at him and stormed away, allowing the soldiers who had been his own personal detachment to come close.

This isn't Helm's Deep.

The enemy wasn't on the outside, attacking the fortress.

The enemy was already inside.

He sat up and immediately witnessed the horror.

Hadar was right.

A Sonarouan, entangled in yards of metallic chains around his extremities, hung like a rag doll from a platform.

A living piñata.

Appearing to be drugged, the body swung slightly, back and forth. What Ned could only surmise as Sonarouan blood, stained his outer garment. His wings, broken and twisted into a mangled mess, lay at his feet.

Another Sonarouan was strapped to a stone slab while Annehegan soldiers struck the prisoner with mallets, as if they were tenderizing meat in an industrial-sized kitchen.

Three others were pinned to wooden lattice boards with large spikes, lining the inside of the tall stone wall. They moaned and whimpered in definite agony. One even resembled Hadar, which made Ned shiver with the thought.

Further to his left, he watched as an Annehegan soldier thrust a long sword into the belly of another Sonarouan standing in front of him with his feet in shackles. The soldier howled in laughter as he stepped away and watched as the Sonarouan grabbed the blade and growled in agony. Then, just as quickly as the soldier impaled the prisoner, he clutched the sword's handle, yanked it out, held it up in the air, and let out a cry. A salute to Solobaid.

The Sonarouan fell to his knees, now grasping his stomach. Blood poured out of the wound, but to Ned's amazement, he didn't pass out.

As a matter of fact, none of the prisoners had done so. They all were still alive. They were still awake.

But they should have been dead.

How can this be?

How can they survive such atrocities?

How can they—

"Take him," the commander said as he approached his regimen. "Solobaid awaits."

Ned snapped out of his nightmarish daydream as two of the soldiers grabbed him by the arms.

"What are you doing to these people?" Ned looked the commander in the eye. "Why are you abusing these people? It's a crime."

"That is where you are wrong," the commander said as his soldiers yanked Ned to his feet. "For there to be a crime, one has to have done something against the law. But here, on Anneheg, there is no law. We abandoned the law a long time ago." He swept his arm around, showcasing the cruelness around him. "With the law still intact, none of this would be possible."

"That's the purpose of laws. To prevent abuse like this."

"We hate laws. They are restrictive. This is what we treasure. We relish pain. We savor trouble and inflicting agony upon others, especially those who aren't Annehegan. We ... *enjoy it*."

"You *enjoy* it?"

"More than life itself." The commander offered a fiendish grin before clapping his hands together. "Take him."

Instantly, his regimen dragged Ned away.

FOURTEEN

SUSPICION

THE SOLDIERS HAULED Ned up a thousand stairs. Or at least, that's what his battered body believed. He ached, and his mouth was parched. He'd asked for something to drink, water actually, but the soldiers simply laughed and repeated his words in derision.

"We do not have water here," one of the soldiers said. "Or anything else, for that matter."

"But I don't understand." Ned grimaced as he spoke. "How do you survive if there's nothing to drink?"

"It makes no sense to you because you do not understand our realm," came a voice from behind him. Ned recognized it as the commander's voice. "If you did, then you never would have come here."

"That makes no sense."

"It will, soon enough." The commander stepped past the group. He knocked on the large wooden door before them with a malformed hammer that hung off to the side from a braided coil that reminded Ned of spider web strands.

The door opened wide, and two huge soldiers, at least three

feet taller than the military team manhandling Ned, stood facing each other, one at the end of each door. They were clad with enough weaponry and shields to start a small war. Ned was forced to stand and walk into a huge throne room on his own.

To his right were approximately twenty rows of bleacher-style seating, filled with soldiers, similar to the ones who had captured him. However, these soldiers were bigger, uglier, and viler. They spewed various forms of hatred at him. Some accused him. Some mocked him. Some warned him of impending doom. Each phrase laced with contemptable profanity and slander.

To Ned's left were another twenty rows of howling, screeching soldiers, echoing the same, vehement vitriol. Both sides continued heaping insults on Ned as he was led to the front of the room and before the huge, dark, foreboding throne.

Suddenly, a trumpet blast filled the room, and all the wretched creatures to his right and left stood at attention, then fell to their faces, bowing down toward the throne.

Before Ned's eyes, a creature stepped out from behind a veil of curtains. His appearance, although Sonarouan in shape, was not blue. Instead, his skin was red, scaly, and splotchy.

He stood at least ten feet taller than the soldiers who opened the doors. His physique was impressive and reminded Ned somewhat of the depictions on Earth he had seen of the devil.

Minus the pitchfork and horns.

As he cleared the curtain, the rows and rows of revolting creatures, still bowing down to the ground, shifted from howling and screeching to chanting something in a language Ned didn't understand.

The creature surveyed the room, closing his eyes and

drinking in the unified words of the abhorrent creatures around him.

Then, without warning, he held his hands up high and spoke. "Silence!"

Instantly, the voices ceased, and all Ned could hear was his own accelerated breathing.

The object of everyone's adoration sat down on the throne and peered at Ned.

The revolting individuals on either side all followed their master.

The commander, who knelt beside Ned, gave a wave at his soldiers. They stood, bent slightly at the waist, and backed away three steps.

"Earthling!" the commander said. "On your knees before the great King Solobaid!"

Ned, peering at the being now sitting on his throne, knelt down on one knee.

Solobaid's voice was low but forceful. "How did you get here?"

"Your soldiers brought me."

"No. That is not what I am talking about. How did you get to Sonarou? It is several light years away from your home planet."

"How do you know where I live?"

Solobaid slammed his fist down on the throne's armrest. "Silence!" His voice echoed throughout the chamber. "*I* am the one to ask the questions of *you*. You will not ask any of me."

"Have it your way," Ned said, finding a resolve that surprised even him. "But you wouldn't believe me, even if I told you."

"Well, go ahead and tell me anyway, and I will decide whether to believe it or not."

Ned spent the next few minutes explaining how they

found the monolith in the woods by Lake Tahoe, how they discovered different languages printed on its sides, about the pulse of light, and his sudden appearance in the middle of the battle on Sonarou.

When Ned concluded, the rows of vile creatures snarled and hurled accusations, calling him a fraud and a liar, attempting to deceive them with his fanciful stories.

Solobaid raised his hand again, and the crowd fell silent. "That explanation sounds farfetched to the others in this assembly. However, I must admit, it makes perfect sense to me."

Ned wrinkled his brow. "I don't understand how it could."

"I have been waging war for quite some time. Two wars, actually. And for several millennia. One here ... a realm you cannot begin to understand, and one on Earth." Solobaid motioned to those present in the throne room. "We are Annehegans now, but I once was a prince. I was a commander of legions in another kingdom. I was ...," Solobaid closed his eyes and smiled slightly. "Glorious. However, there was one who did not see it that way. He was afraid of my power. He was scared I would usurp his throne, so he *excommunicated* me from his kingdom. He said I had become everything he was not, which was a lie, of course. He was simply afraid I would become more powerful and more popular than him, and he cannot stand to have competition.

"As a matter of fact, he fears the same thing about you, Neville Edward Dansbury. He is afraid you and your kind will know the difference between good and evil, right and wrong, and if you do, then you will see what a fraud he his, and how he has been lying to Earthlings for thousands of years. Were you aware of this?"

Ned took a moment and tried to process Solobaid words. "Look, uh, I'm a scientist. I don't go for all that esoteric, spiritual, mumbo-jumbo. Good versus evil. God versus the devil. Angels versus demons. Science has no room for such views. Those beliefs may help give people hope, but if you can't quantify it, can't substantiate it, or can't measure it, then for me, it doesn't exist."

"Finally!" Solobaid said with an air of confidence. "Someone who is after my own heart!"

Those words made Ned shiver. "Uh, I'm not sure what you mean by that, but if you're expecting me to join your team, or get down on my knees with my face to the floor and chant like the goons in this room, then you don't know me at all."

A wry smile formed on the lips of Solobaid. "I know you better than you think. I have been around for a very long time. I have watched countless millions of beings believe in themselves more than anything or anyone else, just as you do. I and my cohorts have encouraged them every step along the way." Solobaid's smile morphed into something a little more sinister. "We pat them on the back when they feel superior to their peers. We convince them their beliefs are right, and everyone else who disagrees is wrong. We tell them truth is relative, and they believe it. Why?" Solobaid lifted his arms. "Because deep down, in the crevices of the heart, for beings such as yourself, you are all *just like me*."

Ned chuckled at the thought. "I doubt that."

"You laugh?"

"Yes."

"But why?"

"All you have to do is look at me. I'm nothing like any of you."

Solobaid let out a hearty laugh. "You think you understand, but you do not truly see. Even your laughter is based on a lie. You are like me more than you will ever care to admit."

"I don't see how."

"Then, let me explain it to you. It's quite simple, actually." Solobaid paused and stared at Ned. "You like your freedom. You believe that freedom will set you free. Free from your enemies. Free from other countries who believe differently from you. Free from the ones who live in your neighborhoods, who have different political views. Free from those who have different viewpoints on morality and religion."

"That's all true, but I still don't see how that makes you and me the same."

Solobaid stood.

Ned flinched, but he tried to remain calm.

"You see, Earthling, all of your varied beliefs clash with one another. They cause strife, division, skirmishes, and even wars. That is why your people create laws. To try and prevent such *atrocities*." Solobaid took a step toward Ned. "You, on the other hand, personally believe, deep down, that if everyone would simply apply science to everything, then you will somehow be free, because your science will debunk all of those beliefs and laws that cause the strife, the skirmishes, the wars." He chuckled. "Even insane religious fantasies, like the ones your mother tried to impose upon you when you were young."

Solobaid took another step toward Ned. "You see, if you stop long enough to think about it, the laws of government and society, *are the problem*. You believe science can debunk the religion, make the politics moot, bring solidarity to the sociological and anthropological issues of your time, and bring into alignment the minds of everyone under one banner." Solobaid lifted his right hand into the air, with his index finger pointing toward the ceiling. "'Truth!' you call it. The kind that is based in scientific fact." He took another step and pointed directly at Ned. "That is what you have based your entire existence upon. Am I correct, or do I exaggerate?"

Ned, still kneeling, peered at the ground. All of a sudden, a wave of uncertainty crashed down on him. A pain, resonating from within, rose from his toes and spread across his body. Not because he was kneeling, or because his hands were bound. It wasn't the injuries he had suffered. It was because there was more truth in Solobaid's words than he cared to admit.

Science had become everything to him. And yes, it was true. Even within the scientific communities, there were laws, protocols, and rules that prevented scientists from digging deeper, trying new things, and experimentation.

Solobaid laughed as Ned continued to stare at the ground. "Your silence is your answer, my friend. And I know why I am correct. It is because you and I are kindred spirits. You are more Annehegan than Sonarouan. You want autonomy. And ultimately, that means you seek liberation from everything. And that is what we have here. Anneheg is living proof that emancipation from everything, including Ahsay, is ultimate freedom. Ahsay wants his people in chains. He wants to control them." Solobaid lifted his arms with a regal flare. "I, on the other hand, wish to let my people go and do whatever it is they wish. So, you tell me, which one is more loving?"

"From what I have witnessed here, in the short time I have been in the presence of your soldiers and the people of Anneheg," Ned said, lifting his eyes to meet Solobaid's, "I believe complete freedom to do what you wish without restraints and compassion for the environment around you, to include your peers, is a fool's errand. A pipedream. Not to mention simplistic."

"So, you view me as the enemy, like the Sonarouans do?"

"I see you as dangerous. We had individuals on Earth who believed in what you do. They slaughtered millions of people who disagreed with them. They believed their ways were better than any other way. They promised freedom to the masses who followed them, but those masses lived in poverty while the leaders themselves lived in luxury and did everything they had to in order to maintain their power."

"Ooh, that sounds a lot like Anneheg, does it not?"

"Yes."

"Do you know why, Neville Edward Dansbury?"

"Because those people are evil?"

Solobaid grinned with an evil flare. "To me, evil is a relative term."

"Well, if evil is a relative term, then that means you have no laws to define it."

Solobaid clapped his hands together in glee. "Now, we are getting somewhere! Now, you are beginning to understand." He slithered down the steps and circled Ned. "It is the law that is the problem. Create one law, and you now know something that is considered wrong. Create two laws, and you have two things that are prohibited or at least limit you in what you can and cannot do. Create a slew of laws, and well, you will have a hard time living up to all the expectations. Thus, the laws do not bring freedom. They bind you, like chains in a prison."

"Only if you believe those laws are unjust."

"Are not all laws unjust when it comes to freedom?"

"Not true freedom."

Solobaid stopped directly in front of Ned and posed, with his arms crossed and a hand on his chin. "And what is *true* freedom? For if your version differs from anyone else's, then whose version is correct?"

"That's my point. The kind of independence you are proposing is what we call *lawlessness* where I come from."

"And the kind of liberty you are proposing, Neville Edward Dansbury, only works if one person or group calls the shots."

"And I suppose that here on Anneheg, that person is you?"

Solobaid allowed a wry smile to form as he turned to face

Ned. "You know what they say on Earth. 'It's a dirty job, but somebody has got to do it.'"

Before Ned could answer, Solobaid clapped his hands again, but this time it alerted the soldiers. They stepped forward and grasped Ned, pulling him to his feet.

"Let me illustrate for you what *ultimate freedom* entails. Then, maybe, when my demonstration has concluded, you will understand fully." Solobaid gave a quick nod at the commander of the group.

The commander gave the order, and Ned was ushered out of the throne room.

FIFTEEN

1

ANNIHILATION

THE ENTIRE ASSEMBLY in the throne room followed as Ned was led back into the open square outside the Palace.

"Tie him down on the open slab!" the commander said.

The soldiers picked Ned up with ease and body slammed him face first before flipping him over onto his back. He noticed a stench rising from the stone slab. Dried blood stains spread across its surface.

Feeling dizzy from the sudden blow to his head, Ned had little strength against his captors. They grabbed his arms and feet, all at the same time. His limbs were pulled taught, to the point of his tendons and ligaments burning with pain as they stretched to their limits.

Finally, those soldiers stepped back, and two other soldiers, who were broader in the shoulders and in possession of forearms and biceps bigger around than Ned's torso took their places on either side of the stone slab. Each one held and large hammer that reminded Ned of his mother's meat tenderizer in the kitchen back home.

"No, no, no. Listen, please, I get what you are saying. You

obviously have the freedom to exact your will over mine because you possess the power to do so."

"Oh, Neville Edward Dansbury," Solobaid said with sorrowful tone. "It is so much more than that. It has nothing to do with me exacting my will against you, or me having more power than you do. I have that kind of power because you *gave* it to me."

Ned blinked and shook his head. *I must be dizzier than I thought.* "When did I give you the power?"

"The moment you left your Sonarouan friends and sought to engage me. Such recklessness. But that was not the only instance. The day you left Earth and came here was another step. Such carelessness."

"Yeah, but that wasn't my fault. We had no idea that monolith would do what it did."

"Ahh, but your scientific curiosity could not be curtailed. Nor could it be reined in. The moment you walked out on your mother's urging to embrace her Christian beliefs is a case in point. Such mockery that was."

"Well, just because I don't believe in the things she does has nothing to do with being one of your followers."

Solobaid motioned for the crowd to part. He stepped through the widening space, laughing as he did so. "Such arrogance." His laughter grew in intensity. "Must I recount every occurrence in your life when you chose me and my ways over the ways of Ahsay, or in your world, the ways of Jesus? To include choosing science as the means by which to explain everything."

"Jesus? How does he factor into this conversation?"

Solobaid bent over so he could look Ned in the eye. "He doesn't. Oh, He had His chances with you. But you rejected Him at every turn, and for that, I applaud you. Instead, I appreciate your commitment to the 'dark side.' Is that not a reference to which you can relate?"

"The *dark side*? Really? So, what? You're the emperor of this little slice of the underworld, I assume?"

"No. I am so much more than that." Solobaid stepped away and motioned for the executioners to proceed.

The one on Ned's right lifted his hammer, and with a large, circular motion, hoisted the weapon behind him, then over his head, then downward with enormous force.

The device struck Ned in the midsection, and he immediately could feel bones crush as the air in his lungs was forced out of his nose and mouth.

Ned couldn't breathe, and a searing, fractured pain radiated from his ribs and shot throughout his body.

The soldier to his left lifted his steel mallet. With the same motion, he slammed his instrument of torture into Ned with even more force.

Solobaid and the soldiers from the throne room howled in laughter and hurled more insults at Ned as the executioner to his right took another turn.

Ned tried to yell out for them to stop, but the words couldn't arise as his flattened lungs struggled to operate.

As the executioner's instrument of torture made its circular trip, a blinding beam of light streaked across the sky and zeroed in on Ned.

As the hammer angled over the executioner's head, light engulfed Ned, and he vanished just as the hammer slammed down on the stone slab with a thud.

LIGHT FLASHED and shot Ned across a grassy area. He struck the ground and rolled until he lay flat on his back again.

He didn't move. He pinched his eyes shut, afraid to open them ... afraid of what he may see.

But he realized he could breathe. And the excruciating pain was gone.

He opened his eyes, pressed in on his chest with his hands, and poked at his ribs. Nothing hurt.

How can that be?

He lifted his head and immediately spotted the monolith. He was laying in the exact spot he had stood when the monolith flashed and sent him to Sonarou.

He sat up as Carter and several park rangers rushed to him.

"Ned! Where have you been?" Carter held his arms out from his side, looking truly worried. "We've been looking all over for you."

"How long?" Ned shook his head wiped his eyes. "How long have I been gone?"

"I don't know. You were gone when I got back from the car." Carter glanced at his smartwatch. "But we've been looking for you for well over a day now."

"And what about Tyler or Everly? Did they go missing?"

"Yeah. All three of you disappeared. But you left your backpacks behind. Your phones too."

"Are they back?"

"Back? Back from where?"

Ned stood. "Are they here?"

"No. I mean, yes. I mean, Everly ... she was here ..." Carter struggled to organize his thoughts.

Ned scanned the growing crowd of people. "Where is she?"

"She, uh, said she couldn't stay. She said she had to leave. She met someone ... some guy named Finn and she needed to get back. I mean, go back ..."

"She went back to Sonarou?"

Carter pinched his brow together and grabbed his curly

hair with both hands. "I don't know where she is. I just know she said she had to get back to wherever she came from. Something about saving that Finn guy. Then, the monolith started doing its thing again and ...Wait!" Carter grabbed his phone from his pocket and manipulated the screen.

"Who's Finn?"

Carter ignored Ned's question and continued tapping his smartphone's screen. "She had me record a message for her. To give to her parents. And I recorded her leaving again too."

Ned faced the monolith. "You have her using the monolith? On film?"

Carter nodded and finally opened the correct file. He tapped the screen one last time.

Ned suddenly heard Everly's voice. He took the phone and watched Everly give her parents a heartfelt goodbye, never knowing if she would ever be back on Earth. She was returning to a kingdom called Lux. To help a person named Finn and another named Kaitlin. Fulfilling a desire to do the right thing before it was too late. A trait instilled in her by her parents, she said.

Eventually, the video stopped, and Ned peered at Carter. "You said there was another video?" he said, clearing his throat. "Of her using the monolith?"

Carter pointed at his phone. "It's the next one."

Ned swiped the screen to his right, tapped the *Play* button, and the monolith blazed with light in the background. Everly took one step toward it but rushed back to hug Carter and thank him for inviting her on the trip to Lake Tahoe. Then, she walked toward the monolith, and it instantly enveloped her.

A loud noise emanated from the sky above, and just like that, she was gone.

Ned held the phone out and waited for Carter to take it. "I need to get back to Sonarou. I need to warn Hadar." He walked up to the monolith and waited, mimicking what he had just watched Everly do, expecting it to zap him as well.

"Saw-naw-roo?" Carter shrugged. "What's that? And who is Huh-dar?"

"Sonarou is the planet *I* was on." Ned examined the monolith. He pushed on some areas with his index finger, looking for a secret button. "Hadar befriended me. She helped me recover from a serious spinal injury."

One of the park rangers standing nearby, listening to the conversation, spoke up. "Sir, we're gonna need you to give us a statement about what happened."

Ned continued to touch the monolith in an ever-increasingly frantic manner. Finally, he stepped back and glanced up at the writing at the top. However, this time, there was nothing there. "That doesn't make sense."

"What doesn't make sense?" the park ranger said.

"Everything." Ned fell to his knees, in the same location where the beam of light had tossed him just minutes before. "And if I can't get back to Hadar, her people will die. And it will be all my fault."

SIXTEEN

1

RECLAMATION

SEVERAL DAYS PASSED before Ned was allowed out of the hospital. He'd told them of his back injury, and as a result, was forced to undergo a barrage of tests as a quarantined patient. He argued against the isolation, but they insisted that if he stuck to the story of being on another planet, they couldn't take any chances on him bringing the Andromeda Strain back with him.

Interestingly, when they did extensive X-rays and MRIs, there was no sign of the creature the healer had attached to his spine. There wasn't even residual evidence of a spinal cord injury to his thoracic region.

Ned also gave statement after statement to the park rangers, to the highway patrol, to the local sheriff's office, and even to the FBI. Yet, despite having the video Carter recorded, they accused him of everything.

Some said Ned was a bona fide nut case. They believed he made up the story so he could appear on network news shows and claim his fifteen minutes of fame. However, Ned denied all the requests for interviews. Not because he was trying to prove his accusers wrong, though. He just didn't know what to say or how much to divulge, without sounding psychotic.

Others believed he was somehow involved with Tyler and Everly's abductions. That this entire story was an elaborate scheme to abduct them for some nefarious purpose. However, no one could come up with any significant evidence that proved such a theory. And Carter, to his credit, stood up for Ned, giving evidence of seeing Everly and hearing her say she wanted to go back to wherever she had been. "Those aren't the words of someone who has been abducted, if you ask me," he said to the sheriff.

Still others believed Ned helped Tyler and Everly escape, possibly together, to some far away destination, to maybe even live happily ever after. Social media pundits accused the two of being secretly in love and wishing to avoid family issues. They said the "kingdom of Lux" was some code name for where they really went.

However, Ned knew the people floating these theories simply had no clue what actually happened. Instead, they were trying to formulate conclusions based on limited, concrete evidence and wild, fanciful stories.

Sitting at the local coffee shop a few blocks from the university campus in Camino, wearing a pair of dark sunglasses and a ball cap and trying to be as inconspicuous as possible, Ned waded through all the so-called reporters' recaps of Crypto Club's exploits in the several newspaper articles about the incident.

He read the last article, folded the paper back to its original form and dropped it on the stack. With a sigh of exasperation, he picked up his coffee cup and took a swig when someone stepped into view.

Ned lifted his eyes, and there, standing beside him, holding a cup of coffee, was Koki.

She pointed to the empty chair across from him. "May I?"

Ned motioned to it. "Of course. Please."

Koki draped her purse over the back of the chair and sat down. "I would ask how you have been doing, but that is such an understatement, considering the circumstances."

Ned smiled at first, and then chuckled slightly. "I think saying it's an understatement is an understatement."

"I do wish my condolences. I know Tyler and Everly were your friends."

Ned chuckled again, but this time as more of a thought than a response. "You know, you're the first person to say that?"

"Am I?"

Ned nodded and took another swig of his coffee.

"How sad."

"Sign of the times, I'm afraid. Everyone was more interested in finding out what happened to them and me than whether or not they are missed." He rubbed his thumb up and down the side of his coffee cup. "I can only hope the authorities expressed condolences to their parents."

Koki pursed her lips. "One would hope."

"So, what brings you to Camino on a hot, summer's day?"

"I heard you were still in town and stopped by the campus. One of your science buddies said you might be here. Although I thought for sure you'd be home with your family by now."

"My mom flew out here just as soon as she learned about the news of my disappearance. She came to the hospital and stayed with me until she believed I was out of the woods." Ned laughed. "No pun intended."

Koki offered a puzzled expression. "You do not wish to be home now that you are out of the hospital?"

Ned scratched the back of his head with his left hand. "I will. Eventually. I just have a great deal to process right now. Being alone helps me do that."

"Oh," Koki said. "I apologize if I intruded." She pushed her chair out from the table. "I can leave and let you—"

"No. Please. Stay." Ned held out his right hand. "This ... actually, has been helpful."

Koki repositioned herself in her chair. "Can I be of any help?"

"You remind me of someone."

"Probably your girlfriend. That seems to be my lot in life."

"No. There's no girlfriend." Ned peered at his coffee cup in a shy manner. "Although now that you mention it, I remember now who it is you remind me of ... and I guess you could say she was a friend, who was a girl."

"Everly?"

"No, no, no. Not her. This person's name was Hadar."

Koki lifted her head slightly and stared at Ned. "She was pretty then?"

"She was in her own way. She was different than us in many ways, so it's hard to compare or find words to describe her."

Koki picked up her smartphone and thumbed the screen. "Her name, if it is spelled the way I think it is, is the Hebrew word for 'beauty and honor.'" She kept swiping at the screen and then typing something until she finally smiled. "Yes, that is what it means. Sometimes it can mean 'to glorify, to ornament, to bring splendor to' as well."

"So, you're a linguist?"

"It's a hobby."

Ned nodded and took another draw from his coffee. "Well, I'm not sure how her name was spelled, but that's how she pronounced it."

"Did she live up to her name?"

Ned paused as he recalled Hadar. "She did. In more ways than just her looks."

Koki smiled and set her phone down. "I would like to meet her."

"Well, that may be a trick."

Koki pointed at the stack of papers on the table. "Was she part of the, uh, experience?"

Ned nodded. "She and her friends saved my life. Then, in my selfishness, I put their lives in danger."

"How so?"

Ned hesitated. "I'm not sure you want to hear the story. It's quite long."

Koki glanced at her smartwatch. "School's out. I don't have any summer classes. And I'm in-between jobs right now, so ..." She started to settle into her chair and stopped abruptly. She held up her cup. "I need a refresh. You? My treat."

Ned shrugged. "Sure."

NED AND KOKI spent the next two hours talking. Ned gave her most of the story, spending a great deal of time describing Hadar and her people. However, it was during the part of the story involving King Solobaid where Koki became very interested and asked a lot of questions.

"Can I ask you something?" Ned finally said after telling Koki all he wanted to describe.

"Of course."

"Why are you so interested in King Solobaid?"

Koki clasped her hands together and rested them on the table. "It's not that I am interested in him, per se. He sounds like the personification of evil, so he scares me a little. But the reason why I asked questions about him and his planet is because the pastor of my church just concluded a sermon series on true freedom in Christ. He talked about how our understanding of freedom is skewed. We view it, here in America, as freedom from tyranny. We get that view from the days of our revolution and war against England. We wanted to be free from a government that was oppressive and taxed us from two thousand miles away."

"And now, we have the same kind of government that we fought against."

"In many ways, yes. But that wasn't the point of the sermon. It was to show how we can only have freedom from sin. And we can only have freedom from sin when we have a relationship—a true relationship—with Jesus. Only He can offer us true freedom."

Koki peered at Ned, and he noticed how her eyes fascinated him. The same way Hadar's eyes did. Her desire to care for him superseded any desires of her own.

"However," Koki continued, "the kind of freedom Solobaid offered was actually bondage, not freedom. We can't have individual freedom because at some point, our rights to that freedom will step on someone else's quote-unquote freedom. And when that happens, fights break out. Wars start. With each person or group trying to impose their freedom over the other."

Ned wanted to speak several times, but he found himself holding his tongue ... remarkably so. Instead, he listened, and what Koki taught him made sense. It made sense because he'd lived it. He'd experienced it. Hadar and Meno spoke of it.

He had his empirical data.

Yet, despite having some hard evidence through personal experience, that wasn't the conclusive part of the equation.

What convinced him more than anything were Koki's words. Her eyes. Her sincerity. Her ability to come back and talk to him, even after he had treated her so miserably in the past.

It was the same kind of demeanor he experienced in the presence of Hadar. These two women were genuinely concerned about more than just his physical welfare.

They cared about his soul.

And except for his mother—and mothers are supposed to do this—no one else had shown such depth of compassion for Ned before.

And here he was, experiencing the same depth twice.

Inside of a week.

Even the scientist inside him couldn't reconcile the "coincidence" of such an occurrence. Especially when you considered the miles that separated the two "women."

There was more at work here than mere happenstance.

"Are you free for dinner tonight?" Ned said.

Koki smiled and brushed a strand of hair from her eyes. "Only if you're free Sunday morning. I want to invite you to come to church with me."

Ned smiled and reached out his hand. The quick gesture astonished even him. "Deal."

Koki took his hand, and Ned sensed a warmth flow from his hand to the rest of his body. The same warmth he discovered the first time he held Hadar's hand.

"Deal," Koki said.

"Thank you." Ned held her hand a little longer than what was customary.

"For what?"

"For seeking me out again. You could have left me all those weeks ago and concluded that I was a first-class jerk, and you would have been right. But you came back, and I thank you for doing that."

"I never thought you were a jerk, Ned." She squeezed his hand. "Today, I was scrolling through some social media feed ... I don't even remember which one, and I read a story about you. I simply felt compelled to drive to Camino and try to find you."

"Well, you found me. And I'm glad you did."

Koki gripped Ned's hand with both of hers. "And once you are truly found in a spiritual sense, then you will fully understand what Hadar was trying to tell you. About Ahsay. About life. About everything."

"You think so?"

Koki smiled. "Did you know 'Ahsay' is 'Yasha' in reverse, Ned? That is a Hebrew form of Yeshua. You probably know that name better as 'Joshua.'" She smiled even bigger. "The Greek transliteration of that name is *Jesus*."

Ned's eyes lit up. "That's too many coincidences again."

Koki nodded. "Way too many. I think someone went to great lengths to get you to open the eyes of your heart. Don't waste it."

"No. No. I intend to pursue it." Ned squeezed her hand. "Will you help me?"

"I believe that is why I'm here."

ACKNOWLEDGMENTS

From Brett:

I'd like to thank my fellow writers Erin and Kevin for the fantastic experience of working together. This has been a blast from start to finish and that's in large part due to everyone's willingness to hear out each other's ideas and try to craft the best stories and books we can. It's been a privilege.

This wouldn't have happened without our publisher, Linda Fulkerson, seeing the potential in speculative fiction and being a fellow fan of it. Her support and offer of this opportunity led to something really special in *The Near Distant* and I can't say enough how much I appreciate it.

My family's limitless support and patience and encouragement make every writing endeavor possible. Especially during the times while writing things out, needing a sounding board or time and space to write/edit/plan, and so many other little sacrifices needed in order to bring a story from ideas to completion. Every book written reflects their hard work and passion as much as mine.

Most of all the grace of God daily to have the phenomenal privilege to write the words He places on my heart, however imperfectly, and give glimpses through them of the Way, the Truth, and the Life and His unfailing love and wisdom.

From Erin:

Isn't it funny how looking back on something later, you can see just how much you needed it at the time? I knew I wanted a story that was more lighthearted, full of magical fun and dare I say it—romance. I just finished writing *Beyond the Gates*, a suspenseful dystopian novel, and I needed to shift gears completely to write this book, but I fell in love with this story and the entire process. I will still write my darker and suspenseful stories you are all used to, but I have a feeling there will be more magical, royal books in the future.

Thank you to the Expanse Books and Scrivenings Press family and Kevin and Beau, who so graciously decided to jump headfirst into this novella collection with me. I had such a blast plotting and planning this collection with you.

Thank you to everyone who helped me through this entire process. Whether you helped me with the plot, critiqued, read, or offered encouragement, it means the world to me.

And thank you to my readers. I hope you enjoy this new adventure with Everly and Finn!

From Kevin:

This may very well be the toughest thing I ever write. It's probably because Sci-Fi supernatural fantasy is a bit out of my wheelhouse as a mystery/suspense/thriller writer. Yet, this story has been one in my idea book from the very beginning. I was so pleased when I had the opportunity to bring it to life.

I want to take this moment to thank those who helped me along the way.

To Linda Fulkerson and Scrivenings Press: Thank you for the opportunity to team up with other SP authors in their novella series. Two hurricanes and many other obstacles later, we have finally accomplished it. No small feat.

To Brett Armstrong and Erin Howard: Thanks for allowing an old mystery guy to branch out and team up with them. If it wasn't for Zoom and late nights, staring at each other, addressing one question after another, I'm not sure we would have been able to pull this off. I know we wanted to do so much more, and if we had not lived in three different states, if we had all been unemployed, and did not have families, then we may have accomplished all the lofty goals we initially set out. But thank God, we have jobs and families, and we can live with the final decisions we made.

To my Word Weavers of Lake County group: Although I did not bring much of this to the group for critique (but boy, do I wish I had now), your encouragement to me has meant more than pointing out all my literary faux pas.

To my family, thank you for all of your encouragement as well: Your constant support keeps me going when my will wavers. And maybe someday, when you ask me if I'm able to retire yet, I can say, "Yes," even if it just means I'm old enough.

And to my wife Cindy: Your input, both literarily and in all other aspects of our lives, speaks to my heart in ways words cannot divulge because they fall short. Instead, my undying love for you will have to be the means by which I show my gratitude.

ABOUT BRETT ARMSTRONG

Brett Armstrong has been exploring other worlds as a writer since age nine. Years later, he still writes, but now invites others along on his excursions. He's shown readers haunting, deep historical fiction (*Destitutio Quod Remissio*), scary-real dystopian sci-fi (*Tomorrow's Edge*) and dark, sweeping epic fantasy (*Quest of Fire*). Every story is a journey of discovery and an attempt to be a brush in the Master Artist's hand. Through dark, despair, light, joy, and everything in between, the end is always meant to leave his fellow literary explorers with wonder and hope. Always busy with a new story, he also enjoys drawing, gardening, and spending time with his wife and son.

ABOUT ERIN R. HOWARD

Erin R. Howard is the YA urban fantasy author of The Kalila Chronicles, and The Gates of Deceit (dystopian) series. She is also a content and acquisitions editor for Expanse Books, an imprint of Scrivenings Press.

She loves playing video games with her husband, watching movies with her children, and fueling her many craft addictions. Erin has a Creative Writing degree and is a member of Realm Makers, RagTag Writers, and Once Upon a Page. She resides in Western Kentucky with her husband and three children.

ABOUT C. KEVIN THOMPSON

C. Kevin Thompson is a husband, a father, a grandfather, and a kid at heart. Often referred to as "crazy" by his grandchildren, it's only because he is. He's a writer. Need he say more? He lives in Florida, sixty miles from either coast, and has been married to Cindy, the love of his life, for over 41 years. He is a former English teacher who has gone over to the "dark side" and is now an administrator at a high school. He has three daughters, three sons-in-law, five grandchildren and zero pets. His children have enough pets to go around, so he can visit the five dogs, multiple cats, and farm full of goats whenever he likes.

Kevin is a huge fan of the TV series 24, *The Blacklist*, *Blue*

Bloods, NCIS, Criminal Minds, Broadchurch, Wallander, and *Hinterland*. He loves the entire Jurassic Park/Jurassic World complex, is a fan of the *Jason Bourne* movies, *Jaws, Gladiator*, loves anything to do with *Star Trek*. He is a Sherlock Holmes fanatic too. But you'll never catch him wearing a deerstalker. He has to draw the line somewhere. Ironically, however, his favorite movie is an older movie called *Hopscotch*, a mystery-slash comedy. Maybe one of these days, he'll write a book like that.

His previously published works include two award-winning novels, *The Serpent's Grasp*, and *The Letters*. He also has written (or is writing) the Blake Meyer Thriller series (adult fiction) and the Oliver Wendell Holmes series (middle grade fiction).

ALSO BY BRETT ARMSTRONG

Quest of Fire Series

***The Gathering Dark**: Quest of Fire Series – Book One*

After a thousand years of light, a teen's world teeters on the edge of utter darkness.

Jason is an expert at running from his past. But when it catches up, he finds himself hiding in a peculiar inn listening to a tale from centuries past.

The story is Anargen's, a teen who is pulled from all he loves to follow his oaths of loyalty to the fabled King of the Realms. Together with his mentor, Cinaed, he rides north on a special quest to mediate peace talks between ancient foes—the men of Ecthelowall and the dwarfs of Ordumair. Nothing goes as planned. Many on both sides of the dispute despise Anargen's Order. Worse, an arcane evil has returned to the North. This "Grey Scourge" seeks to ruin the peace talks and ensure a lost treasure held by the dwarfs is never found by those for whom it is meant.

As Anargen's story unfolds, Jason begins to wonder whether it is truly just a fable. He soon finds himself drawn into the conflict Anargen faced. A battle that has shaped and can destroy his world.

The Gathering Dark was a 2020 Selah Awards Finalist for Speculative Fiction.

Get your copy here: scrivenings.link/thegatheringdark

Succession: A Novella: *Quest of Fire Series – Book Two*

The heir must prove his worth - or die trying

Son of the Northern Realm's Defender, raised among the dwarves of Ordumair, Meredoch was anticipated to succeed his father. Some whispered he would bring the longed-for peace between Ordumair and their ancient foe, Ecthelowall. All of that changes when

Ordumair's Thane is killed and Meredoch and his family are exiled. From prestige to poverty, the young boy must chart a new course.

As the years pass and the idol that was his father's legacy tarnishes, Meredoch's past resurfaces. An artifact of immeasurable worth to Ordumair is found. If recovered by the wrong hands, disaster would befall those Meredoch serves and cares about. Battling creatures believed only myths and racing against evil toward the prize, Meredoch must face the truth of his place in the world and claim his right of succession.

Get your copy here: scrivenings.link/succession

Shadows at Nightfall: *Quest of Fire - Book Three*

The hour has arrived ... with all its terrors.

The shadows of Jason's past have caught him. Having stepped into the Quest of Fire, Jason is pursued by a league of assassins formed of pure darkness. To his horror he discovers these creatures also were contracted to eliminate Anargen and his friends as they sought to understand the Tower of Light's oracle. To unravel the mystery of who wants him dead and how he fits into the ages old quest, Jason must travel the lengths of the Lowlands. In the Ziljafu deserts a secret awaits him that will shake him to his core. He'll have to move fast and cling fiercely to hope, as Anargen's story twists down a bleak path to almost certain failure.

The creatures of darkness in the Lowlands have long waited for men to spurn the High King's laws. With few concerned for the light and everything falling apart around them, Jason and Anargen will face the shadows of night's falling as their world hangs in the balance.

Get your copy here: https://scrivenings.link/shadowsatnightfall

---

Desperation: A Novella: *Quest of Fire - Book Four*

Guarding his nation's last hope, a teen must escape enemy lands.

While Anargen, Caeserus, and Bertinand are held captive in Stormridge, the war to restore Ecthelowall's Commonwealth has been waged for months. Their friend Terrillian is on its frontline and hopes are high.

For Barons Fenwrest and Sornfold the fight is too close to their children, whose union represents the only viable challenge to the Monarchists claim to Ecthelowall's ancient throne. Enter Thomas Fenwrest, an orphan and page to Sir Hurstwell, who is captain of Baron Fenwrest's guard. The pair must escort the teens to Castle Yerst expecting boredom to be their only danger. Everything quickly spirals out of control when the Monarchists somehow deliver a devastating blow to the Restoration army and Thomas and Sir Hurstwell face the increasingly difficult task of keeping their charges alive. Ancient sorcery and bitter grudges combine to ensnare them.

As desperation sets in for the Restoration and Thomas, to where will they turn for hope?

Get your copy here: https://scrivenings.link/desperation

Tomorrow's Edge Trilogy

Day Moon: *Tomorrow's Edge Trilogy Book One*

AD 2039: Eluding authorities, one teen holds the past and future's key.

Prodigious seventeen-year-old, Elliott, is assigned to work on a global software initiative his deceased grandfather helped found. Project Alexandria is intended to provide the entire world secure and equal access to all accumulated human knowledge. All forms of print are destroyed in good faith, to ensure everyone has equal footing, and Elliott knows he must soon part with his final treasure: a book of Shakespeare's complete works gifted him by his grandfather. Before it is destroyed, Elliott notices something is amiss with the book, or rather Project Alexandria. The two do not match, including an extra sonnet titled "Day Moon."

When Elliott investigates, he uncovers far more than he bargained for. There are sinister forces backing Project Alexandria who have no intention of using it for its public purpose. Elliott soon finds himself on the run from federal authorities and facing betrayals and deceit from those closest to him. Following clues left by his grandfather, with agents close at hand, Elliott desperately hopes to find a way to stop Project Alexandria. All of history past and yet to be depend on it.

Get your copy here: https://scrivenings.link/daymoon

Veiled Sun: *Tomorrow's Edge Trilogy Book Two*

AD 2040: Every day the world slips further into lies.

Seventeen-year-old Elliott knows that better than most. Project Alexandria is rewriting history, shaping the world according to sinister goals. To stop it, Elliott must assemble the "Veiled Sun", a secret program written by his grandfather. The only people he can count on are siegers–outlaws who use their coding skills for purposes almost as nefarious as Project Alexandria. Overcoming the schemes and betrayals all around him, he's the world's best hope to save reality, if he doesn't lose hold of it himself.

Get your copy here: https://scrivenings.link/veiledsun

ALSO BY ERIN R. HOWARD

Gates of Deceit

Beyond the Gates by Erin R. Howard

Gates of Deceit - Book One

If playing by the rules means it keeps you alive, then seventeen-year-old Renna James should know better. She is, after all, the one who broadcasts these rules to the Outpost. What lies beyond the gates had always lured her, but her venture outside wasn't supposed to leave her locked out. Now, Renna's one chance to survive the next seventy-two hours just ran into the forest she's forbidden to enter.

Get your copy here: https://scrivenings.link/beyondthegates

The Kalila Chronicles

The Seer

Book One of the Kalila Chronicles

Viktor has one order to follow:

Kill the girl before her eyes are opened.

For thousands of years, his job has been to torment and kill seers: humans that have the gift of seeing the spiritual realm. So it was no surprise when his brother Matthias was once again sent to stop him and protect the girl.

Now the last of the seers' bloodline hangs in the balance, as the estranged demon and angel brothers are forced to work together to save a girl's life and escape to the sanctuary city of Bethesda.

Get your copy here: scrivenings.link/theseer

The Soul Searcher

Book Two of the Kalila Chronicles

Elnora's parents gave her one rule:

Stay hidden away at all costs.

Elnora Scott is used to her survival depending on the decisions of others. Locked away in her safe house, it is easy to follow her parents' dying wishes until an angel, demon, and seer show up on her doorstep. Now, waking up in a dirty cell, she wishes she would have gone with them when she had the chance, because the ones who unknowingly ushered the kidnapper to her location may be the only ones who can save her now.

When Thea learns that Elnora may be in danger, she doesn't hesitate to find her. Thea thought stepping through the portal would be her greatest obstacle, but it only reveals a more sinister threat.

Get your copy here: scrivenings.link/thesoulsearcher

The Silencer

Book Three of The Kalila Chronicles

Sam's parents asked him to do the unthinkable:

And it cost him everything.

When Sam Hart was forced to walk away from everything and everyone he knew, The Kalila became his new home. He thought he could keep the past buried but after an unexpected visit from his brother, a family secret is revealed.

Already reeling from a murder of one of their own, an unimaginable chain of events leaves everyone questioning each other's loyalty. Will Sam, Viktor, and Matthias be able to stop this newest threat before they lose another?

Get your copy here: scrivenings.link/thesilencer

ALSO BY C. KEVIN THOMPSON

The Letters by C. Kevin Thompson

Rachel Hamar—a Manhattan bank teller—lives nothing close to a Manhattan lifestyle. Residing in Washington Heights, NY, the only thing keeping her in The Big Apple is her mother—a long-time patient in a local psychiatric hospital. It's December 2014, and the twentieth anniversary of her high school sweetheart's tragic death. She's not sure how much more heartache she can endure, especially after being told earlier in the day she no longer has a job at the bank. A casualty of downsizing.

In the midst of spiraling depression, Rachel receives a mysterious letter in the mail. When she opens it, she becomes cautious and skeptical of its contents and discards it as a mistake, concluding it's simply addressed incorrectly or a postal worker's faux pas in the midst of a busy Christmas season. But another letter arrives the next day. And another the day after that. Before long, she is in possession of several letters. Each one more puzzling than the last.

Thinking that someone may be playing a cruel game, she contacts the police, and this propels Rachel and the two detectives into one of the most bizarre cases they've ever encountered. Is it a friend's cruel joke? Is it some stalker's perverse idea of manipulation? Or is it something more?

Get your copy here: scrivenings.link/theletters

MORE SPECULATIVE FICTION FROM EXPANSE BOOKS

The Girl with Stars in Her Eyes by Dawn Ford

Firebird Series - Book One

Eighteen-year-old servant girl Tambrynn is haunted by more than her unusual silver hair and the star-shaped pupils in her eyes. Her uncontrollable ability to call objects leads the wolves who savagely murdered her mother right to her door.

When she's fired and outcast during a snowstorm, her carriage wrecks and she's forced to find refuge in an abandoned cottage. There, her life is upended when the magpie who's stalked her for ten years transforms into a man, Lucas. He's her Watcher and they're from a different kingdom. His job is to keep her safe from her father, an evil mage, who wants to steal her abilities, turn her into one of his undead beasts, and become immortal himself.

Can they make it to the magical passageway and get to their home kingdom in time for Tambrynn to thwart her father's malicious plans? Or will Tambrynn's unique magic doom them all?

Get your copy here:

https://scrivenings.link/thegirlwithstarsinhereyes

Kokopelli's Song

Book One of the Four Corners Fantasy Series

New Mexico

When seventeen-year-old Amy Adams finds her father's family and a lost twin brother on the Hopi reservation in Arizona, she stumbles into a struggle between shamans and witches that spans a thousand years. After Mahu is attacked and a Conquistador's journal stolen, Amy and her new friend Diego set out on a dangerous quest to find and perform the ceremony that can stop ancient evil from entering our world.

But Amy and Diego are not alone as they race against time measured by a waxing moon. Kokopelli's song, the haunting notes of a red cedar flute, guides them along the migration route sacred to pueblo peoples: West to Old Oraibi, South to El Morro, East to Cochiti Pueblo, North to Chimney Rock, and finally to the Center—and the final confrontation—in Chaco Canyon.

Get your copy here: https://scrivenings.link/kokopellissong

Stay up-to-date on your favorite books and authors with our free e-newsletters.

ExpanseBooks.pub (an imprint of Scrivenings Press LLC)

CPSIA information can be obtained
at www.ICGtesting.com
Printed in the USA
LVHW072028060623
748977LV00044B/855

9 781649 172600